Praise for *Ruth's Ginger Snap Surprise*

Ruth's Ginger Snap Surprise is a sweet, fas̶ ̶ ̶ ̶ written story that piqued my interest fr̶ ̶ ̶ nected with Ruth, the strong, yet vulner̶ ̶ tender story will win your heart and tug ̶ ̶ that has everything in life that matters. ̶ ̶ must-read!

—Lisa Jones Baker, award-winning author of
the Hope Chest of Dreams series

Anne Blackburne has burst onto the Amish scene with this heartwarming story of love and healing. Sink into this sweet story, and enjoy the rich setting and quirky, loveable characters. Anne Blackburne is an author to watch! I can't wait to see the next book in this well-written series!

—Patricia Johns,
Publishers Weekly bestselling author

Ruth's Ginger Snap Surprise is a beautifully romantic story! Anne Blackburne has created a rich and detailed world full of wonderful and memorable characters. An absolute delight!

—Maggie K. Black,
USA Today award-winning author

THE HEART *of* THE AMISH

Ruth's Ginger Snap Surprise

ANNE BLACKBURNE

BARBOUR
PUBLISHING

Ruth's Ginger Snap Surprise ©2023 by Anne Blackburne

Print ISBN 978-1-63609-689-6
Adobe Digital Edition (.epub) 978-1-63609-690-2

This book is a work of fiction. Names, characters, places, and incidents are either products of the author's imagination or used fictitiously. Any similarity to actual people, organizations, and/or events is purely coincidental.

Cover Design: Kirk DouPonce, DogEared Design

Published by Barbour Publishing, Inc., 1810 Barbour Drive, Uhrichsville, Ohio 44683, www.barbourbooks.com

Our mission is to inspire the world with the life-changing message of the Bible.

Printed in the United States of America.

DEDICATION:

With gratitude to my friends and family who believed in me, and who read the early drafts of this book. Without your encouragement, I might have given up—and we would have missed out on this fun!

CHAPTER ONE

"Just stop blowing for one minute, and I'll be done!" Ruth Helmuth spoke around a wooden clothespin clenched in her teeth, the wind nearly whipping the damp, snowy-white apron out of her hands as she secured it to the line. She reached down into the laundry basket made of beautifully stained maple slats and pulled out another apron, which soon joined the first, flapping in the stiff December breeze. It was above freezing and the sun was shining, so Ruth had decided it was a fine day for hanging out the wash—even if it was a bit chilly and her hands were growing red and numb from handling the wet clothes.

The cold breeze caused the skirts of her long purple dress to billow around her ankles as she hurried back toward the warm house she'd shared with her husband, Levi, until his death nearly one year ago.

But before she could climb the steps into her cozy kitchen with its glowing woodstove, a buggy turned into her driveway.

"Now, who could that be?" Ruth squinted against the morning sun still riding low in the eastern sky.

Her two Great Pyrenees dogs jumped up from where they'd been lying in the brown winter grass and barked a warning.

"Wolke, Heftig, go guard the goats." With a final half-hearted woof from Wolke, the pair took off toward the barn.

As the two-seater buggy drew nearer, she was surprised to recognize the bishop of her district, Abram Troyer, guiding his standardbred mare, Spot, down her drive.

"*Guder mariye*, Ruth," Bishop Troyer said as he climbed from his rig and secured the gentle animal, a former harness racehorse, to the hitching post. He rubbed the mare's velvety nose as he peered anxiously at the dogs. "I'd forgotten about those two great, fierce beasts of yours! My, they've gotten big! Are you sure they're safe?"

"Guder mariye, Bishop. *Ja*, I told them to go inside with the goats, and they'll stay in the barn for now."

He nodded, casting a slightly apprehensive glance toward the barn. "Well, I have something to discuss with you, Ruth, if you have a few minutes?"

"For sure and certain. Please come inside. It's right cold this morning, even with the sun so bright. I've got cinnamon rolls fresh from the oven, and a pot of *kaffi* on."

"I don't mind if I do." Bishop Troyer followed Ruth through the little gate leading from the farmyard into her garden and then up four steps into her kitchen.

Ruth filled two mugs with kaffi, leaving room in one for the cream and sugar she knew Bishop Troyer loved.

"*Ach*, it feels *gut* to sit down in a cozy kitchen with a warm stove keeping the chill away. *Denki!*" Bishop Troyer stretched his long legs underneath the table.

"You are welcome, Bishop." Ruth set a plate of hot rolls before him.

"These look delicious." He selected one and placed it on his plate before licking the icing from his fingers and smiling sheepishly. "My Amelia used to make these for me." He sipped his kaffi before taking a large bite of his roll. Closing his eyes in bliss, he sighed. "Ach. Yours are just as gut, Ruth."

She smiled, well pleased, and sipped her own kaffi. She wondered when he'd get around to speaking of the reason for his visit.

"I'll get fat as a *millich* cow if I eat too many of these!" The bishop wiped the crumbs from his face and fingers, then placed the napkin on the table above his plate. He took another sip of kaffi and then set the mug down and looked at Ruth. "Though, it might be worth it. Do you mind if I have another?"

"Of course not, please help yourself."

He ate another roll with obvious pleasure before sitting back, dabbing at his mouth with his napkin, and patting his slightly rounded belly contentedly.

"I'm sure you're wondering why I came here this morning, and it wasn't to eat your fine rolls, although that was an unexpected pleasure!"

At last! She smiled and waited for him to speak his mind.

"It's been a year since Levi passed, and it's time you thought about what you're going to do next. The other elders and I think that, as a childless widow, you won't want to stay here on this big farm. Especially when you realize there are men who wish to marry and work the land, for whom this farm and house would be perfect. I've come to offer to help you sell the farm. In fact, I know just the man to buy it."

Ruth's lips parted, but no words came to mind. She felt disoriented and dizzy. What did he mean, sell the farm? This farm had been in her family for several generations. How could she possibly consider leaving it?

"...could move his buggy business into the big barn out back. You see? It's perfect!" He smiled and sat looking expectantly at her.

"I...I'm sorry, Bishop, I missed that last part. If you wouldn't mind repeating it?"

He looked a bit annoyed but sighed and said, "Samuel Mast wants to farm, and he's outgrown the shop where he makes buggies. I think he'd buy this place if you'd sell it to him. What do you say?"

She stared blankly at the bishop. He wanted an answer right away? Ruth couldn't think. An odd buzzing was filling her ears. She shook her head to clear them, then stood up abruptly, dropping her napkin onto the floor. She picked up the empty dishes and put them in the sink. When she turned back to the bishop, he stood looking at her in surprise, holding the napkin he'd retrieved from the floor.

"What is wrong?" He seemed truly puzzled by her reaction.

"I. . .I am not ready to sell my house, Bishop, but I thank you for stopping by to discuss this with me. Please let me think about it and get back to you." She walked over to the door and opened it. She had never been so rude in her life—and she picked her bishop for the first time!

He raised his bushy gray eyebrows at her and ran his hand through his chest-length beard thoughtfully. "Well, all right, but don't think too long. Samuel might find another place, and then you might not sell this big house and farm for a long time. Have you thought about how you'll manage on your own?"

"I've been doing fine for a year, Bishop Troyer," she said quietly. "No disrespect intended. But I need time to think. This home is very dear to me. It belonged to my *grosseldre*. And then I lived here with Levi for nearly fifteen years. I don't know where I'd go if I left here. Or what I'd do without my goats."

"Your goats. Right." He walked to the door and took his warm black wool hat from a peg on the wall. "I had forgotten them."

Ruth raised several types of goats and supported herself by selling some of the purebred kids each year. She also sold the rich hypoallergenic goat's milk, the cheese made from it, wool from her fiber goats, and meat from the Boers. She brought in a bit extra by making scented goat's milk soaps, lotions, and candles. It was a modest living but one she knew and understood.

Bishop Troyer put on his heavy black coat and looked thoughtfully at Ruth.

"I understand it is hard to contemplate change. And hard to leave a place we love. But consider letting another family have this place. If you're worried about where you'll go, I have a suggestion for that as well. I hadn't actually thought to mention this idea now, but, well, I suppose I might as well. Perhaps it will help you make a decision."

He looked a bit uncomfortable, and tugged at the collar of his shirt, his eyes cast toward the floor. He took a breath and met her puzzled gaze. "Ruth, I realize I must seem like an old man to you. Ach, in truth, I must have thirty years on you. But you see, I had my Amelia for forty-three years, and I miss her like I'd miss my arm if I lost it. I know I could never really replace her and what we had together. But, well, the fact is, I don't like living alone. And it occurred to me that maybe you don't either."

He looked hopefully at her, and when she just stared back, uncomprehending, he frowned. "You don't have any *bopplin*, and maybe you aren't able to. But that's all right, because I've raised my children, and now my grandchildren are bringing joy into my life. You could enjoy them too, if you were to marry me. That way, you'd have a gut home to go to, and my barn is plenty big enough for your goats. And you'd have a new purpose as my wife, helping the people of our community. Well? What do you think?"

Ruth realized that she was still just staring at Bishop Troyer. He wanted her to marry him? Give up her farm and move into the house he'd shared with his late wife, Amelia, for so long? She had liked and respected Amelia and couldn't even imagine taking the older woman's place in her kitchen, let alone in other areas of her married life. The bishop was a gut man, but he was old enough to be her father—nearly her grandfather.

She realized the bishop was waiting for a response and that he was starting to look decidedly uncomfortable. Sweat had broken out on his forehead, and he took out a handkerchief and dabbed at it self-consciously. It was time to say something. But how to turn him down without hurting his pride or his feelings? Ruth sent up a quick prayer for the right words and took a deep breath before meeting the bishop's eyes.

"Bishop Troyer, I'm very honored by your offer, but this is so much, so fast. I still feel married to Levi, you see. And while I can appreciate that marrying you and living in your home and serving our community with you would be gut, I am not ready to think about such a thing. Can you understand? I'm not ready to leave my home or to remarry."

He looked disappointed, but he grimaced and turned to put his hat on before facing her again. "Ja, I can understand. And I do realize

I'm too old for you. But I could support you, and I think we'd do well together. Please think about it, and think about selling your house to Samuel Mast. He is a gut man and would honor your family land. I believe he's considering taking a wife. He'll need to move out of the bachelor quarters he shares with his brother. Well then."

He walked out the door and down the steps and through the gate, then untied Spot, who was standing patiently in the cold sunshine, one hip cocked.

"I'll talk to you again soon. Meanwhile, I encourage you to pray about this. Denki again for the delicious rolls and kaffi. I could easily become accustomed to having them every morning."

She nodded stiffly, wishing he were already gone so she could think about this unexpected development.

He climbed into his buggy and turned to regard her solemnly for a moment. "Ach. All will work out as *Gott* wishes. Meanwhile, my granddaughter is coming in a few days to visit for a spell. Perhaps you'd introduce her to some of your friends at services? See she's included in the fun things you young people like to do?"

Ruth smiled tightly. "We'll make her *wilkum*, Bishop Troyer."

He nodded. "Gut. Gut." With a gentle snap of the reins, he guided Spot down the driveway before turning onto the road toward his own farm.

She sagged against the doorframe. She hadn't even considered that the elders might think she should give up her farm.

"Of course they do!" she cried, staring blindly out into her farm-yard. "What does a childless, thirty-three-year-old widow need with ninety-five acres of prime farmland, a huge barn, and a five-bedroom house, not to mention the connected *dawdi haus*?"

She had no answer. But she knew where to go with important questions. With jerky motions, she pulled on her warm black woolen cloak. Picking up her laundry basket, she silently asked Gott what she should do about her situation. He would know what was right, though He didn't always give His answers quickly, or clearly.

"Help me, *Vader*," she murmured as she unpinned aprons and dresses and folded them neatly into her basket. "I don't want to be selfish and stand in the way of another family making a home. But I don't want to give up my own home either! Please guide me. If it is Your will, I will do as the bishop asks and sell my farm. But if there is another way, please help me find it. As for marrying Bishop Troyer, I can't see it, Vader. But again, if it is Your will, soften my heart to become receptive to the idea."

She stood holding an apron for a moment before adding, "But Vader, if you want me to remarry, maybe You could consider someone a little younger? I wouldn't mind being a *mudder* before I become a *grossmudder*, if it is possible, and if it isn't too late. But Your will be done. Amen."

She would wait and think and pray, and see what happened next.

Before lunch, Ruth decided to check the mailbox, as she was expecting a letter from her mother. Opening it, she exclaimed happily, "Ah! Here it is!" She was about to cross her quiet rural road again when she heard the *clip-clop* of a fast-approaching horse, and she peered down the road to see who was coming. It was a two-seat black buggy, and she could see that it was a man holding the reins.

She heard the driver call out to his horse, "Ho, Samson!" and the buggy drew to a stop beside her. The driver slid open the window, leaned forward, and tapped his hat in greeting. "Guder mariye, Ruth! Are you enjoying this sunny day?"

Ruth recognized Jonas Hershberger, who owned a basket-weaving company he operated out of the small barn on his farm, only a few miles away. His late wife, Viola, had been in her class in school. They belonged to the same church community but hadn't spoken much at services.

"Ja, denki, I am." Ruth shaded her eyes from the sun with her hand as she peered up at him. He smiled, showing off a pair of dimples she didn't recall noticing before. Maybe he simply hadn't smiled much in recent years, since losing his Viola. Or maybe she hadn't looked properly since losing Levi. How nice it was that he was smiling again. It was a shame to hide those dimples.

A bit flustered by her stray thoughts, Ruth tucked a strand of red hair back under her prayer *kapp* and said, "I managed to get a load of wash done. I was about to iron when I remembered I was expecting this letter from my mudder in Texas. Now I'll have to put off the rest of my chores and read my letters first."

"Shocking," he said with a teasing gleam in his eye.

"Ja, don't tell anyone, okay?"

He mimed buttoning his lips, and she couldn't help grinning in return. His good mood was contagious.

The dogs barked, and Jonas squinted toward the sound, shading his eyes with a gloved hand. "Ach, those dogs are so big since the last time I saw them!"

"They're harmless, unless you're a coyote."

"That's gut to know!" He squinted across the road again. "That's a fine, big barn you have, Ruth. I imagine you house your goats and other livestock there?"

She nodded. "Ja, down on the first floor. I don't use the top floor for much since Levi. . .passed."

He smiled understandingly. "Well, I'll let you get to your letter. Perhaps I'll see you at services Sunday." He touched his hat again and clucked to his gelding. "Giddyap, Samson!"

Ruth stood watching the buggy until it was out of sight and then shook her head.

"Anyone would think I'm *verhuddelt*, standing here like a ninny with nothing better to do than watch someone drive away down the road!"

She hurried up the drive to her warm house. She'd enjoy the letter, then do her chores. What she *wouldn't* do was waste time thinking about a handsome widower with dimples, even if his smile had made her feel something she hadn't felt in a long time—something she was pretty sure she wasn't ready to feel. She'd spoken the truth when she'd told the bishop she wasn't ready to think about remarrying. But maybe she'd stretched it a bit when she said she still felt married to Levi. It was hard to feel married to someone you hadn't seen or touched for a year.

CHAPTER TWO

A mile down the road, Jonas held Samson's reins loosely, trusting the horse to stick to the job of getting them both home. *Ach, how have I not noticed before how pretty Ruth Helmuth is with her fiery red hair peeking out from under her proper kapp, and her sparkling blue eyes?*

Shaking his head, Jonas drove on toward home, located at the point where the old state route grew busier with heavy truck traffic coming and going from the nearby quarry. What used to be a quiet country lane was now dusty and sometimes downright dangerous. And the narrow berm left little room to move out of the way of the big trucks that trundled by filled with heavy gravel.

His young daughter, Abigail, was waiting for him at home—four years old and a handful for a widower like himself. His eyes grew fierce when he thought about how he'd had to defend his right to raise his own child when Viola had died shortly after giving birth to the tiny little girl, fading before his eyes and gone before an ambulance could be summoned. There had been some who'd thought a lone man had no business raising a baby on his own and that he should give her up to some childless Amish couple.

Jonas thanked God every night that his sister, Sally, had stepped forward with the support of her husband to offer to help him with the little girl. He'd been so consumed with grief over losing Viola that he'd hardly known what was happening. Looking back, he was fully aware that without Sally's intervention he would probably have succumbed to the well-meant suggestions that he allow someone else to raise Abigail.

There had been times in the last four years when Jonas had been hard pressed not to weep with heartbreak at both his loss and his little daughter's loss in never knowing her sweet mother. But lately it had been growing easier. He still missed Viola, but it no longer felt like a raw wound. Now when he thought of her, sometimes he found himself laughing at something funny he recalled her saying or doing.

"Ah, Viola, you were a gut wife, and I loved you," he murmured. "But you're gone, and I hope you won't mind if I admit that I'm lonely sometimes now for someone to talk to at night—yes, and to hold."

At thirty-five, he was too young to be alone for the rest of his life. In fact, his sister had started hinting that maybe he should consider finding another wife. He'd thought he wasn't ready to hear that yet. But after spending just a few minutes with pretty Ruth, he wondered if maybe he was ready to at least think about it. If he were fortunate enough to find the right woman, it would be *wunderbar* for Abigail to have a mother too.

A low rumbling drew Jonas from his woolgathering, and he saw a cloud of dust farther along the road.

"Drat," he mumbled. He steered Samson toward the right side of the road as the truck, slowing as it approached the buggy, rumbled past, much too close for comfort. The driver waved, and Jonas touched his hat in response. Samson tossed his head and nickered, blowing the dust of the passing truck from his nostrils. Inside the buggy, Jonas did the same. "It would be nice if the township sprayed down these roads with oil more often," he commented to Samson, who nickered in response to his voice.

A few minutes later, Jonas turned Samson into his driveway, and the gelding headed straight to the barn. The small door on the side opened, and his sister poked her head outside. "Finally! I was starting to worry. What took so long?"

"Well, as it happens, I ran into an old friend and stopped to chat for a few minutes." Jonas unhitched Samson from the buggy and led him around to the big door and into the back half of the barn, where he housed his stock.

Sally followed him as he let Samson into his stall before grabbing a rag and going to work on his coat, making sure he was well dried off from his exercise.

"Well? Who was it?" She rested her elbows on the stall door.

"Patience," Jonas said as he grabbed a brush and gave the horse a good brushing down before patting him fondly on the rump and exiting the stall.

"Hmm. I can't think of anyone with that name around here."

"Well, it surely isn't you."

Sally rolled her eyes, well used to her brother's teasing, and watched him scoop up some oats and dump them into Samson's feed bucket. The horse nickered his approval and tucked into the meal. After making sure Samson had plenty of fresh water, Jonas closed the stall door behind himself.

"If you must know, I ran into Ruth Helmuth on my way home." Jonas busied himself with a couple of small chores but noticed his sister raise her eyebrows in an interested manner.

"Really," she murmured. "And?"

He shrugged. "And nothing. We caught up for a few minutes. I was in school with her late husband, and she was in school with Viola. We made small talk, the way people do. That was it. Now, let's talk about that new wine basket we're starting production on next month."

He headed out of the barn, and Sally caught up the skirts of her long royal-blue work dress and hurried after him. "Jonas Hershberger! You can't get away from me that easily. I saw the gleam in your eye when you mentioned Ruth. And why not? She's a lovely woman, and the right age for you. I'd be surprised if you didn't take notice of her."

Jonas stopped and turned to face Sally so abruptly that she squeaked and pulled herself up short to avoid running into him.

"Don't torment me about Ruth, Sally. I'm not interested in matchmaking, *fashtay?*"

Sally rolled her eyes. "*Ja*, I understand."

He looked intently at her for another few seconds, then turned and strode toward the door leading into the basket-making shop.

"We have more important things to worry about right now, anyway." Jonas gestured to the stacks of wood slats and boxes of other basket-making supplies piled up around the walls of the small barn their business was rapidly outgrowing. "Such as where we're going to store all this stuff until we need it. It can't stay in here—we won't be able to walk from one side of the room to the other. I suppose we could put some of it in the basement of the house, but I don't like the damp down there. It might warp the wood."

Sally frowned and looked at the supplies that had been delivered the day before and been stacked hither and thither around the space. "It does seem to be more crowded than it used to be in here. What happened?"

"We're growing, that's what happened," Jonas said, sidling around a stack of boxes filled with glue and linseed oil. "This barn was perfect when we started the business a few years ago, but now, with the extra people working for us and the additional supplies we need to keep up with our orders, there's simply not enough room. We're going to have to find something bigger—and soon."

"It's been so convenient having it right here, close to home. I don't suppose we could build something?"

Jonas thought about Sally's suggestion. It had merit—no surprise, as his sister was a smart woman. There was room enough in the field behind the little barn. But with so much of his capital already sunk into inventory and wages, he didn't see how he could swing a large new outbuilding at this time.

He shook his head. "*Nee*, it's a gut idea, Sally, but I don't have the cash, and I don't want to take a loan. I'll look for something we could just remodel to suit us. We can last a while longer."

Sally puffed some air from her cheeks. "I guess you're right, *Bruder*." She stepped over a pile of wood slats as she headed into the back of the shop. "But if we wait too long, they'll have to send in search parties to find us. We'll be buried in baskets!"

Jonas laughed and started figuring out what was needed for that day's project. That was one of the things he liked about working with his sister. She had a terrific sense of humor, and she didn't sweat the small stuff.

"She's not wrong, though," Jonas mused as he sat down at his desk in the tiny back room to go over the books. "We do need a bigger place. And sooner rather than later."

But where would he find something that was affordable, convenient to home, and suitable to their needs—or at least not too tough to convert? Though he pondered the question for several minutes, nothing occurred to him.

"I'll leave it in Gott's hands for now," he decided. "He's never let me down before."

Unfortunately, as soon as he stopped worrying about his business, Ruth's pretty face, tilted up to look at him in the buggy, a hand shading her eyes from the sun, and wisps of red hair peeking from beneath her cap, popped into his head. Jonas groaned. At this rate, he wouldn't get a thing done. Impatiently, he forced his mind away from the intriguing widow. He wasn't interested.

Was he?

CHAPTER THREE

Later that afternoon, Ruth was responding to her mother's letter when she again heard a buggy pulling into her driveway. Reluctantly, she set aside her pen and went to see who was calling.

"Oh! It's Lydia!" she exclaimed happily as she saw her good friend Lydia Coblentz pulling up to the hitching post in her buggy. Ruth slipped on her shoes, hurried outside, and exclaimed, "Now this is a gut surprise!" She tied the horse, a sweet but elderly gray gelding, to the rail.

Lydia stepped stiffly down to the ground, stretching a little before patting her horse on the flank and then walking around to the steps.

"Ach! I'm not as young as I was. I get stiff riding a few miles these days!"

"Well, come inside where it's warm," Ruth urged her elderly friend. "The sun was out earlier, but it seems to be clouding up now."

She followed Lydia's slow progress up the steps, noticing her friend carried a small, closed basket with her.

"Would you like some kaffi?"

"I never say no to kaffi, as you well know," Lydia said with an impish grin, for her doctor had suggested a bit less of the stuff might not do her any harm.

Ruth poured mugs of hot kaffi, added a plate with a few snickerdoodles, and sat down with her friend. As she savored the first taste of the strong brew, Ruth happened to glance down at the basket by

Lydia's feet and was startled to see it move slightly.

"Lydia! What's in that basket?"

"Oh, just a little something I thought you might enjoy." Lydia picked up the basket and unlatched the hook holding the wooden lid closed. She lifted the lid, and a tiny orange head popped up, tip-tilted golden eyes surveying the room. The wee pink mouth opened wide, and it emitted an indignant squeak.

"A kitten!" Ruth murmured, charmed.

"One from Hephzibah's last litter." Lydia lifted the little animal free and set the basket back on the ground. It squeaked again, its mouth opening wide, obviously complaining about something.

"Is it hungry?"

"Probably. He's only been weaned a few days."

Ruth looked askance at her friend. "Lydia, did you bring him for me?"

Lydia smiled smugly. "Yes, indeed! You've lived alone long enough."

Ruth sat back and crossed her arms over her chest. "I don't live alone. I have a barn full of animals right across the yard. And the dogs—I can't step outside without Heftig and Wolke running up to see if I've got a treat in my pocket."

"You live alone in here, with no one to talk to, so this little boy is just what you need."

"I need a cat that isn't old enough to go outside by itself?"

"Oh, Hep's kittens are all inside cats," Lydia said seriously. "I won't have one of my kittens smushed on the highway. If you take him, you have to promise he'll live in the house. If you can't promise that, I'll find him another home. But I really do think you and this kitten were made for each other, Ruth."

The idea of an inside pet was unusual for an Amish household, although not as much as it used to be. But then, Lydia was known to be somewhat eccentric by Amish standards.

In fact, Ruth knew her friend was planning on spending gut money to have her cat, Hephzibah, spayed in a few weeks. The vet had said she'd had enough litters of kittens, and that was all Lydia needed to hear.

Ruth studied the kitten currently using its sharp little claws to climb up Lydia's sleeve onto her shoulder, where it sat and began batting at the strings of her kapp.

"He is awfully cute," Ruth said, weakening. Reaching out absently to scratch the small animal on his head, she said, "I'm glad you came by, Lydia. Something happened this morning that I wanted to discuss with you."

"My, this sounds serious." Lydia's eyes twinkled.

Ruth nodded distractedly, watching the kitten scamper down Lydia's arm and settle in her lap, open its mouth wide in a silent yawn, and effortlessly go to sleep.

"Ja, it may be," she said, and told her friend all about the bishop's visit.

When she was finished, Lydia sighed and leaned back in her seat. "Ja. I'd heard some talk of this," she admitted. "Although I didn't see the proposal coming."

"What? Then why didn't you warn me?"

"I only heard it recently and haven't seen you since." Lydia gave a dismissive wave. "You have to admit, from the bishop's point of view it makes perfect sense for you to sell out to a man who wants to farm the land. And Samuel Mast has that buggy business that would do nicely in your big barn." She sipped her coffee thoughtfully. "As far as proposing marriage, the old fool is lonely, and he has a sweet tooth. He probably came up with the idea over a plate of your cinnamon rolls. They'd have reminded him of Amelia's. It wouldn't occur to him that he needs a wife thirty years younger than he is like he needs a toothache."

"So, do you think I should sell?"

Lydia held up a hand. "I only said I can see the bishop's point. It's gut to be able to see things from various points of view. Helps you understand why people do what they do."

Ruth chewed on her bottom lip. "But maybe I should consider it?"

Her friend shrugged and finished off her kaffi. "It's always gut to consider your options, dear. Why don't you sleep on it and pray to Gott for guidance? He will help you make a decision in gut time."

"I'm not sure Bishop Troyer is willing to wait for Gott to point me in the right direction. He wanted my decision right away. On both questions!"

Lydia pushed herself to her feet, cradling the sleeping kitten in her hands, and Ruth stood as well. "I hope you let him down gently."

"You mean the marriage proposal?"

"What else?"

"I told him I was honored but that I wasn't ready to consider marriage again yet."

Lydia's rich laugh rolled out, and she put a hand on her ample stomach while she wiped tears out of her eyes. "Honored! Oh, poor Abram. I'll bet that hurt."

Ruth stared at her friend, dismayed. "Did I say the wrong thing? I wouldn't want to offend the bishop!"

"No, child. If Abram Troyer wants to remarry, he should look to a woman more his own age. But men aren't always sensible creatures, are they?"

Ruth smiled wryly. "No, I guess they aren't." She hugged her friend. "Denki for listening." She laughed when she felt tiny claws climbing up her arm.

"Ouch! This little ginger has sharp claws!" She plucked the baby off her sleeve and held him gently against her stomach, stroking his knobby little head with one finger. The kitten closed his eyes and emitted a surprisingly loud, rumbling purr.

"Listen to that engine!" Lydia reached out and gave the baby a gentle rub under his chin. "I thought you said two 'somethings' happened today. What was the other?"

"Oh! Well, it's nothing, really. Just that I saw Jonas Hershberger today while I was getting my mail." Ruth busied herself clearing the dishes with one hand, holding the kitten against her body with the other.

At this, Lydia pursed her lips thoughtfully. "Jonas, eh? A good-looking boy, that one, and a hard worker. What did he want?"

"Want? Nothing. That is, he was driving by on his way home from the market, and he stopped to pass the time, that's all."

Lydia studied Ruth with her keen old eyes. "Hmmm."

"Hmmm? That's it?" Ruth said.

Lydia's dimple flashed as she smiled at her young friend. "That's right. Hmmm."

"Now don't go making something of this, Lydia. I know you too well. It was nothing, honestly."

"If it was nothing, he could have driven by with a polite wave. But he stopped and spent valuable time talking with you on a workday? Hmmm."

Ruth rolled her eyes. "Fine, think what you want."

"I always do. Meanwhile, don't fret about the bishop. He's a gut man, just watching out for his flock, including you," Lydia admonished her friend. "And he'll get over the rejection. He's not a young man to have his heart broken by something like that."

"I know. By the way, he mentioned his granddaughter is coming to visit from New York."

"Is she? Interesting. Her parents are probably hoping she'll find a husband here."

"Oh, do you think so?"

Lydia shrugged. "Could well happen. I remember she's a pretty girl. If she has a modicum of sense, she should do well here. Now, come with me, if you don't mind. I have a few things you'll need out in my buggy, if you'll put the kitten down on the chair and help an old woman outside?"

Ruth chuckled and followed Lydia outside. "If I see an old woman, I'll be sure to help her. What do you have in the buggy?"

"This and that." Lydia rummaged in the buggy, then handed Ruth a large bag. "There's a litter pan, cat litter, a scoop, a bag of kitten food, a few little toys for him, and a blanket that smells like his mama and siblings. Don't wash it for a couple weeks."

"My goodness, Lydia, this is a lot!"

"It gives me comfort knowing you'll be good for each other." She climbed into the buggy. "Ruth," she said before driving off, "Jonas

Hershberger is a very gut man. You could do far worse, if you're interested in marrying again. And he isn't old enough to be your grandfather, like some, which is a plus."

She held up a hand, forestalling Ruth's protest. "I know how much you loved Levi. But he's gone, and you're too young to spend the rest of your life alone."

Ruth frowned. "I don't know, Lydia. It isn't just how I felt about Levi that's keeping me from thinking about marrying again."

Lydia looked puzzled. "Then what?"

Ruth bit her lip, wondering if she should tell her old friend her deepest, most secret fear. Lydia waited patiently, her eyes kind and her mouth closed.

Finally, deciding there was no point in keeping the matter to herself when Lydia might be able to offer some wisdom, she sighed and admitted, "It's me, Lydia. I can't have bopplin."

"Child, you don't know that."

"After fifteen years of marriage without any babies, it seems pretty obvious, don't you think?"

Lydia shook her head. "No, I don't. You don't know that it was you who couldn't have bopplin. It could just as easily have been Levi. Besides, Jonas has a child, and if he wants you, it'll be for yourself, not for your ability to make bopplin."

Ruth swallowed hard. "I'll think about it, Lydia," she whispered. "But it isn't as if it's a secret in the community. Even the bishop mentioned it today. He said he knew I couldn't have children, and that was one of the reasons he thought I should marry him. He has grandchildren I can enjoy. But Lydia, I don't want grandchildren yet. I want children of my own."

"Goodness, child. Of course you do. And you'd make a wonderful mudder. But remember, a beloved child doesn't always come from one's own womb. And Jonas has that beautiful little girl who needs a mudder. Listen, I have to run. But you're not too old to find happiness with another man—a young man. We'll talk more about this later."

She squeezed Ruth's hand and then took up the reins.

Ruth stood on the bottom step of the house, watching her friend drive away. She'd forgotten about Jonas' child. Annie? Alice? No, it was Abigail. She'd seen her in church, but as the child was one of many, she hadn't taken much notice. Before she could consider the matter further, she heard a scratching and climbed the steps and peeked in through the storm window to see the kitten trying to climb the metal door.

"Look out, silly." Ruth carefully let herself into the house and closed the door behind her. "I'll have to decide where to put these things," she said, taking the kitten supplies out of the bag.

Bustling around seeing to her new housemate's needs, Ruth forgot to worry about the bishop's visit, or whether or not she should forever turn from the idea of one day finding happiness with a second husband. When she realized this, she frowned.

"Maybe I'll enjoy having you around after all," she told the tiny creature. An idea occurred to her. Wouldn't it be lovely to give something thoughtful to Lydia in return for the gift of the ginger kitten? But what would she need, or want?

Ruth thought about it as she set about the afternoon's tasks, the kitten scampering around behind her trying to grab her shoelaces.

"Silly little thing, I'll step on you!" she chided. But the kitten ignored her and kept on playing.

Ruth smiled. She realized that she hadn't known she'd been lonely before this minute. "That Lydia," she whispered, tossing a little woolen mouse she'd found in the bag for the kitten to chase. "She always knows."

CHAPTER FOUR

Jonas lifted his small daughter from the old-fashioned claw-foot tub and wrapped her snugly in a large white bath towel. His regular babysitter, Selma, had offered to bathe the child, but Jonas liked to do the little day-to-day chores for his baby whenever he could. He felt as if it somehow made up for the lack of a mudder for her. He knew that was silly, and nothing could make up for that. On the other hand, how much could his daughter grieve for what she'd never known?

He shook his head. Overthinking was one of his faults. He needed to remember that their situation was Gott's will, and it wasn't for him to understand it, necessarily, but simply to accept. That didn't mean he had to like it, though.

Small hands cupped his face, and his attention was drawn back to the subject of his musings.

"*Dat*, are you woolgathering again?" Blue eyes twinkled into his own, and all his cares evaporated.

"You caught me!" He scooped her up and carried her into her bedroom, which was furnished simply with sturdy pine furniture that was nevertheless pretty with its warm honey tones.

A quilt made by Viola when she was carrying Abigail covered the bed, cheerful yellow-and-white daisies pieced on a grass-green background. A braided green-and-yellow rag rug was Sally's contribution to the room, and pretty green gingham curtains made by Viola's mother made Jonas think of a summer field. Framed and hanging on one wall were quilt squares in various patterns in shades of green, yellow, and blue pieced by various women in the community. They'd presented them to Jonas after Abby was born, as a way to express their love and sympathy for the loss of the well-loved wife and mother.

He swallowed hard as he gazed around the room, well aware of all he had to be thankful for in his life.

"Dat, you seem sad tonight," his observant child commented as he set her gently on her bed and went to the little dresser to get her a clean nightgown.

"Sorry, Abby. I was just thinking about your mudder."

"Why does that make you sad? You said *Maem* is with Gott, so we should be happy for her."

Jonas paused, a small white nightie held in his big, work-roughened hands. "Ja, that's true. But I still miss her sometimes, and that makes me sad."

He sat down on the bed and unwrapped the towel from around his child before popping the nightie over her head. Then he got a comb from a basket he'd made on the dresser top and began carefully combing through Abby's long blond hair.

"I'm sorry you're sad, Dat. But you do a gut job combing my hair. You're a gut vader."

"I'm mostly not sad, just sometimes." Jonas put the comb aside and picked Abigail up and walked to the rocking chair in the corner of the room. A little table with an oil lamp stood beside the chair. Jonas carefully lit the lamp and picked up the small selection of children's books from the table. "What story would you like tonight?"

"Tom and Pippo, please." Abby snuggled into her father's arms and popped a thumb into her mouth.

"Abby, remember you're trying to give up sucking your thumb," Jonas gently reminded his daughter, who shrugged and kept on sucking her thumb. Jonas sighed. It was a fairly harmless habit, he supposed, and she'd give it up when she was ready. At least that's what Sally said.

He read about a little boy named Tom and his stuffed monkey, Pippo, and their trip to the zoo. This was one of Abby's favorite books, and it was becoming dog eared with use. When he was finished with the book, Abby begged for him to read it again, but he closed it, placed it on the table, and carried Abby to bed, where he tucked her in and kissed her tenderly on the forehead before picking up the damp towel from the floor.

"Remember to say your prayers, Abby," he said. "Good night." He turned off the oil lamp and left the room, leaving the door cracked the way Abby liked it.

"Night, Dat," he heard, and he peeked through the crack in the door to see his child snuggled safely in her bed, eyes closed, the Pippo doll given to her by her indulgent maternal grandparents clutched in her arms.

"Night, *Dochder*," he whispered before walking into the bathroom to hang up the towel, and then heading downstairs for some reading before his own bedtime arrived. Morning came early enough—not as early as it did for some of his friends and family who had working farms, but Abby would be up with the chickens even if he didn't have to get up and get ready for work.

Thinking about farms brought Ruth Helmuth to mind again. He imagined that with all those goats to milk, she was up before dawn. It must be hard on her, doing it all by herself. He frowned. Did Ruth have anyone to help with the heavy chores? He couldn't think of any immediate family in the area.

"It would be neighborly of me to stop by and see if there's anything she needs help with, as she has no *brudders* or *onles* in the area," Jonas mused as he poured himself a glass of milk and placed several of Selma's large oatmeal cookies on a plate. Then he recalled another excuse to see Ruth. Sally had brought over a box of saltwater taffy she got on vacation in South Carolina that summer, that she said she'd been meaning to give Ruth. He thought that seemed a bit suspicious, but he wasn't one to look a gift horse—or box of taffy—in the mouth.

He carried his milk and cookies into the living room. "Ja. I'll do that tomorrow morning on my way into town. And why am I going into town tomorrow morning?" He laughed at himself as he plopped into his favorite reading chair and deposited his snack on the table by the chair. "Apparently so I'll have an excuse to stop and see Ruth!"

With a grin at his own foolishness, and feeling more settled than he had all day, Jonas opened the Louis L'Amour western he was rereading for the umpteenth time and lost himself in his story.

CHAPTER FIVE

Loud barking alerted Ruth to the presence of a visitor the next morning. She opened the kitchen door and was surprised to see Jonas Hershberger standing by the gate, keeping a nervous eye on the dogs.

"Guder mariye," she called.

He turned his gaze to her, not moving.

"Um, hello again, Ruth." Jonas slowly moved his arm up to touch his hat brim. "Do you mind calling off your dogs?"

Amused, she surveyed the situation. She supposed Wolke and Heftig were a bit intimidating, if you didn't know them. "They're just saying hello. They won't hurt you. You're not a coyote, remember?"

"Right. Are you sure they understand that?"

"Pretty sure." Taking pity on him, she said, "Go guard the goats, guys," and smiled at his sigh of relief as they ran off, tongues lolling. "Not a dog person?"

"Not really," he admitted sheepishly. "Guess we just didn't keep them when I was growing up, so I never really got to know one."

"That's funny. Bishop Troyer was here yesterday, and he's afraid of them too. I just see my babies when I look at them."

"Pretty big babies," Jonas muttered. Glancing toward the barn to make sure the dogs weren't returning, he held up a paper bag. "My sister, Sally, asked me to drop this off for you since I was going to be driving right by on my way into town."

"That's kind of her." Ruth walked across her small courtyard and met him at the gate. He handed her the bag, and their fingers brushed, causing her to experience an odd, unsettling jolt of awareness.

What on earth? She lowered her lashes and dipped her chin so he wouldn't see she was *ferhoodeled*. Opening the bag, she forgot all about her confusing reaction to Jonas in her delight at its contents—a pound of saltwater taffy from the Carolina coast.

"Oh! I love this stuff!" she exclaimed, reaching in to choose a piece. "How kind of Sally to remember!"

She held out the bag, but he shook his head. "I have my very own bag."

"Lucky me." Ruth unwrapped a green candy. "I get credit for offering, and don't actually have to share!"

He laughed. "Maybe I'll change my mind."

"Too late!" She whipped the bag behind her back. They stood grinning at each other across the gate for a few moments, until Ruth, realizing she was admiring his dimples again, felt awkward. She cleared her throat. "I was just dusting," she said, holding up a Swiffer duster she'd tucked under her arm. He nodded, his eyes not leaving hers. She looked away, unsure how to handle the feelings he awoke in her.

"You must be very busy, Ruth," he suddenly blurted. "What with the house and the livestock and all and nobody to help you out."

Her eyes flew to his. Had he been talking to the bishop? Did he also think she should sell her farm? Maybe he was a friend of Sam Mast and was going to pitch his qualifications as the next owner of Ruth's land. "I do all right," she said stiffly.

Jonas frowned. "I can see that. I only meant, maybe you could use another pair of hands around here occasionally. You know, with the heavy lifting. If so, I'd be glad to offer mine."

"I. . .I couldn't really afford. . ." she began in a fumbling manner, but Jonas interrupted.

"No, no, not for pay." He dragged a hand through his hair, obviously frustrated and at something of a loss as to what to say. "I meant as a friend."

"A. . .a friend?" Ruth stammered.

"Ja! Like, a *nochber*—you know, the neighborly thing to do." Jonas grabbed on to the explanation with both hands. "I was just thinking yesterday that you don't have any family in the area, do you? So who helps you out around the place? It's awfully big for one woman—or man!" He recovered quickly when he saw her eyes flash. "But if this is a tender subject for some reason, forget I brought it up."

Ruth's shoulders drooped. She'd overreacted, and she knew it. "I'm sorry, Jonas, I'm not usually so prickly. It's just that recently it was suggested that I should sell out to a man who wants to farm and raise a family, that I was selfish to keep such a large house and so much prime farmland to myself."

"Really? Who said so?"

"Bishop Troyer," Ruth whispered, watching to see if Jonas would take their church leader's side. After all, as Amish they were taught to go along with what the community wanted, and the bishop pretty much spoke for the community. But Jonas surprised her.

"Was that why he came by yesterday?" At her nod, he looked perplexed. "Huh. I don't think it's selfish of you to live here. Hasn't it been in your family for generations? I respect the bishop, but sometimes he forgets we live in more modern times than when he was a young man."

Ruth's eyes flew wide open. "Yes! Exactly! I wouldn't go against the *Ordnung*, but I'm just making a living as best I can on my own property. I don't think I should be judged harshly for that."

Jonas nodded thoughtfully. "Did you explain to Bishop Troyer all you do here? He may not realize how much of this farm you utilize in your operation."

"I reminded him of my goats, but no, I don't think he fully understands how I use the place for my herds, my crops, and my soap and lotion making. He just sees a big house with one woman in it, a dawdi haus standing empty, and ninety-five prime acres with a big barn."

Jonas' eyes went to the barn, and he recalled her saying she only used the bottom floor, leaving the top story of the barn empty and unused.

Suddenly, the germ of an idea began to take root in Jonas' mind. He frowned at the barn as he considered it and must have stayed quiet for too long, for Ruth interrupted his thoughts.

"Maybe I should have explained in more detail?"

"No, that probably wouldn't have made a difference. Abram Troyer is like a mule headed home after a day's work—you won't turn him easily from his goal. Let me think about this, Ruth. I've just had an idea that might help you out. It might help both of us, in fact."

"An idea? What idea?"

"Nee, let me cook it for a day or two, and then I'll come back and tell you what I'm thinking if it has any merit." He glanced at his watch and frowned. "Meanwhile, I have to run. We have a delivery of wood slats arriving today, and I'm not sure where we're going to put them all!"

"Well, thanks for bringing the taffy. Be sure to thank Sally for me."

Jonas touched his hat, turned, and climbed up into his buggy. Ruth watched him drive away, wondering what his big idea was all about. And how could it help both of them out?

"*Ach vell*, the dusting won't finish itself." She carried her taffy inside and decided one more piece might give her energy for housework. She unwrapped it, then, glancing down at the kitten playing on the kitchen rug, crumpled the wax paper and tossed it on the floor for him to bat around.

"I'm throwing trash on the floor now," she mused. "I've lost it."

Shaking her head, she retrieved the duster from the counter by the kitchen door and got back to work.

CHAPTER SIX

Jonas thought about the idea he'd had yesterday at Ruth's as he forked soiled straw out of Samson's stall into a wheelbarrow. He'd been thinking of little else since yesterday morning and had slept little last night as he turned it over and over in his mind like a smooth, perfect stone.

It had occurred to him as he and Ruth were discussing the bishop's suggestion that Ruth's barn was very large indeed. She'd said she only used the ground floor, which meant the cavernous upper level was going to waste. He imagined where he'd place all the elements of his basket business if he had a space that large. The business was bursting out of his much smaller barn, and the need for a larger space was growing urgent. He wondered what Ruth would say if he asked her if he could rent the space for his business?

As he finished his barn chores, the idea took shape in his mind, and the more he thought about it, the more convinced he became that that big red barn was what he needed for his growing business. . .and he couldn't think of a single reason not to go and put the idea to Ruth.

"Why not?" Determined to ask her this very day, Jonas poked his head into the shop where his sister was already at work, although their employees hadn't arrived yet.

"Sally, I need to do something. If it works out, it will be gut for the business. I'll be back in a while. Can you hold down the shop?"

"Sure, but Jonas, where are you going?"

He gave her an enigmatic smile. "To see Ruth Helmuth." And out the door he went—but not before he heard her say to herself, "Gut for the business, gut for my bruder. Well, it's just a gut day all around!"

"I hope I baked enough," Ruth fretted as she pulled a sheet of fragrant cookies from the oven.

She glanced at the clock above the sink, removed the apron she wore over her indigo dress, and hurried to prepare a fresh pot of kaffi.

Today was a special day. Several of her friends were coming over to sew clothes for a family who had lost their home to a fire. Everyone had gotten out safely, but they'd lost most of their possessions. Today they were going to make a set of clothing for the two youngest children—a baby just a few months old and a three-year-old girl.

She turned to place cream on the table and nearly tripped over a bundle of orange fur streaking across the room.

"Oh! You're going to either kill me or get squashed under my feet, cat!" He zipped behind the potato bin, apparently under the impression that he was hidden there.

"I can't blame him for getting under your feet, if those cookies smell as gut to him as they do to me," a voice said from the doorway. Ruth spun toward the door and squeaked in surprise when she saw Jonas standing there, a big grin on his handsome face and his hat in his hands.

"Sorry, I was going to knock, but I saw through the window you were getting the tray out of the oven, and I didn't want to startle you and make you burn yourself, so I just opened the door."

"Oh! That's okay, come on in! I can't visit long, though. I'm expecting company."

Jonas closed the door, hung his hat on the peg, and sat down. A small sound from the direction of the trash can caused him to glance in that direction, and surprise crossed his face at the sight of the small orange bundle crouched behind the plastic bin.

"So, you have a kitten?"

"Right the first time," she laughed.

"In the house?"

"Right again. Lydia Coblentz gave him to me the other day. He's from her cat Hephzibah's last litter."

"But why do you have him in the house? Is he sick or injured?"

"Nee. Lydia brought him to be company for me in the house. She doesn't allow any of her kittens to be outside cats. I promised her I'd keep him inside."

"Huh. I guess that's all right."

"So happy you approve," Ruth said acerbically as she sat down and placed a mug of hot kaffi in front of Jonas.

"Sorry, that came out wrong. Of course you can do what you please in your own home. I just don't know many people who have animals in the house. Don't be mad."

Ruth shrugged and took a sip out of a second mug. "Ouch. Burned my lip. I'm always too impatient to wait for it to cool." She rubbed gently at the small hurt.

Jonas' gaze moved to Ruth's mouth, his own mug arrested halfway to his own lips. Catching his eye, she felt a blush creep over her face and neck, and she wondered later what she would have said or done if the sound of buggy wheels in the gravel driveway hadn't interrupted the moment.

"It's my friends," Ruth gasped. "Remember, I said they were coming. We're sewing clothes for a family that lost their home to a fire. Either they're early, or I lost track of time!"

Jonas stood and cleared his coffee cup to the sink. "I'll see you another time, then. Sorry about the kitten. Honestly, sometimes my foot goes right into my mouth."

Jonas plucked his hat from the hook by the door, tossed a salute her way, and went down the steps to her yard.

Anna Stolzfus and Rebecca Beachy, with Elizabeth Miller riding in the back, were pulling up to the hitching post as a second buggy pulled into the driveway. Rebecca hopped out and waved at Jonas when he tied the horse for her while Anna and Elizabeth carried several sewing kits into the house.

"Thanks, Jonas," Rebecca said. "Don't leave on our account."

"I just stopped by to discuss some business with Ruth, not realizing you all had plans." He looked at Ruth, who was hovering in the doorway. "I'll stop another day, Ruth. You all have a nice afternoon sewing. I'm afraid there are a few less cookies for you to eat than when I got here."

"That's a shocker," Rebecca laughed.

Jonas helped tie up the second buggy, driven by Mary Yoder with Jane Bontrager riding in the passenger seat. He then walked around to open the door for Mary and reached in to help her alight. Mary had been in a buggy accident as a child and had been lucky to regain any use of her legs. She walked with the aid of two crutches and carried her supplies in a clever backpack her stepfather had made out of sturdy leather. She worked for Jonas in his basket business, weaving intricate designs into baskets. She grinned at him as she climbed slowly from the buggy.

"Thanks, boss!" she said, accepting the crutches from Jane and turning toward the house.

"You're welcome, Mary!" Jonas said. Ruth watched from the kitchen door, thinking that her petite friend was the sunniest-natured woman she knew, in spite of living with what some would consider a heart-breaking disability. But Ruth knew Mary could put in a full day's work as well as most, and better than many.

A final buggy pulled up, containing Lydia, Katie Lapp, Miriam Zook, who was driving, and a young woman Ruth didn't recognize. She wondered who the stranger could be and watched as Jonas tied up the buggy and then helped the women out. The stranger gave him a brilliant smile, and Ruth could have sworn she batted her eyelashes at him.

"She's batting her eyelashes at him, the little flirt," Jane murmured in Ruth's ear. "Who is she?"

"I don't know," Ruth said, feeling an unreasonable dislike for the girl, considering she'd never met her. At that moment, Elizabeth, swinging a basket as she headed toward Ruth's back door, called out, "I have a new recipe I want to try out on all of you!"

Ruth watched as Jonas waved goodbye, climbed into his own buggy, and headed for the road. With a sigh, she closed the door and smiled at her friends.

"What did you make today?" Ruth asked Elizabeth as she welcomed everyone inside, including her unknown guest, a tiny, blond woman of about eighteen or twenty years.

Before Elizabeth could answer, Ruth's kitten suddenly came flying out from behind the potato bin—it had been more successful hiding there this time, Ruth thought with chagrin—and climbed with lightning speed right up Elizabeth's apron onto her shoulder, where it clung with sharp little claws as Elizabeth craned her neck and regarded it with alarm. "Ouch!"

There was a moment of silence in the kitchen, broken first by Lydia's delighted chuckle, before all the ladies began talking at once.

"I'm so sorry! I never know what he's going to do!" Ruth hurried over to remove the kitten from her friend's shoulder.

"Oh my goodness, he's just the same age as my new kitty!" Elizabeth cried, reaching out to stroke the fluffy mountaineer with a finger. "Only mine is a little tabby cat!"

"You too?" Miriam asked. "Mine looks just like a Holstein cow!"

One by one the others exclaimed about the kittens they'd just gotten. Finally, Mary looked at Lydia, who was smiling smugly at all the fuss.

"Lydia," Mary said softly, "did you give us each a kitten?"

"As it happens, Hephzibah gave birth this last time to ten kittens. And I wanted to be sure each of them went to just the right home. I've known all of you since you were bopplin, so I knew you'd be excellent partners for my babies. When I realized the number of my young friends matched perfectly with the number of my kittens, it seemed as if it was meant to be!"

"She made me promise to keep Blackie inside," Anna said. "My kitten is a little black one, in case the name didn't tip you off," she added with a little laugh.

"My mother thinks I've lost my mind, but I'm keeping my little calico inside," Mary admitted. "I'm living in the dawdi haus, since it seems unlikely I'll marry, so she isn't in anyone's way." At the exclamations of protest, she raised a hand. "No, I'm fine with it. And my parents won't want it for years probably, so I'm living there with my cat, Hope."

"Still, Mary," Ruth said, "you're only twenty-nine."

"And you're, what, thirty-three?" Mary said. "You could remarry."

"You know, it's funny that none of us are married," Jane said, looking around at her friends.

"Well, you're only twenty. You've got time," Ruth said.

"Yes, but who?" Jane asked.

"I thought you had your eye on that Samuel Mast, the buggy maker," Elizabeth teased. Ruth stiffened slightly at this—how odd to think that if Jane and Samuel married, and Samuel bought her farm, Jane could soon be the mistress of her home! She bit her lip. Hopefully she would be able to find a way to keep that from happening—as much as she liked Jane, she didn't want to give up her home.

"Ach!" Jane said with a grimace, interrupting Ruth's thoughts, "He is fine looking, and a gut man, but he doesn't seem interested," she said sadly. "He never talks to me."

"Do you ever talk to him?" Miriam asked.

"Well. . ." Jane hedged.

"Jane! Talk to him," Miriam said. "I happen to know he's terribly shy."

"I met him the other day, and he didn't seem shy to me," a voice piped up from the vicinity of the door. Ruth glanced over and saw that it was the strange young woman who had spoken up.

"I'm terribly sorry!" Ruth exclaimed, horrified at her bad manners. "Here we are all carrying on, and we haven't even introduced ourselves! I'm Ruth Helmuth, and this is my home," she said, smiling in welcome and extending a hand. The young woman stepped forward and shook Ruth's hand with a small smile.

"I know who you are. My grandfather told me all about you."

Ruth saw Lydia grimace but couldn't ask what was wrong. She looked back at her new guest and smiled again. "Really? Who is your grandfather?"

The young woman smiled smugly. "My grandfather is Bishop Troyer. I'm Evelyn Troyer. I'm visiting from New York for a few weeks. Grandfather mentioned that you're selling your farm and that Samuel Mast might buy it. And that he's looking for a wife!" The girl giggled. "Maybe I'll let him find one—me!"

There was a small distressed sound from Jane. Ruth looked at Lydia, who sent her an apologetic look, saying, "The bishop dropped by this afternoon with Evelyn, and mentioned she was here for a few weeks and wanted to meet young people. Naturally I invited her along tonight."

"Of course! I'm so glad you did. Your grandfather mentioned to me that you'd be coming, Evelyn, and asked me to be sure to include you in community events, so welcome to our little party!" Ruth squeezed Jane's arm, jolting her friend out of her momentary shock at hearing the stranger plotting to marry the man she'd admired for years.

Jane smiled gratefully at Ruth, recovering herself and, ignoring the impertinent younger woman, said, "What about you, Miriam? You're twenty-two, and you've had a crush on that Miller boy since school. What's his first name? Ah! David!"

"Your cousin, right, Elizabeth?" Ruth asked, relieved to turn the topic away from Samuel Mast and whom he might or might not marry. . .or where he and his hypothetical bride might live.

"Ja, but I haven't seen him in several years," Elizabeth answered.

"Since he moved away," Miriam said, nodding sadly.

The women were silent a moment. Declining to be baptized in the Amish church when he came of age, David Miller had instead decided to go live in a Mennonite community outside of Indianapolis, where he was working as a journeyman carpenter. Since he'd gone before being baptized, he could come home whenever he liked, but he didn't seem interested in returning.

"He writes his parents often," Elizabeth said. "He's a gut man. He just wasn't ready to promise to live by our church rules yet." Several of the women nodded. It could have been much worse—they all knew of young people who had gone quite wild during their running around, or *Rumspringa*, time. Some had gotten involved with drugs and alcohol, and a few had not been able to find their way back to a healthy way of living.

"Wait, he left the community? And you're still pining for him?" Evelyn snorted indelicately. "I don't know why you'd waste your time on a man like that."

"What do you know about it?" Miriam spat, stung at this unfair criticism.

Evelyn shrugged carelessly. "Nothing, really, except that I wouldn't want a man who turned away from our way of life. He should be shunned."

"He wasn't baptized!" Elizabeth came to the defense of her cousin. "He's living as a Mennonite. He didn't do anything to deserve shunning."

"That is sort of harsh, Evelyn," Mary said in her soft voice.

Evelyn frowned at Mary, who was seated at the kitchen table, her crutches leaning on the table's edge. "Well, I wouldn't want to risk displeasing *Gott* by breaking His laws, that's all," she said.

"Of course not, child," Lydia soothed, trying to defuse the growing tension in the room. "But David did not break any laws, as he left before being baptized. So all is well, and he can return if he likes. Your grandfather, the bishop, agrees." There were nods from the other women, and Rebecca spoke up, breaking an awkward silence, "And if he doesn't, someone else will catch your eye, Miriam."

"Ja, I suppose so," Miriam said.

"Maybe that handsome man who was here when we arrived! I'm looking forward to getting to know him a bit better," Evelyn exclaimed. "Who was he?"

Ruth felt another stab of jealousy, which she immediately squashed. She had no claim on Jonas, and if this girl caught his eye, who was she to stand in the way?

"That was Jonas Hershberger," Mary said. "I work for him. He's a widower with a small child, and he owns a basket-weaving business. Seeing as he was here this morning, I wonder if he's taken a shine to our Ruth?"

Evelyn's eyes narrowed meanly, and she spoke up loudly over the chitchat of the others. "I hope you weren't alone here with him. That would be very unseemly."

"Ruth is not a young girl, and her behavior is always above reproach," Lydia said, a bit sternly for her, Ruth thought. She tried to be ashamed of the pleased feeling it gave her when the girl frowned.

"Well, I'm just saying, we have to be careful of our reputations."

Lydia had evidently had enough of the growing hostility in the room. She clapped her hands briskly to gain everyone's attention. "None of you is exactly over the hill," she said. "I'll see you all married and raising bopplin yet! The kittens will be gut practice for you!"

"So, Lydia," Ruth said, sitting down near her friend, very willing to see the conversation turned in a new direction, "there are eight of us. If we each got a kitten, where are the last two? You said there were ten."

"Well," Lydia said sadly, "one didn't make it."

There were murmurs around the kitchen.

"Where is the last kitten?" Jane asked.

"Actually, I have her yet," Lydia said.

"So all of you have cats living inside your homes? That is so odd!" Evelyn said, shuddering. "They really aren't very hygienic, you know. And if they're living inside, that means they're going to the bathroom inside! Disgusting!"

Ruth frowned at the younger woman. "Can you smell my kitten's litter?"

Evelyn's nostrils flared as she inhaled deeply, and she seemed to consider the question. "Well, no, I can't, now that you mention it."

Ruth smiled at her and turned to the other women. "I thought we were here to make baby clothes?"

The morning flew by, with everyone, including the prickly new-comer, having a good time sewing and talking, and when they were done there was a complete wardrobe for each child, including diapers for the baby. They laughed when Ruth's kitten tried to sneak up on the table to sample a cookie.

"He wants my ginger snaps!" Elizabeth exclaimed.

"Oh, keep him off the table!" Evelyn cried, picking up her cookies and coffee to protect them from contamination. Ruth picked him up and set him gently on the floor, where he began batting at her shoelaces.

"What's his name, anyway?" Rebecca asked, gathering up her sewing supplies and placing them into a little wicker basket.

"I haven't thought of one that seems right yet," Ruth admitted.

"What! You've had him for days," Anna said. "I named Blackie right away."

"It sounds like it!" Katie said with a laugh.

"Oh, well." Anna laughed too. "It fits him."

"Say, what about Ginger Snap?" Elizabeth suggested, watching the kitten sniffing interestedly at an invisible spot on the floor. "He's the right color to pull off the name."

Ruth considered it a moment, then smiled. "I like it!" She picked up the kitten and looked into his golden eyes. "Are you Ginger Snap?" she asked. The kitten opened his mouth wide and issued a very loud "Yow!"

"Well! That's that, then!" Lydia said. "Ginger Snap has spoken!"

"It was such a surprise to me that this little boy fit right into my life, Lydia," Ruth mused, still holding her tiny kitten and stroking the velvety fur on his head with her finger. "I like the name too, Elizabeth. It fits him."

"Then Ginger Snap it is." Miriam laughed. "He's your little Ginger Snap Surprise!"

Ruth set her newly named kitty on the floor. As if showing off his new name, the kitten dashed under the stove and emerged with his little toy mouse, which he batted madly around the room. The women all giggled, and Ruth smiled at her friends. "Oh, he's full of surprises, all right!"

"Who ever heard of naming a cat after a cookie?" Evelyn wondered as she took her warm cloak from a hook by the door.

"I think it's perfect," Lydia said. "But that may be because I have a weakness for cookies!"

Outside, Lydia threw Ruth an apologetic look as she climbed up into the buggy, and Ruth winked at her. They'd discuss Evelyn Troyer and her uncensored opinions later.

Ruth waved as the ladies steered their buggies down the road, but as she turned to go back inside, her grandmother's old greenhouse caught her eye. It was covered with dead vines and looked forlorn and abandoned.

"I should do something with that building." She brushed a stray lock of hair out of her eyes as she regarded the mostly glass building her grandmother had used for growing seedlings. "Later. Right now, it's time for chores."

She'd only taken a few steps toward her barn when once again the sound of an approaching buggy caught her attention. Perhaps one of her friends had forgotten something?

But to her surprise it was Jonas Hershberger who turned into her driveway. What was he doing back so soon? For that matter, it occurred to Ruth to wonder what he'd stopped by for earlier—he'd said business, but she didn't know what he could mean.

He secured his horse to the hitching post before turning to greet Ruth, removing his hat, and running his hand over his hair. "Gut afternoon again, Ruth," he said. "I need to talk to you about something, if this isn't a bad time? I passed your friends on the road, so I thought I'd stop by since I knew you wouldn't still be entertaining."

"Oh. Of course not," Ruth said. On a sudden impulse, she turned toward the greenhouse. "I was actually just going to take a look at my *grossmammi's* old greenhouse. Would you like to go with me? I could use a second opinion on its condition."

"Sure," he said, and fell into step beside her.

"My grossmammi grew vegetables, houseplants, and herbs for sale, and started her garden plants in there every winter." She glanced at

Jonas as they walked. "But it hasn't been used in years. I doubt it's in very good shape.

"It's an interesting building. We'll soon see if it's sound." They made their way along a flagstone path to the greenhouse, which was really quite large. "So, I got to thinking the other day. . ." Jonas started to say, when, spotting them from where they were lying outside the barn, Wolke and Heftig ran over to check out what they were up to.

"Oh!" Jonas said, obviously startled. "Here are your polar bears!"

Ruth laughed and said, "They're really very gentle. Here, let's introduce you to them."

"If you think so," he said. Ruth turned and made a hand gesture, and the dogs dropped to their haunches. Jonas raised an eyebrow. "Wow. You've got them well trained."

"That was a must for them to be able to do their jobs. Wolke, Heftig, this is Jonas. He's a friend." They wagged their tails and looked between the two humans, tongues lolling, eyes bright with intelligence.

"Now hold out your hand, palm down, fingers curled under, and let them get your scent." He took a hesitant step forward and did as she said. The dogs sniffed his hand and wagged their tails politely but remained seated.

"Okay, now you can pat them on the head," she said. He looked unsure, and she impulsively took his hand in hers. She swallowed, surprised again at the shock of sensation resulting from the contact. She placed his hand, palm down, on Heftig's head. He stood for a moment, a look of uncertainty on his rugged face, and then moved his fingers in the dog's fur.

"Why, it's as soft as fleece!" he exclaimed. The dog wagged harder, and Wolke reached over and nudged Jonas with his nose, insisting on his share of the attention. Jonas tentatively scratched Wolke on his head. He relaxed a bit when neither dog seemed in the mood to have him for dinner. "They really are friendly, aren't they?"

"They really are. Shall we look at the greenhouse?" Ruth released the dogs from their sit, and the big animals sniffed their way up the path ahead of Ruth and Jonas, then danced around Ruth when she stopped outside the structure to look up at it with doubtful eyes.

"I haven't been in here for several years." She pushed open the door, which squeaked on its hinges, and she and Jonas entered into a large space which was warmer than the outside air. They stood for a minute, taking it in.

Jonas sifted his hand through some dry soil, down to the bottom of the tray which held nothing but crumbling, dead plants. "The trays still look good, if you look past the dead weeds."

"Yes, not bad," Ruth said, a bit surprised. She walked down one of the gravel pathways between stands of growing trays. "Look! There's a big woodstove in the back."

She could remember the smells of the woodstove mixed with rich earth and growing plants, the warmth of the sun coming through the windows, and the fun of digging into bags of soil and helping her grandmother plant seeds and transplant little seedlings.

"I used to love it in here."

"Then why aren't you using it?" Jonas asked, going over to try out one of the Levolor windows, which opened with long cranks to let out excess heat in the summer. It protested with a creak, but it opened.

"These still work," he said with a satisfied smile. "And the glass didn't fall out when I opened it. I think the old place is fine. A little oil, a bit of a cleaning, and you could use it again."

"And a lot of tearing vines off the outside!" Ruth said with a look up through the glass at the Virginia Creeper covering much of the glass roof. "Or no sun will be getting in here." But then she frowned.

"What are you thinking?" Jonas asked.

"Well, what would I grow?"

"You can think about it, now that the idea is in your head. And pray about it. I'll bet something will occur to you."

"Yes, that's a gut idea."

"I'll come back and check that stove for you another day," he told her.

Suddenly self-conscious, she shook her head. "That isn't necessary,

Jonas. I can call for someone out to check it."

"Remember, I was just saying the other day that I'd like to help you out around here, since you don't have family nearby? Don't make me look unneighborly, Ruth," he chided gently.

"Oh! I didn't mean to do that," she said, feeling a blush steal across her cheeks. "But I know you have your own business to run, and I don't want to take up your valuable time."

"Actually, that's what I wanted to talk to you about when I stopped by earlier."

Ruth was confused. "Your business?"

"Yes. My business, and how I think we can help each other out."

"Oh, right, I remember you said something to that effect the other day."

"Well, I thought and prayed about it, and I think it would work." He looked at her expectantly.

She giggled. "Maybe you should explain, since I can't read your mind?"

"Good grief, of course." He smacked himself on the forehead. "So, my business is doing very well. We're growing fast—too fast for the space we're currently occupying—a small barn on my property."

She was beginning to suspect his plan. "You make baskets, right?"

"Ja! And at the moment, we're overrun with supplies stacked all around the place. We don't have room to work. Let's go outside." He opened the door, and they stepped back out into the colder air and walked toward her barn.

"When you said you only use the ground floor of this big barn of yours, I got to thinking that with a little work, the upper floor might make a wonderful new home for my basket business. That way I have room to keep growing, my people won't be stepping on top of each other, and you'll be able to show the bishop that you're earning income from your barn." He smiled at her. "What do you think?"

"Let me be sure I understand. You want to rent my barn. . . ."

"Only the second floor."

"Right. The second floor. But it's just a big open space. How will that work?"

"We'll use a lot of the space unchanged, but our workspace will need to be closed in. So we'll frame out and drywall part of the space. It won't be hard."

She considered it. "I can picture it. It should work. But will my animals bother you downstairs? They can be loud. And they might smell funky."

"No way. We're all farmers. We like those sounds and smells."

She laughed. "Me too. Okay, so, let's look at the barn so you can be sure it'll work."

"I'm pretty sure. But let's take a look."

They walked in companionable silence up the ramp to the second story of the large red barn, and he opened the man door cut into one of the huge double barn doors, then stepped aside for her to enter first.

The interior of the barn was vast and mostly empty except for a couple of pieces of farm equipment Levi had parked there. "Oh, I forgot the plow was in here," Ruth said.

"No problem. There's much more room than we currently need." He wandered through dusty sunbeams across wide-plank oak floors, his eyes taking everything in as he silently plotted out the configuration of walls and ceilings he'd need to build.

"This is perfect. We'll build our work area in this corner. I'll put in a large workroom and a couple of smaller storage rooms for supplies that need to be in a climate-controlled area."

"How will you heat it?"

"I'll put in an outside wood burner. They're safer than having a woodstove inside, and they do a really good job of heating a space. In fact, if we put it between the barn and the greenhouse, we could heat both and forget about that big old wood burner in there."

She considered. "Maybe. I'm not sure about the expense just now."

"It won't cost you anything. I'll need to install it for my business, so you might as well take advantage of it."

"Jonas, what if things don't work out? If for some reason we don't get along or something, and you pull out. What happens to your improvements then?"

He shook his head. "You get to keep everything. That's how it works. I improve the space as I need, and pay you rent. If it doesn't work out, you can rent it to someone else or use it yourself."

"Just like that?"

He nodded. "Ja. But I'm betting we'll get along just fine, and you won't have to worry about it."

"So how would we proceed, if I agree to this?"

Jonas took off his hat and scratched his head, gazing into the distance. "Well, I'd need to assemble a crew, and we'd have to get supplies—drywall, lumber, an electrician to run some wires in the new walls, and a plumber for a small kitchen area and bathroom. It'll take me a couple weeks to get it all together. Then we'd come and knock it out in about a week. After that, it would just be a matter of moving the business from the old location to the new one, which would take a couple days. All told, if we agree to move forward on this, Hershberger Baskets could be up and running in your barn within about a month."

Ruth's eyes widened. "Wow, that's fast. But then, I don't suppose, once you've decided to move on something, there's any point in delaying, right?"

Jonas smiled. "Right."

Ruth thought about it for a few moments. It was a risk, sure, but wouldn't it be nice to have people around the place every day? She missed knowing that she would see another human face every day. Plus, she'd be utilizing more of her farm and bringing in new income. Maybe she'd look into buying a couple llamas with it, or even alpacas.

"Ja," Ruth said very softly, almost to herself. "And then Bishop Troyer will see that I'm utilizing my property and forget about his plan to make me sell out."

Jonas turned and looked at Ruth, a puzzled frown turning his well-shaped mouth downward. "What did you say?"

Ruth snapped out of her momentary reverie, embarrassed to realize she'd spoken the words aloud. "Oh, it's really nothing. Come, I'll show you downstairs where you can stable your horses when the snow is deep or it's too cold outside."

She hurried to a staircase leading down to the ground floor of the barn, and Jonas followed after her. She showed him around the area, presently empty of animals as they were all outside enjoying the mild day, and then they exited the big building through the first-floor door. Once they were outside, Jonas took her elbow to make her turn and face him.

"Hold up, Ruth, are you still worrying about Bishop Troyer trying to force you to sell out?"

She frowned at her feet, noticing that she'd soon need a new pair of everyday boots, as the toe was wearing out on the left foot of her current pair. "Oh, dear," she murmured. "I didn't mean to say anything. But yes, I can't seem to stop thinking about how he and the other church elders think I should sell my home and property to a man who wants to settle down and farm and raise a family. To Samuel Mast, in fact!"

Jonas regarded the big barn thoughtfully. "Samuel is a friend of mine, and a gut man, and I sympathize with his interest in your property. If you are interested in selling, he would be a gut one to sell to, as he'd take gut care of it all."

"But that's just it!" Ruth cried, throwing her hands up in the air and turning to walk briskly toward the house. "As I told you before, I'm not interested in selling! I couldn't believe it when Bishop Troyer suggested it!"

Jonas hurried to keep up with Ruth, who stomped up the steps to her kitchen and went inside. He followed, removing his hat inside the doorway and waiting for her to invite him to sit. She started to make kaffi and got out a tin of cookies, which she set on the table.

"Sit, sit! I'm sorry. This subject really has me upset. I've prayed but so far, I'm not sure what to do!"

Jonas hung his hat on a hook and took a seat at Ruth's table, saying nothing, just letting his own calm wash over her.

She took a deep breath and joined him at the table with two mugs of kaffi. She doctored hers, and he sipped his black. She handed him the cookie tin, and he helped himself to two delicious-looking oatmeal raisin cookies before she finally spoke again.

"That's not even all of it." She glanced up at him, blushing. "He proposed to me!"

Jonas' hand with his first cookie stopped halfway to his mouth. "He what?"

She nodded. "You heard me right. He said..." She swallowed hard, then continued. "He said since I probably can't have children, I could marry him, and neither of us would have to be alone, and I could enjoy his grandchildren. And he said he likes my cooking. It reminds him of his late wife's." Her eyes flooded with unshed tears, and she wiped impatiently at them.

Jonas handed her a napkin, which she took gratefully, dabbing her eyes and blowing her nose before laughing shakily. "You must think I'm being pretty silly."

"No, not at all. I'd be pretty upset if my bishop suggested I should sell my house so another man could farm my land and raise his family in my home." He regarded her seriously for a moment. "I imagine you know that when Viola died, there were those in the community who thought it was unseemly for a widowed man to raise a new baby. They put pressure on me to give Abigail up to another family to be raised."

She nodded, and he smiled humorlessly. "If not for my sister and her husband, who helped me through that time and promised to help me with Abigail, I might have caved in to pressure. And I would have regretted it for the rest of my life. So I understand holding on to what is yours. I understand very well."

She stared at him, aware that he'd given her a gift by trusting her with that private story. "Jonas, from what I've seen and heard, you are a very gut father. I'm glad things worked out for you."

"Denki, Ruth. I didn't mean to make this about me. I wanted to show you that I understand that sometimes you have to go against what others think is best for you. You know what is best for you better than anyone else."

Ruth gave him a watery smile. "Thanks. That helps."

He took a sip of coffee. "As for the rest of it, the bishop is a gut man. But he's lonely. And you really are a very gut cook! Still, if he wants to remarry, he should probably look at women closer to his own age."

"That's what Lydia said."

"She's wise. Listen to her."

She nodded. "I'll try. Meanwhile, to make matters even more interesting, the bishop's granddaughter is visiting from New York, and seems to be interested in both Samuel Mast and my home!"

Jonas frowned. "His granddaughter from New York wants to marry Sam?"

She shrugged. "Who knows? You actually met her. She was the young lady you helped down from the buggy earlier." Ruth glanced at him to see his reaction. Seeing none, she continued. "She told everyone that Bishop Troyer had told her I'm selling, and that Samuel is thinking about buying. And that he's looking for a wife. She said she might volunteer for the position."

"Huh. Your day was way more interesting than mine. I just sorted some inventory."

"It made one of my friends feel bad. She likes Samuel. But of course, she has no claim to him."

"Hmmm. It's a complicated situation, eh?"

"Ja! I know Miss Troyer is young, but I'm sorry to say she did not make a gut first impression on me and my friends today! She said several ill-considered things. And she has me feeling pretty un-Christian. I hate when that happens."

"Hmmm. You'd better pray about it." At her quick glare, he held up his hands. "I was joking! It'll work out. You'll see."

"That's what Lydia said."

Jonas looked thoughtful. "Ruth, back to the subject of selling. Just because you live here alone doesn't mean you have to sell out, or get married again, no matter who does the asking. And look at the bishop's proposal this way—it's a compliment."

Ruth gave a tearful laugh. "Ja! He wants me for my cinnamon rolls."

"Well, that's a perfectly legitimate reason to get married!"

She laughed again, and he reached out and covered her hand with his own, giving it a comforting squeeze. "Things have a way of working out, Ruth. Keep the faith."

She nodded mutely and stared at his large hand covering her smaller one, and after a few moments he pulled his hand away and stood. "Well, I'd better be getting back home."

Ruth followed Jonas outside. He glanced at the sky. "Storm's coming. Shouldn't amount to much, though."

She nodded and watched him untie Samson, climb into the buggy, and turn the horse before waving and heading down the driveway. When he turned onto the road, she sighed. Storm coming? Oh, there were so many possible storms on her horizon! Hopefully, with Gott's help, she'd be able to weather them all!

As for what they might amount to, well, she'd just have to wait and see.

———————————— ⚘ ————————————

Later that day, Jonas signed a delivery slip for a shipment of wood shakes. Sally stood next to him, checking off the boxes in the shipment against a packing slip.

"Where are we going to put all this?" Jonas muttered, frowning at the stacked boxes which filled the front of his workshop. "We barely found room for the last shipment."

Sally shrugged. "Gut question, big brother. That's why you make the big bucks. You're the one who has to figure out all the tough questions."

"You're right, little sister. I guess we'll have to ask Ruth Helmuth if we can store it in her big barn, since I've rented it from her and we'll be moving the business there next month anyway."

Sally's jaw dropped and she stared at her brother. "Are you serious?"

He grinned. "Ja! We came to an agreement today. That's where I went earlier. It'll be the perfect place for our business to grow."

Sally let out a loud whoop and threw herself at Jonas, who caught her in his arms. "Now you'll have to admit your older bruder is brilliant and deserves fresh baked apple pie for dessert tonight."

"You'll have the pie, but you may be pushing it on the brilliant part," she laughed, giving him a last squeeze before pulling away. "So, we'll be working over at Ruth's every day. Nice work! You get the big barn and you can talk to the pretty widow every day without raising any eyebrows."

"That was not my design," Jonas said, casting a stern eye at his sister, whose eyes were twinkling merrily.

"Maybe not, but it'll be a nice side benefit. Remember to ask Ruth if we can start storing materials in her barn, okay? Maybe we can have the next delivery sent straight there."

"I'll ask her tomorrow. Meanwhile, you make sure everything is here. That's what you get the medium bucks for, little sister." He tugged playfully on the string of her kapp.

"If I stick my tongue out at you, I'm afraid *Mam* will show up and chastise us both for reverting to childhood."

He grinned at that. "Well, if you don't stick your tongue out at me, I won't steal your kapp and ruffle your hair."

"Deal. I don't have time to fix it. Please don't forget to ask Ruth! If she says yes, she'll save us from having to suck in our bellies while we're walking around in here for the next month."

"Will do." He picked up the design for their newest basket and looked it over as she took her clipboard and started sorting through the delivery.

It didn't escape him that in order to ask Ruth about storing stock in her barn, he'd have to go see her. A win-win for him.

CHAPTER SEVEN

Over the next few days, Ruth spent so much time thinking about how to use her grandmother's old greenhouse that she barely registered what she was doing from one hour to the next.

"Maybe I should start garden seedlings for sale," she mused as she scrubbed out the trough in the barn. "But there are already two other greenhouses in the area doing that. So would there really be enough business for a third?" She rinsed the trough once more before filling it with fresh clean water. "Would people drive here to tiny little Willow Creek? Just to come to my greenhouse?"

"I think they would," a deep voice said from behind her. Startled, Ruth whirled around and saw Jonas smiling at her, those dimples of his catching her eye again. "But it might be a better bet to come up with something different, something that isn't already being done in the immediate area."

"Jonas!" she exclaimed, drying her hands on her apron. "I didn't hear you come in."

"You were busy talking to your goats," he teased, looking around at her herd.

"They say you don't need to worry unless they answer back, right?" she asked, a reluctant smile tugging at the corners of her mouth.

His eyes dropped briefly to that mouth, and she felt her smile falling away as confusion washed over her.

Jonas snapped his eyes back to hers. "So, are you going to introduce me?"

She looked around. "To the goats?"

"Ja, I already met the dogs outside. They didn't even try to eat me."

"I told you."

Across the barn, one of her Angora nanny goats bleated for attention, and Ruth walked over and scratched her head. "Say hello to Mildred."

He walked over and patted the goat. "Mildred?"

"Ja. She's my favorite nanny goat."

"Her hair is very soft. What breed is she?"

"She's an Angora."

"They aren't all the same breed, are they?"

"No, there are several different breeds, serving different functions."

"I recognize the Boers over there." He looked around and walked over to the pens holding her Nigerian Dwarf goats. "Some of these ladies are as wide as they are tall," he said, reaching in to scratch a goat on the head.

She laughed. "They're all pregnant, and as they've got a while to go, they'll get even wider before they're done."

"What about these beauties?" he asked, sounding truly interested.

"Those are my Nigerians."

"I've never heard of these. Some of them have amazing blue eyes."

"They're really gut milkers. Levi and I took months deciding whether to go with this breed. I took a class at the Ohio State University extension office and found out they produce a very high-quality milk with a lot of butterfat. It makes really gut cheese. That's what sold Levi—he loved cheese."

He nodded. "I remember now when you bought your first goats, some of the old timers around here thought you were *narrish*, going with that odd little breed. I thought if you and Levi had chosen it, it must be gut."

"Denki, Jonas. It's true, most cheese producers around here prefer Nubians or Saanens. But I haven't had any cause to regret my decision."

"Don't you have regular weekly orders to fill all summer for your cheese?"

"Ja, spring, summer, and autumn, as long as they're producing milk."

"Sounds like it was a gut decision, then. What breed is this?" Jonas asked, running his fingers through the hair on a fat, placid nanny.

"That's a Nigora. They produce wonderful fiber, and they're a cross between the Nigerian dairy goats I already had, and Angoras," she said. "Though I soon found out the Angoras are pretty, but they're hard to keep. Picky and fragile. But since Levi and I couldn't find a breeding pair of Nigoras, we decided to breed our own. So we went ahead and bought three Angora does, and bred them to Fat Harvey over there, my Nigerian buck."

"You started your own herd of a pretty new type of goat, then?" He whistled. "I'm impressed. Risky and bold. And it worked, because here they are!"

"Ja," she said, smiling as she looked around her barn. "Thanks to Fat Harvey. He's a trooper. And now I make extra money selling Nigora kids every spring, because I can't possibly keep them all."

"And they're hardier than the Angoras, right?"

"Ja, they are. So, as you see, I kept the Angora does for their fiber and to breed more first-generation Nigoras, and I do love them, especially Mildred, the imp, but I won't buy more of them once these three are gone."

"I don't think anyone else in the area breeds the Nigoras," Jonas commented.

"No, not yet. I've sold kids to people as far away as New Mexico and British Columbia. They'll catch on soon enough, I'm sure."

"Probably. But the point is, you had a vision of what you wanted to accomplish, and you pulled it off. You and Levi, it's true. But the goats were your thing, right?"

"Well, yes, but I couldn't have done it without his support."

"Maybe not in the beginning, but you're doing it all on your own now. Bishop Troyer should recognize the important contribution you're making to the agricultural scene, both locally and farther afield. And he should see that you're more than capable of making gut use of this farm and land. And of taking care of yourself, Ruth." He looked away, as if embarrassed by his impassioned speech.

"Denki," she said, pleased that this man, at least, was treating her like a competent adult.

He smiled. "You're welcome. So, when did you decide to add the meat goats?"

"Well, the milk and fiber goats were doing really well, so I suggested to Levi that we might do well to add the Boers. I knew it would be difficult to raise the cute animals and then sell them to market. But I grew up on a farm, and I'm careful not to become too attached to the meat animals. I keep around ten of them, as you see."

"How have you done with the not-getting-attached thing?" he asked, watching her scratch one of the little goats on the head.

"Mmmm, so-so," she admitted with a smile. "But I keep on trying!"

"So when did you get the polar bears?" he asked, straight faced.

She stared at him, and then comprehension hit. "Oh! Wolke and Heftig! I bought them with the first year's profits."

"You gave them interesting names. Imaginative."

"The male is Wolke, which is German for *cloud*, and the female is Heftig, German for *fierce*, which she always has been."

"How did you learn to train them?"

"A local sheepherder taught me. I spent hours working with them on commands, obedience, enemy recognition—actually, a lot of it is pretty instinctive."

"They're very gut dogs. It's obvious how much time you devote to them."

"They are, but they're outside animals. Not house pets like Ginger Snap."

"Ginger Snap?"

"Ja! I named my kitten!"

"And after one of my favorite cookies!"

"Mine too."

They grinned at each other, and he asked, "Are you going to church at the Beachys' Sunday?"

"Ja, of course."

"Will you stay for the singing afterward?"

She considered. "I suppose I could. Will you be staying?" she asked as casually as she could.

"Ja, my daughter, Abigail, and I enjoy the singing. We often stay, if it isn't too late when they start."

She nodded, thinking of his pretty little daughter.

"Maybe I'll see you there, then," she said. He nodded, and shortly after that, he climbed back into his buggy and turned toward home.

"Wait!" she called as he pulled away. "You still haven't told me what you came to talk about!"

"Oh, right! I've been trying to get back over here to ask you for several days, but we've been swamped. If you don't mind, I was wondering whether I could start moving some supplies into the back of the barn? We're bursting at the seams, and can do without some of our inventory until the move."

"Sure, that's fine. Move it in anytime. When will you begin construction?"

"Probably right after Christmas, at this point."

"Ach! Christmas is nearly here! I have so much to do."

"Don't we all? Well, I'll see you soon, Ruth." He tipped his hat and drove off down the driveway.

Despite her promise, Ruth did not show up to services at the Beachys' Sunday. Jonas was worried. He tried his best to sit still through the three-hour service, but when everyone began heading to the kitchen to load up their plates for lunch, he couldn't wait any longer.

He looked around the crowded room and saw his sister, with Abigail beside her, talking to Mary Yoder and the bishop's granddaughter.

What had Ruth said her name was? Evie?

"Jonas! You're just in time to meet Evelyn Troyer, visiting from New York for a few weeks," Sally said. Jonas glanced at the young girl, who was looking frankly back at him with large blue eyes.

"We met unofficially about a week ago at Ruth's." He politely touched the brim of his hat. The girl simpered—Jonas was sure that was the word for the expression on her face—and gushed with enthusiasm, "Oh, this is a wonderful community! So many handsome men. And is this pretty little girl yours? Oh, are you married?" She looked so obviously disappointed Jonas almost laughed. Sally stepped into what could have been an awkward moment, saying, "Jonas is a widower, Evelyn. This is his daughter, Abigail."

Abigail smiled. "It's nice to meet you, Miss Troyer."

Jonas was proud of his child. But then she acted her age, tugging on his sleeve and loudly telling her dat that she was starving, and couldn't they please eat?

"I'm sorry, Abby, but we need to leave. There's something I need to do. Sally, I'll see you at work tomorrow. Nice to meet you officially, Evelyn."

"Oh dear, what can be so important that you have to leave before lunch?" Evelyn asked as Jonas was taking Abigail's hand and turning away. Reaching for patience, he turned back and said, "A friend didn't come to services, and since she'd said she was coming, I'm a bit worried." Sally looked at him sharply and started to speak, but Evelyn quickly asked who his friend was. He couldn't think of a way to dissemble without outright lying, which he wouldn't do, so he muttered, "Ruth Helmuth."

"Oh, I know her!" Evelyn said. "I'll go along with you in case she needs a woman's help."

Jonas felt momentary panic at the thought, but Mary came to his rescue, putting her gentle hand on Evelyn's arm and saying, "Oh, Evelyn, that wouldn't be proper, a young girl like you riding alone with an older, unmarried man. Please stay and have lunch with us. I'm eager to hear about your home. I've never been to New York."

As he pulled Abigail toward the door, Jonas was sure he heard Evelyn complaining that all the handsome men were gone, and who was she going to sit with? The last thing he heard was Mary Yoder assuring the girl she could sit with her group of friends.

"I'm going to have to give Mary a raise," he told himself as he helped his daughter into the buggy.

"Why couldn't we eat before we left, Dat?"

"Sorry, Abby." He pulled onto the road and pointed Samson toward Ruth's farm. "I'm worried about Ruth Helmuth. She didn't come to services today, and she said she'd be there. I promise I'll get you lunch as soon as we check on Mrs. Helmuth, all right?"

Jonas was surprised at the magnitude of relief he felt when, turning into Ruth's driveway, he saw her making her way from the barn toward the house.

———————— ⚜ ————————

Shortly after 1:00 p.m., as Ruth left the barn finally confident that her pregnant goat Ethel was going to be okay along with her unborn kid, a buggy turned into the driveway. Ruth swiped the back of her hand across her forehead, peering toward the approaching vehicle, and groaned when she recognized Jonas through the windscreen.

"Perfect. I'm sweaty and smelly, and here comes Jonas." She stood waiting as Jonas climbed down from the buggy, then reached in to lift a small child from the vehicle. Ruth recognized his daughter, Abigail.

"Hello!" he called, walking toward Ruth with the child's hand in his. "When you didn't come to church, we got worried, so we decided to stop by on our way home and make sure you were all right."

"Oh! Yes, I'm fine, denki," Ruth said, wiping her dirty hands on her apron. "One of my goats took ill this morning, and I had to stay home and tend her."

"Your goat is sick? Will it be okay?" the child piped up.

Ruth smiled down at the little girl, whose sunny hair peeked out from under her crisp Sunday kapp. "Ja, denki, she'll be fine."

She stood regarding her unexpected guests, wondering whether to invite them in, when Jonas said, "Well, that's gut, then. We were worried, so we wanted to make sure."

"Dat, I wasn't worried. You were, remember? I wanted to eat lunch, but you said we had to leave right away and check up on Mrs. Helmuth."

Ruth had never before seen Jonas blush. "Um, well...you said you'd be there, so when you didn't come, I thought maybe something had happened to you," he muttered.

Ruth smiled. "Ah. So, then you two haven't had any lunch?"

"No! And I'm hungry. There was gut food after services. My tummy is grumbling."

"Abigail. Don't be rude," Jonas said quietly, and the child's face took on a comical expression that mixed contrition with stubbornness.

Ruth took pity on her. "Well, if you don't mind that I smell like a goat barn, I could probably put together a couple of sandwiches."

"Dat! Could we stay?" Abigail looked beseechingly at her father, who still had high color riding on his cheeks.

"I'd enjoy the company. And you can tell me about services, since I missed out today."

"Well, okay then, denki," Jonas said.

They followed Ruth inside, Abigail chattering to her as they entered her warm kitchen.

"Oh, it's so pretty in here!" Abigail exclaimed, looking around with wide eyes. "Look, Dat! The place mats are so nice! Did you make them, Ruth?"

Ruth looked at the blue-and-white quilted mats that she had made a few years before to go with her pretty blue dishes. "I did, yes, and thank you."

Jonas looked a bit embarrassed. "We don't have a lot of pretty things, I guess."

"That doesn't really matter," Ruth said. "Pretty things aren't important. A loving home and family are what matter. After all, we are supposed to be plain people."

He nodded and smiled. "Ja, that's true. Sometimes I forget that in the day to day."

"Still, pretty things are nice too," Abigail said with a serious expression. Ruth nodded in agreement. "Ja, I think they lift the soul." As Ruth scrubbed the grime off her hands, Abigail said, "There was a new lady at church today! She was pretty."

"Ja?" Ruth asked, taking sandwich makings from the propane-powered refrigerator and setting them on the counter.

"Ja, it was Bishop Troyer's granddaughter, visiting from New York," Jonas said. "I believe you've had the pleasure of meeting her already?"

Ruth shot him a look to see if he was teasing, but he gazed back at her innocently. "Yes, I have. I believe you met her yourself when she was here just the other day."

"Why, yes, now that you remind me, I recall that," Jonas said, laughter in his eyes. "But today I had an official introduction. She was very happy to attend services today and to hear her grandfather speak. She was disappointed that some of the young men are away on a mission trip, though."

"Oh? Such as Samuel Mast, maybe?" Ruth asked.

"I believe his name did come up."

"But she liked you, Dat," Abigail pointed out helpfully. "She was sad we weren't staying for lunch. I heard her tell Mary Yoder that she was going to sit with you, and hoped I'd sit with Mary."

"Did she?" Jonas asked, smiling at Ruth as she placed a sandwich she'd cut into small triangles in front of Abigail, who dug in eagerly.

"Ja," she said around a mouthful of sandwich, "but before Mary could answer, you said we were leaving."

"Hmmm, don't talk with your mouth full, Abby," Jonas admonished. "She did offer to come along and make sure you were fine, Ruth," he added with a teasing gleam in his eye.

"How nice," Ruth said, biting into her own sandwich.

"I thought so," he said. "Obviously a mannerly girl."

Ruth snorted, and they talked of other matters, of people they knew, and about the speakers in service that day. After lunch, Ruth thanked Jonas and Abigail for stopping to check on her and was about to wave them on their way when Ginger Snap bounded into the kitchen.

"Dat! A kitten! An orange kitten!" Abigail sat on the floor in her coat and bonnet and coaxed Ginger Snap into her lap. He purred loudly as the little girl petted him gently on his head, and he made her laugh when he batted at her bonnet strings.

"Oh, Dat! Isn't he funny? I wish, wish, wish we had a kitten of our own!" She hugged him a bit too hard, and the kitten squeaked and slipped out of the little girl's arms and scampered away to check out his food bowl.

"Whoops, don't squeeze the kitty too hard, Abby," Jonas admonished.

"I'm sorry, I didn't mean to hurt him," the child said, looking tragic with big tears filling her eyes.

Ruth knelt down before her and gave her a hug. "Nonsense. You didn't hurt him. Just remember to be gentle, like you would with a *boppli*, okay?"

The child gave her a watery smile and wiped her nose with the back of her hand. "Okay," she sniffed.

"Time to go, Abby." Jonas scooped his child up in his strong arms and carried her out to their buggy.

As she watched them disappear down the road, Ruth reflected that the interlude had felt like a family lunch. She was very comfortable with Jonas, except when he made her very uncomfortable. And his daughter was a clever little sweetheart. She rubbed her chest over her heart as she turned to go inside and clean up the lunch dishes. There was a lonely little ache there, and part of her wished Jonas and Abigail had stayed longer. Maybe forever?

CHAPTER EIGHT

Monday passed in chores, and on Tuesday Ruth decided to take another look at the greenhouse. As she was bundling up to go outside, Ginger Snap wound around her ankles and meowed loudly.

"Do you want to go with me, you little darling?"

A loud "Rowr!" seemed to confirm her interpretation of the kitten's demands, so she laughed and scooped him up and headed out the kitchen door. She greeted Wolke and Heftig when they ran up to see what she was doing, and Ginger Snap hissed at the dogs, who wagged their tails and butted Ruth with their big square heads but eyed the little orange fluff ball with doubt and decided to keep their distance from his sharp claws. They were no strangers to cats.

Once inside the greenhouse, she closed the door firmly behind her, then placed the small cat down on one of the growing trays. She stood looking around, unwinding her scarf as she absorbed the trapped warmth of sunshine.

She wandered over to the old cash register and noticed a couple hooks on the wall. "Handy." She shrugged off her cloak and hung it and the scarf on a hook, then poked a couple buttons on the machine. The drawer opened with a clatter, and Ruth saw that there were a few quarters inside and a couple packets of old seeds.

She picked up the seed packets and smiled: zinnias, marigolds, snapdragons, chrysanthemums. How she loved flowers! Especially the traditional, old-fashioned ones. They were so cheerful. Nothing brightened a yard like a row of sunflowers turning their heads all day long to follow the progress of the sun through the sky. And tall, colorful zinnias standing guard over a thick row of fragrant orange and yellow marigolds always made her happy.

As a girl, she'd loved squeezing the sides of snapdragons to make their mouths open wide. And in the fall, gold and russet mums looked lovely bordering a hedge, walkway, or driveway, or vying for space inside big pots on a porch. And they came back year after year, growing ever larger if one was careful to choose a hardy variety.

Ruth stilled as a thought formed in her mind. Chrysanthemums. Hardy mums would overwinter in a farm field. Old Mrs. Atkins, an *English* woman in Sugarcreek, used to grow a large field full every year, and people would come from miles around to dig their own mums. Mrs. Atkins had been famous for her healthy, strong flowers, guaranteed to make it through a frigid Ohio winter and come back bigger and better year after year.

"Mums!" she whispered. "I could start them in here in the winter and move them outside after the last frost."

There were actually two fields where she could plant the flowers. Maybe she'd only harvest one the first year, and then the second year the other field would be filled with larger flowers, for which she could charge more. And she could then rotate the fields, always having a second-year crop to harvest after the first year.

The idea grew in her mind.

"I have to talk to somebody about this! I'll go see Lydia. She'll be home this morning." Ruth returned Ginger Snap to the house, shaking a few kitty treats onto the floor before hurrying out to the barn to harness her mare, Buttercup. A former racehorse like many Amish horses, she was a palomino, and the name suited her.

"Are you up for a little drive, girl?"

The horse nickered, and Ruth guided her out of the barn and hitched her to the single-seat buggy she kept.

Buttercup moved out smartly, trotting down the road toward Lydia's farm. Soon Ruth was tying Buttercup to Lydia's hitching post.

The kitchen door opened, and her friend stood there in a pretty blue dress, drying her hands on a dishcloth.

"Guder mariye!" Lydia called. "What a nice surprise! I was just about to take a break for kaffi and cookies. I hope you'll join me?"

"I will!" Ruth said, hurrying up the steps to give Lydia a hug. They went into the house, and Ruth hung her cape and outdoor bonnet on hooks by the door and took a seat at Lydia's table.

"Well, what brings you out today? I haven't seen you since your work party. By the way, I heard that the Johansen family were very happy with the little clothes and things we sewed that day."

"I'm glad to hear it!"

"What did you think of the bishop's granddaughter?" Lydia asked with a sidelong glance at her young friend.

Ruth sighed. "Lydia, I think she's very young."

"She is that, but I'm afraid her unguarded way of speaking is going to create trouble for her."

"I wouldn't be surprised. She upset Jane and Miriam that day."

"Hmmm. She caused a stir at services Sunday too."

"I heard a bit about that too." Ruth frowned. "Fortunately, it isn't our problem, right?"

"You've never been much of a gossip, Miss," Lydia said. "Which is as it should be. We'll hope she does better as she settles in here, or the bishop may have his hands full, and no woman in his house to guide her."

Just then, Hephzibah wandered into the kitchen, accompanied by a tiny white kitten with blue eyes. "Oh! Is this the famous kitten that you're holding in reserve for a mysterious recipient?"

"Ja, that's her."

Ruth scooped the baby up and stroked her soft head with a gentle finger, making the kitten squeeze her eyes closed and purr loudly. "Not to change the subject, but I've had an idea that might allow me to keep my property."

Lydia reached out to pat Ruth's hand. "Ruth, no one can make you leave your property. It's up to you whether to stay or sell out. The bishop is just making a suggestion."

"That's what Jonas said, but I still feel as if I'm defying him, Lydia!" Ruth said. "I guess I'm used to doing what my elders tell me." Concentrating on the kitten, Ruth missed Lydia's raised eyebrow at her mention of Jonas.

"Well then, do what this elder tells you and stop worrying about this. It'll all work out as the Lord intends. Good grief, it isn't as if you don't utilize that property, what with all those goats you raise and your kitchen business. Now, pour us some kaffi, and then tell me your big idea."

Ruth jumped up and poured them each a mug of coffee and, at Lydia's direction, got out some cookies baked just that morning.

"So, by Jonas, I'm guessing you mean Jonas Hershberger? You've been talking with him about your situation?" Lydia asked casually, taking a sip of hot coffee.

Ruth looked surprised. "Oh! Did I mention Jonas?" She tried for an offhanded tone, but Lydia knew her too well. The older woman raised an eyebrow, and Ruth smiled sheepishly.

"Okay, yes, we've been talking a bit, but that's all, Lydia, just talking. So don't go reading anything more into it."

"I wouldn't dream of it! Although he is a very nice young man, if you want my opinion," Lydia opined. "And he has such a beautiful child! The poor, motherless waif." At Ruth's exasperated look, she smiled innocently and said, "You were going to tell me about your idea?"

Ruth took a deep breath and told Lydia all about her idea for growing mums in the fallow fields last used by Levi to grow food crops.

Lydia listened carefully and then nodded decisively. "I think this is a very gut idea, and well thought out."

"You do?"

"Well, yes! You're a gut businesswoman, Ruth. You've run your goat herds for years now, and you make a profit. Why wouldn't I believe in an idea of yours?"

Ruth jumped up and hugged her friend.

"Well, now," Lydia said, pleased. "That's enough of that. Come, let's talk of practicalities. If you're going to get this off the ground—or in the ground, so to speak—you'll need to move fast. It's nearly Christmas, and you'll need to order seeds, and learn about fertilizer, and just everything. You'll need catalogs!"

Ruth was filled with happiness. Perhaps the bishop wouldn't agree that this was a gut idea. But she thought it was, and Lydia did, and Jonas did. And for now, that was enough.

CHAPTER NINE

Two weeks had passed since she'd had to miss the biweekly Sunday services, and this time no sick goat would keep Ruth from attending. It was her gelding Tom Sawyer's turn to pull the buggy the short distance to the Yoder farm. Once there, she grabbed the large pot of corn chowder and the pan of cornbread she'd made for the meal that would follow the service, and she headed for the house where she was greeted by her friend Mary Yoder.

Mary waved Ruth over to the kitchen door with a broad smile. "Guder Mariye, Ruth! I hope that's your corn chowder. Yours is the best in the county."

"It sure is—my chowder, that is! I don't know about it being best in the county, but denki!" Ruth placed the soup on an empty spot on the stove just as Edie Yoder, Mary's mother, bustled into the kitchen from outside, carrying two pies. "Ach! Ruth, take one of these pies Mrs. Stoltzfus just brought. She's right behind me with two more."

The door opened again, and stout Mrs. Stoltzfus, the acknowledged baker of the best raisin pies in the area, came in, red faced.

"Here are two more, Edie!" she called. "There you are! Ruth, my girl, take these as soon as you have free hands and put them in the pantry. Denki! Denki! Now I'd better sit down and rest a few minutes. A body gets tired faster than it used to!"

She carefully set her pies on the Yoders' kitchen table and took a seat, fanning herself with her hand. The door opened again, and Jonas pushed in carrying a case of soda in a wooden crate, followed by Abigail, who was lugging a six pack with both hands.

"Dat and I got soda at Orme's!" the little girl exclaimed excitedly. "It comes in lots of different flavors!"

"What a treat!" Mrs. Stoltzfus said. "My Joe loves the Zombie Grape best. I like it too, but I usually can't get a bottle before Joe drinks them all up!"

Jonas smiled and set the case of soda down in the corner of the kitchen and placed a bottle of Zombie Grape in front of the woman, who exclaimed in delight. Jonas' sharp cornflower-blue gaze, so like his daughter's, landed on Ruth, who was standing by the stove stirring her corn chowder. Smiling widely, he took a step toward her, and the kitchen door opened, admitting Evelyn Troyer, who carried a pie covered in a piece of cheesecloth.

"Hello! I've brought my famous raisin pie!" She bustled over to the table, where she made room for her offering by stacking one of Mrs. Stoltzfus's pies on top of the other. Mary gasped, but Mrs. Stoltzfus, casting a withering glance at the bishop's granddaughter, picked up her pies and handed them to Ruth, who hurried to take them from her. "I'll just put these in the pantry, Mrs. Stoltzfus."

"Thank you, dear," Mrs. Stoltzfus said. Turning to Evelyn, who seemed oblivious to her faux pas, she said, "I'm sure you didn't realize you were crushing my famous raisin pies, dear."

"Hmmm?" Evelyn, who was staring at Jonas, turned to Mrs. Stoltzfus and, seeing Ruth carrying her pies, said, "Oh, sorry, ma'am. I guess I'm so excited to be here, I wasn't thinking. Hello, Jonas! I hope you'll have a piece of my raisin pie. My grandfather the bishop says it's the best in two states!"

Mrs. Stoltzfus sat back, looking somewhat sour, and Jonas said, "Oh, well, I'd enjoy that, Evelyn, along with a piece of Mrs. Stoltzfus' raisin pie! I'm a lucky fellow to have two bakers of my favorite pie here today."

Ruth returned from the pantry. "The pies are fine, Mrs. Stoltzfus."

"What a gut, considerate girl you are, Ruth," the older woman said. "Jonas, did you know Ruth brought her delicious corn chowder?"

"Ach, I'm likely to eat too much today!"

Feeling uncharacteristically shy, Ruth smiled. "It was one of Levi's favorites, and it's easy to make, so. . ." She stopped talking, thinking she sounded like a ninny.

But Jonas didn't seem to notice. "We'll have to be sure to be near the front of the line or we might not get any, Abigail."

The child smiled up at Ruth with shining eyes.

"I like corn chowder," she said. "My maem used to make it."

"I've told her a lot about Viola," Jonas explained.

Ruth smiled at the pretty child. "I remember," she said. "Your maem's chowder was right tasty."

"For sure and certain it was!" Mrs. Stoltzfus exclaimed with a firm nod and a sideways glance at Evelyn.

Not to be outdone, Evelyn stepped over to Jonas and Abigail and said, "Well, maybe your dat will get married again soon, and you'll be able to try someone else's cooking. Wouldn't that be nice?" She smiled sweetly at Jonas, who stared back, as if at a loss for a reply.

"It's almost time for service! We'd better finish up here or we'll keep the bishop waiting," Edie Yoder interjected, ending the awkward moment.

Ruth was relieved that Mary's maem had interrupted before she found herself saying something she'd probably regret to the impertinent young miss.

"The elders just now went in to meet, so we have a bit of time yet," Jonas said.

"Dat, who am I sitting with today?" Abigail asked.

"That's right, your grosseldre and your Aunt Sally aren't here today," he said, looking stumped.

Evelyn took Abigail's hand and said, "She can sit with me! I'm very gut at modeling proper behavior for *kinner* in services."

Ruth found herself surprised yet again by the girl's boldness and wondered how Jonas would react. Evelyn was, in her opinion, both too young and too brash to interest Jonas. But she was pretty enough, so who knew?

"Oh, well, that's very kind of you, Evelyn," Jonas began, when Abigail pulled her hand from Evelyn's and took Ruth's instead.

"I want to sit with Mrs. Helmuth, Dat!" she said, smiling sweetly at a surprised Ruth.

"That's a smart girl," Edie said. "She figures she'll be more likely to get some of that corn chowder that way!" The woman laughed and took off her kitchen apron and hung it on a peg.

Jonas looked slightly embarrassed. "Would it be okay if Abigail sat with you, Ruth? She's a gut girl, and knows to sit quietly during service. And I'll be close if she needs me. If not, Selma is probably here, and Abigail could sit with her."

"Ja, of course she can sit with me." Ruth smiled at the child, who grinned back, displaying dimples much like her dat's.

Evelyn frowned but quickly recovered, saying, "I'll sit with you both, since I feel as if we're already friends, Ruth."

Ruth could only nod, and Evelyn smiled triumphantly.

The door opened, and a young boy poked his head into the kitchen. "The elders are returning, time to go be seated! They told me to tell you," he said, then bobbed his head respectfully and left again.

"Well!" Mrs. Stoltzfus pushed to her feet with a groan. "Time to go, then. We'll come back during the last hour and help you finish getting ready," she told Edie. They walked to the Yoders' large barn, where rows of backless wooden benches had been set up for services, and took their places, Jonas on the men's side, the women on the ladies' side.

Once they were seated, Ruth between Edie and Abigail, with Evelyn on the child's other side, Ruth peeked toward the men's side and saw Jonas looking back at her and his daughter. He smiled and nodded, and Abigail, knowing how to behave in services, smiled quietly back and folded her hands primly in her lap. Ruth smiled uncertainly as well, then turned her attention to the service, enjoying the songs they sang from the *Ausbund* and the messages delivered by the ministers who took their place at the front to preach Gott's word. She sighed peacefully. She truly enjoyed church and the message of Gott's love she was able to hear and absorb each week, always noticing new ways it applied to her own life. Holding tightly to the living hope of salvation while accepting whatever came as Gott's will, as was the Amish way, had helped her through some very hard times.

Then a small hand slipped into her own, and she glanced down to see Abigail smiling sweetly back up at her, and she felt, somehow, more complete than she had before, even if it was only for a couple of hours. Smiling, she glanced over Abigail's head and found Evelyn glaring at her. Taken aback, Ruth returned the girl's look calmly before returning her attention to the front of the room. She had no time for silly behavior of that sort. But she could feel Evelyn's jealous regard from time to time throughout service. It was. . .disconcerting.

————————— ⚓ —————————

Jonas couldn't help taking his attention from the preaching to look at his daughter sitting with Ruth. They made quite a picture, he thought— the confident young widow sitting straight and slender on the bench, holding the hand of the small, delicate blond child snugged up next to her. As he watched, he saw Ruth glance sidelong at his daughter, a look of gentle wonder and sadness flitting across her face.

She wants a child! The realization, as obvious in retrospect as it might seem, hit him like a board upside his head.

Ruth wanted to be a mother. It was the one thing, it seemed, that she hadn't been able to have with her beloved Levi.

Was it too late for her to realize this most basic of maternal dreams?

Ruth and Abigail look so natural together, he thought. Almost like a real mother and daughter.

For a moment, gazing across the room instead of paying attention to the service, he allowed himself to imagine he, Abigail, and Ruth were a family. It felt like a gut fit. And what if she couldn't have any more kinner? Would that bother him? He frowned. He would like more children, perhaps a *sohn* to help on the farm and to pass the basket business to—and because he loved being a vader. But if it wasn't in Gott's plan, he thought he'd be all right with that.

At that moment, Ruth happened to glance over and caught him staring. Her eyes widened a bit, and he smiled at her. She smiled back, then quickly looked away.

Maybe. . .

Then Evelyn Troyer, seeing Ruth sneak a peek at Jonas, turned to smile at him too. But her smile made him uneasy. Jonas sighed. He was probably going to have to set that girl straight about his intentions before long. He glanced back at Ruth and was just about to turn his attention toward the speaker, where it belonged, when old Benjamin Bontrager, seated to his right, nudged him.

"Eyes, front, Sohn," the old man said, smiling knowingly at Jonas. "She's pretty enough, but you're here for the service. Time enough for romance later."

Jonas nodded at the old man and turned his eyes forward, wondering which young woman he thought was "pretty enough." He hoped nobody else had heard Benjamin's teasing remarks—that would be all he needed! One more quick glance showed Ruth, Abigail, and Evelyn looking at the speaker. Jonas schooled himself to pay attention. Benjamin was right—time enough for whatever he might be beginning to feel for Ruth later.

———————— ⚓ ————————

Ruth and the other women who had promised to help Edie Yoder prepare the meal slipped quietly out after the second hour of the three-hour service, and Abigail went with them. Evelyn stayed behind, accompanying the men into the kitchen after services.

Ruth made certain that both Abigail and Jonas got generous bowls of her chowder, and after serving the other members of the church, she took a seat at a long table set up in the Yoders' basement and enjoyed a bowl along with a piece of Mrs. Stoltzfus' delicious raisin pie.

"That looks gut!" Jonas said, sitting down beside her with his plate piled high with good things to eat.

"*Ach, ja*, it is," she said, eyeing his plate. "Didn't you just eat an entire bowl of my soup?" she asked, astonished at how much food he planned to put away. "And do you have two pieces of raisin pie?"

"Ja." He smiled sheepishly. "But I'm a hardworking man, and I have to keep up my strength! Besides, you know I had to take two pieces of raisin pie to avoid offending anyone. I'm only being a gut nochber."

"Mm-hmm, of course." She grinned. Then she savored her pie while Jonas ate everything on his plate.

"Here, try a bite of Evelyn's raisin pie too," he said, forking up a piece and holding it up to her lips. She had no choice but to open her mouth and accept the offering. It melted on her tongue, the flavors complementing each other, the crust flaky and delicious.

"That is excellent," she remarked. "I thought she was kind of young to be famous for her pie, but after tasting it, I have to accept the possibility." Just then, she looked up and saw Evelyn staring at them, an odd expression on her pretty, young face.

Always fair-minded, Ruth steeled herself and said, "Evelyn, your raisin pie is very, very gut. It melted on my tongue, and the crust is one of the best I've had."

Evelyn looked surprised but then smiled a little. "Denki, Ruth. It was my mudder's recipe. I've made it since I was a girl. Sometimes, when I miss her especially, I make it to feel close to her."

Ruth found herself sympathizing with the younger woman, and smiled. "Ja. I understand. This chowder was my grossmammi's recipe. It makes me feel as if she's here when I make it."

Evelyn nodded and then looked at Jonas. "I see you had some of my pie too, Jonas. What did you think of it?"

"It was gut," Jonas told her truthfully.

She smiled with pleasure. "As gut as Mrs. Stoltzfus'?"

"Ja, I'd have to say so, but don't tell her, please! You'll go back to New York, and I don't want her refusing to give me any pie!"

"Maybe I don't have to go back to New York," Evelyn said, smiling coyly at Jonas. "My husband will have my pies every night."

Ruth gritted her teeth and regretted the moment of sympathy she'd felt for the girl.

"Are you going to stay for the singing?" Abigail asked, pulling on Ruth's apron and distracting her from Evelyn's bold comment.

"Abigail. Don't pull on Mrs. Helmuth," Jonas chided his daughter.

"It's all right," Ruth said. "I don't know... I thought I'd head home soon," she told Abigail.

"We are staying, aren't we, Dat?"

"Well, I thought we might," he said. "Just for a while. I do love singing."

Evelyn said, "Oh, Ruth, don't you have to go take care of your sheep?"

Mary Yoder, who had taken a seat with their group, rolled her eyes and said, "Evelyn, Ruth has goats, not sheep."

Evelyn waved her hand as if it were no consequence. "They all smell bad, if you ask me."

Ruth looked at the younger woman, a small smile tugging at the corner of her mouth. She did need to milk her goats, and Ginger Snap would be getting up to mischief, of that she had no doubt. But...there couldn't be harm in staying another hour or so. And she was big enough to admit to herself that the fact that it would irritate Evelyn was a bonus. The girl was starting to get on her nerves. She'd have to pray about it later.

"Okay, I'll stay an hour. Then I have to go milk my sheep," she said. Mary chuckled, and Jonas shook his head at her silliness.

"Gut!" Abigail said, bouncing in her seat. Jonas also looked pleased.

Evelyn did her best to hide a scowl. "Oh, gut! We'll have such fun!"

"It's almost time for the singing!" Abigail cried, tugging on Jonas' hand. "Let's go get gut seats."

"You two go ahead. I'll be there in a minute," Ruth promised.

"We'll save you a seat," Abigail said, leading her father across the room to where the singing would take place. Ruth turned to ask Mary if she'd like to join them.

"That would be nice." Mary smiled. Evelyn narrowed her eyes at the evidence of Ruth and Jonas' friendship and said, "I suppose Jonas is looking for a second wife and a mother for his child. I might consider him, since he owns his own business and has a nice big house."

Before Ruth could say anything, Mary, usually the most even tempered of all her friends, turned and looked at Evelyn with distaste. "Whether Jonas is considering marrying again is none of your business, Evelyn. And if he is, I assure you he'll be looking for a woman who can be his equal partner, not a spoiled girl who doesn't understand boundaries and has no regard for gut manners."

Ruth's mouth dropped open in surprise. Evelyn's eyes filled with angry, embarrassed tears, and she turned and fled the room. Ruth looked after her, unsure whether she should follow the girl, but a hand on her arm stayed her impulse. She looked over and was surprised to see Bishop Troyer standing by her side. "I'm sorry, Ruth. My granddaughter speaks before she thinks. I'll take her home. You two enjoy your evening." He walked slowly out of the room, and Ruth stared after him, biting her lower lip.

"Now don't waste any sympathy on that girl, Ruth," Mary admonished. "And don't go feeling guilty. I refuse to, and I was much ruder than you!"

Mary pushed to her feet, picked up her crutches, and slung her backpack over her shoulder. "Too bad the bishop had to hear, but I doubt he heard anything that surprised him. Come on, let's go sing."

Ruth and Mary walked over to join their friends, Ruth considering whether Jonas might be actively looking for a second wife.

For some reason, the idea of Jonas finding a new mother for Abigail seemed depressing to Ruth.

Abigail turned and called to her, "Come on! You're going to miss the first song!"

Jonas looked at her helplessly as she sat down beside him. "I'm afraid being raised by a bachelor is turning her into a hoyden."

"No, she's fine, just high-spirited and eager," Ruth said, looking at the child fondly.

She turned to Mary, seated on her other side by the aisle. "Are you sure you're all right? I hardly ever see you get angry," Ruth whispered.

Mary nodded. "Ja. It's just that the girl has no boundaries. I'm sorry if I embarrassed you."

"Ha! You said what I was thinking. So I guess we're both heartless."

Mary reached out and squeezed Ruth's hand, and Ruth felt the glow of happiness warm her. She was a fortunate woman. She had gut friends and a gut life. Was she greedy to want more? Glancing at Jonas and Abigail, she knew that she did want more. She just wasn't sure it was all right to want that, especially in her situation.

It wasn't long before a strong voice began a song and was quickly joined by other voices raised in praise to God.

Ruth enjoyed the way Jonas' rich tenor harmonized easily with the other voices. Abigail's sweet, childish soprano lilted along with the adults.

They sang song after song, many in four- and sometimes eight-part harmony, until they were growing hoarse, and Edie Yoder came into the barn and clapped her hands. "You all sound so gut!" She beamed. "Now come have some coffee and dessert. You must have worked up another appetite with all that pretty singing!"

Ruth, Jonas, Abigail, and a few other friends sat down in the living room with their food.

"That was gut singing!" said Rebecca Beachy, who had a piece of rhubarb pie on her plate.

"Rhubarb!" cried Mary Yoder, making her way in from the kitchen with Mrs. Yoder following, carrying her plate. "I didn't see that!"

"That's because I took the last piece," Rebecca said with a smile, forking a bite into her mouth. "Better luck next time!"

At that moment, a little calico kitten with long beautiful fur wove her way into the room and twined around Mary's ankles.

"Oh! Look at the kitty!" Abigail said, putting her plate down on the coffee table and dropping onto the floor at Mary's knee.

"May I hold her?" the child asked.

"Looks like you may!" Mary laughed as the kitten climbed onto Abigail's lap, purring, and kneaded her tiny claws on the little girl's dress.

"Ouch!" Abigail said, picking the kitten up. "You have sharp claws!"

"What a cute kitten," Ruth said. "She must be the one Lydia gave you?"

"Yes," Mary said. "And I don't know what I did before I had her! She keeps me such gut company in the dawdi haus. Maem doesn't mind her coming over here, though."

"I wish I could have a kitten, Dat," Abigail said wistfully, hugging the calico kitten to her chest. "I miss Snowflake."

"I know," Jonas said. "Remember, I told you I'll think about it." He looked at the women and sighed. "Her cat was killed on the road recently. It was pretty tough on her."

"A new kitten would be good company for her, bruder," Jonas' sister, Sally, said, smiling slyly.

"Denki, I'll keep it in mind," he said with a mock glare at his younger sister.

"You did say you're a cat person the other day, I recall," Ruth said teasingly. After finishing her pie, she stood. "I've stayed longer than I intended. The goats will wonder what has happened to me."

"We're ready to leave too, Ruth," Jonas said.

Outside he held out a hand to help Ruth climb up into her buggy, and she tentatively placed her small hand into his much larger one. It felt odd having a man help her this way. It had been a long time since one had offered. She thought she kind of liked it.

"Good night, Ruth." He smiled warmly and held her gaze.

"Good night, Jonas." He nodded, stepped back, and waved, and so did Abigail.

Jonas' buggy followed behind Ruth's, making her feel safe and watched over, until she turned into her driveway. He stopped a moment and opened his window to call a good night, and Ruth waved back.

Jonas and Abigail continued down the road, and Ruth drove to the barn to unhitch Tom Sawyer. She rubbed him down and gave him some feed, then took care of the goats and other animals. As she worked, she wondered again whether enjoying the feel of Jonas' hand holding hers somehow cheapened her memories of Levi. On the other hand, she wasn't sure she cared. It felt like maybe she was about ready to move on. And that was kind of a scary yet exciting feeling.

CHAPTER TEN

"Here, chick chick chick!"

Ruth's hens came running, along with George, her fat rooster. She threw the feed in wide arcs across the yard, and the birds ran this way and that, clucking and competing furiously for the plentiful grain.

"There's enough for all of you! No pushing. George, be a gentleman!" She scattered the last handful and then upended the bucket and gave it a shake.

"You're lucky I'm so fond of you, Mr. Greedy," she chided the old rooster, that seemed to be about as tough as shoe leather at his age. "Or you'd have been the feature in a stew pot ages ago."

Before she could move on to the next task, a buggy turned into her driveway. She tucked the bucket beneath her arm, held up a hand to block the western sun, and squinted to see who was coming. She smiled when she saw it was Jonas and Abigail.

"Dat!" Abigail said. "There's Ruth! She must be feeding her chickens! Look at the big red rooster! What kind is that?"

"He's a Rhode Island Red, Abby," he replied absently, pulling the buggy up to Ruth's hitching post.

"Because he's red, ja?" Abigail asked, bouncing in her seat.

"Hello, Abigail! You're full of energy!" Ruth called.

"We've had such a busy day!" Abigail chattered. "We fed the stock, and I got to pitch the hay to the horses! Then we went to town so Dat could order more feed, and on the way back we stopped here! Where are your goats?"

"She's a chatterbox and full of curiosity," Jonas said.

"I don't mind," Ruth said. "I enjoy children. I just took a pan of cinnamon rolls out of the oven. They need to be iced, and then we could each have one with a cup of kaffi or a glass of milk. Who wants to ice them?"

"I do!" Abigail cried. Then, catching her father's disapproving glance, she folded her hands before her and smiled sweetly at Ruth. "May I, please?"

"You may, if it's *oll recht* with your dat."

Jonas nodded, and Ruth led the way to the house.

They took the path through Ruth's kitchen and herb gardens, asleep for the winter. Abigail stopped at the sight of the gazing ball. "Ohhhh, this is so pretty!" she breathed, moving closer so her face looked large and silly in the glass ball. She giggled. "What is it?"

"It's a gazing ball, but my late husband called it crow scarer," Ruth said. "The crows take a look and fly away in terror!"

Jonas grinned. "Ah, so that's how you ended up with something so fancy!"

"Ja," Ruth admitted sheepishly. "It's obviously a necessary piece of farm equipment."

Jonas chuckled, and Abigail made a face in the ball, giggling madly.

Inside, Ruth had Abigail stand at the counter on a little step stool so she could reach. She gave her a spatula and the bowl of icing and showed her how to spread it evenly on a warm cinnamon roll. After that, Abigail happily iced the other eleven rolls while Ruth set the table.

"All done!" Abigail said, obviously pleased with her handiwork.

"Gut!" Ruth took the spatula from the child and helped her down from the stool. "Nice job. Now take a seat, and I'll pour you some milk. Nothing is as tasty as cold milk with a warm cinnamon roll!"

Abigail sat politely while Ruth poured milk into her glass and kaffi into mugs for herself and Jonas. She then sat down and honored Jonas by looking to him to lead the prayer before eating.

He bowed his head, signaling the beginning of the prayer, which all three recited silently in their heads. Then there were a few more seconds of silence, in which a person could add personal thanks, before Jonas raised his head, signaling the end of the prayer.

How like a family we seem, Ruth thought. Breaking the spell, she picked up a roll and took a bite. Jonas did likewise, and his eyes grew big as the confection melted on his tongue. "Oh my, this is very gut!"

"It's my mudder's recipe," Ruth said, pleased at his praise. "I think the hint of cloves adds an interesting touch."

"Mmm, they're some of the best cinnamon rolls I can recall having," he said, taking a sip of kaffi. "I can see why the bishop was compelled to propose."

"Very funny," Ruth growled as she doctored her kaffi with cream and sugar—lots of cream and sugar.

"Got a bit of a sweet tooth, ain't so, Ruth?"

"Levi used to say that to me!" she laughed. "He liked his kaffi black, like you. Said there was enough sugar in the rolls."

"He was a gut man."

"Your Viola was a gut woman."

"That was my mudder!" Abigail chimed in. "She died when I was born."

"Yes, I know. I'm sorry," Ruth said.

"Aunt Sally says it's Gott's will, but I don't understand it," the child said.

Jonas' eyes met Ruth's, and she smiled gently at the little girl. "Nee, I don't understand either. I guess we just have to accept that Gott has a plan for our lives, and He understands well enough for all of us."

"That's what my Aunt Sally says too." Abigail munched her roll and washed it down with milk.

"She sounds like a very wise woman," Ruth said seriously. Abigail shrugged and took another bite of her roll. "Ja, she's pretty smart. She knows all kinds of things, like when it's time to put out the bird feeders for the winter. We just did that. I like watching the birds, especially the pretty red cardinals."

Jonas finished his roll. "The time passes on, especially on a farm, one season carrying one into the next, and years go by. And the living go about their days—and Gott's business."

Ruth nodded. "Ja, true and wise."

"Thank you for the roll, it was very gut!" Abigail said, licking icing off her fingers. "May I have another?"

"What do you say, Abby?"

"Please, Dat. May I please have another, Ruth?"

"Sorry, Dochder. You'll spoil your supper. Your smart Aunt Sally will have it waiting when we get home."

"Aww."

Jonas smiled. "But one roll just before supper is better than none, ain't so?"

Abigail gave a sheepish smile and nodded.

"Let me get you a wet cloth. That's sticky." Ruth went to the sink to wet a dish towel, which she took back to the child. Kneeling, she took Abigail's hands and wiped the icing off.

"You have a little on your nose," she said. "Let me get it." Then she swiped at the little girl's nose and made her giggle.

"Silly!" Abigail squealed.

"I just don't want the bees to come land on your nose because of the icing!"

"The bees are sleeping, Dat said, because it's nearly winter." Abigail looked a bit worried.

"I reckon he's right," Ruth said, looking as if she were considering it. "Yes, I don't believe I've seen any bees lately, so he must be."

"That's gut," Abigail said. "Bees are scary."

"But you like the honey they make, don't you?" Jonas asked.

"Well, yes, I do," the little girl said. "But I don't want them on my nose. I might get stinged!"

"Then it's a gut thing I wiped the icing off!"

At that moment, Ginger Snap, having just awakened from a nap, sauntered into the kitchen, sat down, and looked around, blinking sleepily.

"There's Ginger Snap! Oooo, he's so little and cute!" Abigail said, her face suffused with joy. "May I please pet him?"

"Sure, but remember to be gentle," Ruth said.

Abigail sat cross legged on the floor. She reached over and with one finger gently scratched the kitten between his ears. Ginger Snap closed his eyes and let out a loud purr before standing up, climbing into Abigail's lap, and turning in a few circles before settling down and promptly falling asleep.

"He sleeps a lot," Ruth commented.

"He's so little," Abigail said. "I promise not to squeeze him too tight like last time. If we had a kitten inside, it could sleep with me!"

"You are very gentle with him, I noticed," Ruth said, smiling at Jonas.

"Hmmm," Jonas said.

Ruth remembered that she'd meant to speak to Jonas about a gift for Lydia.

"Jonas, while we're on the subject of cats, I was thinking it would be nice if I gave Lydia something as a thank-you gift for my kitten. I thought maybe a cozy basket for her cats would be perfect. Do you make anything that might work as a cat basket?"

He thought for a moment. "Well, we don't, but that doesn't mean we can't."

She nodded. "Gut. I can make a little cushion to go inside. It will be nice and cozy for an elderly cat or two to relax in. Just give me the dimensions when you figure it out, please."

They chatted for a few more minutes, and then Ruth said it was time to milk the goats.

Abigail walked over and hugged Ruth. "Thank you for the cinnamon rolls, and for letting me put icing on them and hold Ginger Snap!"

Ruth's breath caught as she looked back at the beautiful child. She hugged her hard for a moment before letting go reluctantly. She caught Jonas watching and blushed. He smiled, and she wondered if he could tell how much she wanted a child. . .and how much she was coming to enjoy spending time with his child.

Jonas took his daughter's hand and led her to the door.

"Christmas is next week," Jonas commented as he helped Abigail into her coat. "We're going to be spending part of the day at Lydia's house."

"So am I! I'm looking forward to it," Ruth said.

"I am too," he said, putting on his own jacket.

"I still have some presents to make, though. I've been busy, and I'm a bit behind," Ruth said.

"I'm making presents too!" Abigail squealed. "They're secrets! But I'm making something special for Ginger Snap!"

"When did you decide that?"

"Just now." The child grinned at her father, who shook his head and grinned back.

"I'm sure it'll be wunderbar, whatever it is," Ruth said. "He's not very picky, so don't go to too much trouble, okay?"

She donned her barn jacket and followed Jonas and Abigail out the door so she could tend her goats. "I'll see you soon, then," she said, waving them on their way.

Jonas touched the brim of his hat and lifted Abigail into the buggy before climbing in himself and turning to smile at Ruth. "Ja, soon!"

She watched them drive away before heading to the barn and her chores.

Once Jonas had the buggy moving down the road, Abigail turned and gave her father a hug.

"What's that for?" he asked, ridiculously pleased.

"Just because I love you, Dat," she said. "See? I won't squeeze you too hard either. I would be a gut mamma to a little kitten because I'm gentle! Ruth said so! I love Ruth too. She's so nice. I'm glad we're going to see her on Christmas. I need to make her a present!" She smiled sweetly up at her father. He felt his eyes blur with tears. Children loved so freely and readily. They were unafraid to take risks with their hearts.

"She is very nice, baby," he patted the little girl on her head. "I'll help you make her something."

"Denki. It has to be something pretty and useful. When we move our basket business into her barn, I'll get to see her all the time!" Abigail clapped her hands together, grinning at Jonas.

"I guess you will."

"I wish Ruth was my mudder," Abigail suddenly said. "I think she would tell gut stories, and she makes really gut cinnamon rolls, doesn't she, Dat? Maybe you should ask her."

"To be your mudder? Um, I'll think about it, Abigail. But it's complicated."

"Why?" she asked, looking up at him.

"Well, uh, to be your mudder, she'd also have to be my wife."

"Okay," Abigail said simply.

Jonas was stumped. "It's not that easy, Abby. It's a grown-up thing. You'll understand someday."

"Okay," she said, accepting his reasoning, and he felt like a jerk for not having a better answer. "But if you figure it out, I'd really like her for my mudder. Then we'd live with Ginger Snap too!"

"Do you mind very much that you don't have a mudder?" he asked after a minute, dreading her reply.

She considered a moment, then shook her head. "No, I have Aunt Sally and Selma, and you're a very gut dat. So I don't mind too much. Sometimes I think it would be nice, that's all."

"Sometimes, I think so too," he murmured, then clucked to Samson and hurried toward home. He hadn't given the idea of marrying again serious thought. Sure, he found Ruth lovely and fun to be with, but that was a far cry from marrying her. But now that the child had suggested it, the idea seemed to take root and grow. He shook his head. "Too much, too soon," he muttered to himself.

He'd have to do some serious praying about whether the idea of making Ruth Abigail's mudder in reality would be a gut idea—for himself, as well as for his child.

CHAPTER ELEVEN

Christmas morning dawned clear and cold, and Ruth was delighted by the glaze of frost that turned the countryside into a whitewashed fairyland. The sun hitting the frost caused it to sparkle and glitter with Yuletide magic.

She hurried through her morning chores, then loaded a bag into her buggy, hitched Tom Sawyer to the traces, and drove to Lydia's house, where she'd been invited to share Christmas breakfast.

"*Frohliche Weihnachten!*" Lydia called as she threw open the door for her young friend, wishing her a joyful Christmas.

Ruth set her bag down and hugged her friend. "Frohliche Weihnachten!"

She hurried to pull the door closed behind her, shivering dramatically before removing her warm cape and cold weather outerwear bonnet and hanging them on hooks.

"It's cold out this morning! But so beautiful, ja?" Lydia exclaimed, bustling about her warm kitchen. "Christmas morning always makes me feel like a child again. Did you put your horse in the barn?"

Ruth nodded, and Lydia gestured her toward the table. "Sit, sit! It's just the two of us this morning, but after breakfast my daughter and her family are coming, and we've invited Jonas and Abigail to join us. They'll spend the afternoon with us and then go to his sister's for supper."

"Yes, he told me the other day. I like Jonas' daughter. She's wunderbar bright and very happy."

"Told you, did he? And when was that?"

"He stopped by to talk about the barn, that's all," Ruth said. "And it was cold, and Abigail was with him, so I invited them in for kaffi and warm cinnamon rolls. That's when he mentioned it."

"Ah. And his sweet daughter was there too?"

"Ja. She iced the rolls."

"She's a gut little girl, like her mother, who was always cheerful and generous." Lydia set a steaming white teapot on the table.

"Yes, I always liked Viola."

"I think in this modern age even we plain folk forget that sometimes people simply can't be saved, and we're shocked by the sudden nature of our own mortality. But it was hard on Jonas, being suddenly alone, grieving for his wife, and with a baby daughter to raise. Sally has been a big help. And my daughter, Lisle, living on the next farm, also helps out as needed. And of course, there's Selma, who stays with Abigail during the day and cooks and cleans for them too. She's a widow, and her children are far away in Belize. I think it does her good to have Jonas and Abigail to fuss over."

"Belize? Isn't that near Mexico?"

"Ja, in the Caribbean. Too hot for me! But I hear they like it fine. Anyway, the fact is that Jonas is a very nurturing man, and sincerely wanted to raise his own child. Some men would have been overwhelmed, but Abigail seemed to give him an anchor to cling to, and helped him get over Viola's death all the faster. She was a godsend, literally."

Ruth swallowed painfully past a lump in her throat. How much easier would losing Levi have been if she'd had kinner to care for and to give her a strong reason to fight her grief when he'd died? She shook her head. She'd never know.

Lydia, sensing her sudden sadness, patted her hand. "Gott has a plan for you, child, you'll see. There's joy ahead for you. Just open your heart to possibilities."

Ruth smiled and took a bite of quiche. "Mmmm, this is delicious, Lydia, as always. You're a wunderbar gut cook!"

"Denki." Lydia smiled.

"You know, little Abigail is determined to have a kitten of her own," Ruth said, making conversation.

But Lydia smiled mysteriously and said, "Hmmm, we'll just see what we can do about that!"

"What do you mean?" Ruth asked, finishing her quiche and getting up to pour another mug of kaffi.

"Sorry, it's a Christmas secret!" Lydia smiled. Ruth smiled back and let it go. But she had an inkling of just what that Christmas secret might prove to be!

They finished breakfast, sadness forgotten, chatting about people they knew and plans for the winter. Lydia was going to take a bus down to Florida and spend a couple of months visiting her oldest son, Ike, who had a winter home there with his wife, Alma, in the small Amish community of Pinecraft, near Sarasota.

"Won't that be nice! You'll escape the worst of the winter weather!" Ruth exclaimed.

"Yes, though the bus ride is very long," Lydia said. "Nearly twenty-four hours! It's hard on my old bones!"

"But worth it to find yourself in the warm sunshine with palm trees and beaches nearby?"

"More than!" Lydia laughed.

"But who will watch the cats?"

"I'll take them with me. They'll be fine. The vet gives me a little something to keep them calm on the drive."

"I suppose you could fly?"

Lydia shuddered delicately. "No, thank you very much. We'll just stick to the good firm earth, if it's all the same to you."

"I'm telling you, Lydia, I flew to Beesville, Texas, to see my parents, and it was so easy and so fast! Amazing, really. You should try it."

"I'm not going that far, child. The bus will be just fine. You go ahead and try out these newfangled ideas if you like."

"Come on, Lydia. Flying has been around since before you were born! It's hardly newfangled!"

"Whatever, I'm not doing it," Lydia said, waving a hand and closing the subject.

They worked together to clear breakfast and then moved into the living room. Lydia sat down in her comfy recliner, and Ruth took the old maple rocking chair next to it. They sat looking at the flames dancing merrily on the hearth.

"So, Ruth, your second Christmas without your Levi," Lydia commented. "How are you faring?"

Ruth sighed. "It's not as hard as last year, of course, but I do still miss him."

"Of course you do. You always will. But in time, that missing will be softer, and the memories, instead of causing pain, will feel more like an old quilt one takes comfort from. And then, perhaps, you'll be able to open your heart again and consider finding someone else."

"It is already easier—softer, as you say. Sort of out of focus from what it was like at first. I can still make it hurt if I think too hard, kind of like when you bite your tongue and then keep touching it to a tooth to see if it still hurts. So these days, I simply try not to touch the pain, and it really is less."

Lydia nodded understandingly. "Ja. That's how it is for me too."

"Did you ever consider marrying again?"

"Oh no, child. I was much older than you when my Ben passed on. Our children were all grown. And I'm not really alone, am I? Not when I have my children nearby, and friends like you, and my cats. Though sometimes I worry people will start to think of me as a crazy cat lady!"

Ruth laughed. "Don't you need around twenty cats in the house to qualify as a crazy cat lady?"

"Well, when there are kittens, I'm halfway there!" Lydia said, a twinkle in her eye.

Ruth smiled. "I guess I'm a crazy goat lady, then."

"Are you considering moving the herd into the house?"

They laughed, and then Ruth said, more seriously, "Ginger Snap brings me comfort. He's funny and good company. Thanks for bringing him to me, Lydia. It really was a lovely surprise, even though I may not have seen that right at first."

"Gut! Now then, hand me that red bag by your chair. There's something in it I need."

Ruth reached down and picked up a red cloth bag from the floor and handed it to her friend. It was lumpy and mysterious.

Lydia rummaged inside and came up with a small package wrapped in brown paper, and she handed it to Ruth. "Merry Christmas, Ruth!"

Pulling away the paper, Ruth gasped with pleasure. Inside was a lovely crazy-quilt wall hanging in autumnal colors of cats sitting, lying down, running, pouncing—in short, doing all sorts of cat things. It was corduroy—warm and soft.

"Oh! I love this! You are so creative and gut with a needle, Lydia!"

Lydia smiled. "Denki. It'll help keep your living room warm in winter."

"It will! I know just where I'll hang it. Denki, Lydia." She got up and pressed a kiss to the older woman's soft cheek and then sat down and picked up her own bag. She reached inside and took out a small package, wrapped similarly to Lydia's. She handed it to her friend.

"Ruth, you didn't have to make me anything!" Lydia said. But Ruth saw the gleam of pleasure in the older woman's eyes.

"Scented soaps! You know how I love these. You make the very finest soap in the area. Thank you!" She sniffed the bars, which were each wrapped in pretty pieces of calico.

"Mmmm, lavender, rose, sage, and vanilla. These will make me think of warm summer days in the garden whenever I use them." At that moment, the back door opened, and a woman's voice called, "Maem! We're here!"

"Lisle!" Lydia cried, pushing to her feet. Ruth followed her into the kitchen, where Lydia's daughter held the baby, a little boy not yet a year old, wrapped warmly in her arms, as her two daughters and her other son pushed into the room. Lisle's husband, Joseph, followed them inside, having put the horses into the warm barn.

"Lisle! Joseph! Welcome! Frohliche Weihnachten! Come in, come in, it's cold outside! Oh, look at that boy," she said, whisking the baby from her daughter's arms. "He's getting so big and heavy, soon I won't be able to lift him!"

"Like me, Grossmammi!" the older boy, Josh, who was nine, cried, hugging Lydia around her comfortably padded waist.

"That's right, Josh, like you. Frohliche Weihnachten, girls!" she said to the two little girls, who were three and five. "There are some fresh cookies and some cold milk for good children! Lunch won't be for a couple hours yet, Lisle. The meat loaf is in the oven."

"That's gut, Maem," Lisle said, directing the children and her husband to place the pots and bowls they'd carried inside for her on the table and counters.

"Here are the potatoes, ready to cook, and we baked a strudel."

"We helped!" piped up the older girl, Charity. Her sister, Hope, nodded solemnly, a finger planted in her mouth as she watched the goings on with wide-eyed wonder.

"I can hardly wait to taste it!" Lydia said.

"And here are the noodles," Lisle said as Joseph placed a large pot on the stove.

"So let's visit a bit in the living room, and then you kids can play board games while we women cook a tasty Christmas dinner!"

Before they could retire into the living room, the sound of another buggy pulling into the drive reached their ears.

"That'll be Jonas and Abigail!" Lisle said. "Gut! This will give Joseph another man to talk with. They'll keep each other entertained."

"I'll be entertained plenty beating the children at Parcheesi!" Joseph said, a twinkle in his eye.

"Dat! You always win!" Josh said.

"That's because I'm older and wiser," their father said.

"Oh, you," Lydia said, opening the door and calling to Jonas that there was still room in the barn for his horse. Abigail ran to the house while her father stabled the horse, and she was greeted with a big smile and a hug by Lydia. "Welcome! Merry Christmas!" she cried, stepping aside as Abigail skipped up the stoop into the kitchen, a basket over her arm. Jonas followed a few minutes later, carrying two pies.

Abigail handed her basket to Lydia and shyly said, "Merry Christmas and denki for having us over for dinner!"

Lydia took the basket, her eyes filled with joy. "Oh! Did you make this, Jonas? It's lovely, and look at the lid! So clever!"

"Open it!" Abigail said, obviously having trouble containing her excitement.

Lydia put the basket down on the table and opened the lid, which was fastened with a wooden toggle through a leather loop. She lifted the lid, and inside she found another basket. Smiling, she lifted it out and opened it to find a third basket. She opened this one and discovered a pot of honey taken from Jonas' beehives that fall.

"Jonas, Abigail, these are lovely gifts. Thank you so much for thinking of me!"

"Dat made the baskets, and I helped gather the honey and put it in the jar!" Abigail said. "I made sure not to get any on my nose!" She giggled.

"You're a big girl," Lydia said, patting the child's head, which was covered by a snowy-white prayer kapp.

Then Abigail reached into the pocket of her apron, pulled out a small package wrapped in calico, and shyly handed it to Ruth.

"I made this for you and Ginger Snap," she said. "I hope you both like it!"

Touched, Ruth carefully opened the gift. Inside, she found a little oval made of wool, sewn together. There were a few strings attached to one end, and Ruth realized they were whiskers, and the oval was a little mouse. It was attached to a length of string. A cat toy for Ginger Snap!

"Smell it!" Abigail said.

Ruth lifted it to her nose, sniffed carefully, and smiled. "Mint?" she asked.

"Catnip!" Abigail said. "Ginger Snap will love playing with it!"

"We grow some to make into satchels to sell to the tourists, mostly," Lisle said. "It's a variety of mint."

"What a thoughtful gift, and all the more special because you made it for us," Ruth said, hugging Abigail. "I'll play with Ginger Snap later today and tell him you made the little catnip mouse for him."

She met Jonas' gaze, and he regarded her with a strange, intense expression. She dropped her eyes, feeling a blush steal over her cheeks.

"Frohliche Weihnachten, Ruth," Jonas said softly, as Abigail followed the other children into the living room.

"Frohliche Weihnachten," she whispered back, darting a glance into his smiling eyes.

"Thank you for your kindness to Abigail."

"Nonsense! Her gift was so thoughtful! I love it, and so will Ginger Snap."

"I made you something too," Jonas said. "I'll give it to you later."

"Oh! I didn't make you anything!" Ruth said, dismayed.

Jonas touched her cheek briefly, aware of the others in the next room. "Ruth, today is about Jesus. It gave me pleasure to make you something, but I don't mind if you didn't do the same. I'm not keeping score. We're here to celebrate Christ's birth."

"You humble me, Jonas," she whispered. He smiled and gestured for her to precede him into the living room, where they all sat for a while and exchanged small handmade gifts in the Amish way. Christmas, after all, wasn't about presents; it was Christ's day—literally Christ Mass.

After a while, the women went to the kitchen to prepare the meal, while the men stayed in the living room playing board games and cards with the children.

When it was time, they all gathered at Lydia's large table, and Joseph led the silent prayer. Then they shared the delicious meal, which included meat loaf, fried chicken, noodles with sausage balls, pickled beets, green beans, and Chow Chow.

"I thought you might fly to Texas to see your family this year, Ruth," Lisle said.

"I thought about it, but who would take care of my goats? I have to milk the does twice a day, though we're almost done for the season. I invited my parents to come visit, but my father hasn't been feeling well, so they decided not to come. Maybe next year I'll find someone to take care of my animals and go for a few days."

While they ate, Hephzibah wandered into the room and sat politely on the rug by the door, washing her whiskers. After a minute, the little white kitten Ruth had met once before gamboled into the room and pounced on her mother.

"Oh, look! A kitten!" Abigail cried. The other children craned their necks to see the kitten spinning around chasing her tail.

"That's Hep's last baby," Lydia said. "All the others have gone to their new homes."

"May we play with her after dinner? Please?" Abigail begged.

"Yes, Grossmammi, may we, please?" Charity and Hope asked.

"You may," Lydia said. "But this kitten is special. She can't hear. So you'll have to be gentle with her. You can't sneak up on her, or you could scare her."

"How do you know she's deaf?" Jonas asked curiously.

"Most snowy-white cats with blue eyes are," Lydia said. "And when I had Hep fixed, I had the vet check the kitten, and he confirmed it."

"Poor kitty," Abigail said.

"Nonsense," Lydia said. "She'll be perfectly fine. She won't know what she's missing. But we'll have to take extra care with her is all. And she can never go outdoors. She'd be much too easy for a coyote to catch, and she wouldn't hear cars coming on the road."

"Ohhhh," Abigail sighed, no doubt thinking of her lost cat. The other children nodded their understanding.

After dinner had been cleared away and the dishes washed, they all went back to the living room to sing Christmas carols.

"Dat, is it all right if I play my harmonica?" Josh asked. Joseph looked at Lydia, who nodded and smiled widely. "That would be wunderbar, Josh!"

So Josh pulled a harmonica from his pocket and played along quite well. They all sang for about an hour, going through every carol they knew, and then Ruth reluctantly stood. "Time to milk the goats."

"We should too, Maem," Lisle said. "The cows will all be at the gate, and our neighbors will wonder what happened to us."

"Yes, Sally will be expecting us soon, Abby," Jonas said.

Everyone stood to leave, with Lisle, Joseph, and the children being the first out the door. As Ruth was about to go, Lydia caught her arm.

"Ruth, do you mind taking Abigail outside so I may speak with Jonas for a moment, please?"

Ruth looked at her friend searchingly but nodded. "Of course." She kissed Lydia's cheek. "Denki for having me today. It means so much to me that you include me in your family, Lydia."

"It's because I think of you as family. Now go on, before I water up."

Ruth took Abigail by the hand and led her out to get her settled in her buggy with a hot-water bottle and a warm, woolen blanket.

Jonas looked expectantly at Lydia.

"Now, Jonas, I know what you'll say at first, so just don't answer right away."

"You've got me curious, all right," he said, quirking an eyebrow.

"You've done well raising Abigail. I know Viola would be pleased. She is very responsible for a girl her age. That's why I'm going to offer to give you my last kitten." She held up a hand before Jonas could speak. "I know! You don't want a cat—much less a house cat, which this one must be."

"You're a mind reader?" he asked wryly.

"Don't get cheeky with me, young man. Now, Jonas, think about this for a few days, please. Hep's already got this kitten litter trained. A child needs a pet."

He stared at her, as if unsure how to respond. She patted his cheek, opened the door, and ushered him out.

"Think about it! Promise!"

He nodded slowly. "I'll think about it. That's all I'll promise."

She smiled, her eyes twinkling, and called, "That'll do. Denki for coming! It was very merry with all of you children here. I'll see you soon!"

She closed the door, leaving Jonas standing on the stoop. He slowly went down and walked to the buggy.

"What did she want?" Ruth asked. "If you don't mind my asking."

Jonas felt a bit as if a steamroller had mowed him down. "To give Abigail her last kitten. The deaf one."

"Oh! That's wonderful! She must really like Abigail and trust you both, to offer one of Hep's kittens."

When he just looked at her, she smiled and patted his arm.

"I get it. You don't see it as wonderful. Well, don't decide now. Come visit me a couple of times and see how Ginger Snap gets on, if that'll help you make up your mind."

"Cats don't belong in the house," he muttered, feeling decidedly outnumbered.

"I know. But sometimes it's okay to do something different."

"Maybe," he allowed. "Hey, I made you something. Wait here." She stayed with Abigail while Jonas fetched their horses from the barn and hitched them to the buggies.

"At least you don't have any plans to move inside my house," he muttered to Samson as he led him to the buggy.

"I heard that, Jonas!" Ruth laughed. Abigail poked her head out the buggy window. "Are we going soon? I want to play with my new jacks and color in my coloring book, Dat."

"Just a moment, and we'll be on our way," he told the child, who disappeared back inside and zipped the window closed again.

He reached into the buggy, pulled out a large flat object wrapped in brown paper, and carried it to Ruth.

"I thought you might like to have this," he said. "I didn't see one in your kitchen."

Curious, she felt the package.

"Quit feeling it and open it!" he urged.

Smiling, she tore off the brown paper and made a sound of pleasure at what she found inside. "Ohhh, Jonas. This is so beautiful!"

It was a pizza board, for sliding pizza onto from the oven. It was made of carefully fitted sections of variously colored, natural hardwood, beveled at the edge, with a long, narrow handle to hold while removing a pizza from the oven.

"You like it? You don't already have one?" Jonas asked anxiously.

"I love it, and I don't have one," Ruth said. "I'll have to make my homemade pizza for you and Abigail soon!"

"That would be great!" Jonas said, grinning in relief that she liked his gift. Impulsively, he leaned in and gave her a quick, chaste buss on the cheek. She parted her lips in surprise, and he grinned even more. "Well, hop on into your buggy and head home. Goats to milk, you know!"

Bemused, she did so. He held the door for her while she climbed in.

"Well, I'll be seeing you, I guess," Ruth said, smiling at Jonas.

"Ja. You owe me a pizza. Merry Christmas, Ruth," he said, reaching out and touching her arm.

She smiled shyly at him. "You too, Jonas!"

She snapped her reins as Jonas climbed into his buggy beside Abigail, and they both turned their horses toward the road.

Ironically, considering how little he wanted a kitten in his own home, Jonas felt glad Ruth had Ginger Snap waiting for her. At least she wasn't going home to an empty house. He looked at Abigail, who was happily examining her jacks. A kitten might be gut for her. And that might be worth bending the rules a bit.

Ach. He'd think on it later. "Gee-up, Samson!" he called, snapping the reins. Samson was very happy to pull them toward home and a measure of sweet oats.

CHAPTER TWELVE

"Merry Christmas, Ruth!" said Mrs. Richart, an old friend of Ruth's mother. It was several days after Christmas, and the Richarts, an elderly English couple, were the last stop of the day for Ruth, who had spent the morning dropping off gifts of food and socializing with friends.

Mrs. Richart seated Ruth at the kitchen table and poured her a cup of the delicious hazelnut coffee she always seemed to have ready at hand.

As Ruth added a splash of hazelnut creamer, she didn't see any reason to mention this was her sixth cup that day, or that the slice of apple pie was her third. That was what the morning was about.

"Heard tell that young Samuel Mast bought himself a spread," Mr. Richart said, wiping away a bit of pie from his chin.

Ruth blinked in surprise. "He did? Where? Last I heard, he was looking for a farm."

"Yep, heard he's buying the Parson place, over by Berlin. It's an English couple selling the place, so he'll have to take the electricity out of the house, but it comes with two big barns, one that would be just right for his buggy business. And he can farm the land—good farmland, that. And some nice pastures for his stock."

"And it comes with a very nice home, big enough for a family when he's ready to settle down." Mrs. Richart smiled.

"Well, that all sounds very gut," Ruth said. "I'm happy for him."

"And I heard his cousin Jonathan is going to move his farrier business into the smaller building Samuel has been using, so everyone's happy as pigs in mud," Mr. Richart finished.

Ruth wondered if this meant the bishop would give up trying to convince her to sell. Or would he simply come up with some other family looking for a farm like hers? Even more worrisome, would he renew his proposal of marriage, forcing her to actually turn him down, which could prove awkward since he was her church leader?

She had a feeling Bishop Troyer wouldn't give up so easily.

On the way home, she impulsively detoured to Lydia's house and was surprised to see Jonas' rig in the yard.

The kitchen door opened, and Jonas, Abigail, and Lydia came outside. "Good morning! What brings you by?" Lydia asked brightly.

"I've been out visiting, and I have an apple pie with your name on it," Ruth said, hopping out of the buggy and reaching for the pie.

"Oh no, dear, I've already got five pies here! I'll be fat and diabetic if I eat them all! I'm already trying to figure out how I can regift them without anyone being the wiser. But I bet Jonas and Abigail would like to see what a fine pie you bake," she suggested coyly.

Ruth was startled. Was her friend matchmaking?

"I never say no to apple pie," Jonas said. "And in fact, I already know Ruth is a fine baker and cook." He gave her a slow smile that warmed her from her toes to her ears.

"I like apple pie!" Abigail said, breaking the spell.

"Well then, it's a gut thing I have this one!" Ruth said, smiling at the child and handing the pie to her father. She kept a wary eye on him and was careful not to touch his hand.

Then he winked at her and said, "Denki! We'll enjoy this tonight with dinner. And I'm glad we ran into you. I wanted to ask you if you'd like to stop by and see my basket operation? I believe you were interested in a particular project, and I can show you similar items."

Ruth looked at Jonas, and his eyes were dancing with secret laughter. She decided to ignore it and answered his question. "Oh! Yes, I would like to do that. When should I come?"

"We'll be working the next three days getting a large order ready, so feel free to stop by anytime."

"Guess what!" Abigail said. "Miss Lydia is giving me her little white kitten! Dat said I can have her inside the house so she'll be safe. I'm naming her Alaska, because it snows there a lot, and snow is white, and my friend's aunt went to Alaska and said the ice there is blue, like the kitten's eyes."

"Apparently glacial ice is blue," Jonas explained.

"My goodness, that is big news!" Ruth said.

Jonas looked a bit sheepish. "Ja, I decided it would be gut for her to have the responsibility of caring for the creature."

"I'll look forward to visiting Alaska when I come to see your father's basket business, Abigail."

Lydia's eyes sparkled as she looked on. "That's the last of Hephzibah and Zed's kittens accounted for and placed into a gut, safe home. I'll see you after you get the things we discussed, Jonas."

Jonas climbed into the buggy and waved as he drove away.

"What's he getting?" Ruth asked.

"Oh, cat supplies."

"I could make a little bed for her. I made one for Ginger Snap," Ruth said, considering the leftover fleece she had from making a warm sweater for herself that fall.

"That would be very nice," Lydia said. "Well, time for my lunch. Would you care to join me?"

"Denki, but I'm full of pie and kaffi from visiting folks this morning. I'll see you soon!" Ruth climbed into her own buggy and turned Buttercup toward home.

———————— ⚜ ————————

"Abigail, don't run ahead," Jonas warned in a low voice as they walked through the aisles of Orme Hardware in Berlin a short time later.

She slipped her hand into his and smiled up at him. "I won't, Dat, but please try to hurry! I don't want Alaska thinking we aren't coming back."

Jonas smiled and followed Abby into the pet care aisle, and then gazed in amazement at the array of items available.

"Dat! Look at all this stuff!" Abigail's eyes were huge as she scanned the shelves of pet toys, pet beds, pet food, cat litter, dog leashes, and fish tank decorations.

"Remember, Abby, we're just getting a few things," he said, pulling Lydia's list out of his pocket. He read the list, then looked on the shelves for the items. "Here's the cat litter she recommends," he said, grimacing at the price. "And there is a plastic litter pan and scoop." He put them into his cart. "Now, where's the kitten food?"

By the time they had all the items on Lydia's list, which included vitamin drops and a lint roller to remove cat hair from his upholstered furniture and dark clothes, Jonas was wondering what he'd gotten himself into.

"Mr. Hershberger, Abigail, it's nice to see you!" The owner of Orme Hardware smiled from where she and a store employee were working on a display of wine-making items near the checkout aisles.

"Hi, Mrs. McCoy," Abigail said. "I got a new kitten, and her name is Alaska because she's all white, and she can't hear, and we bought what Lydia said, and now we're going to go get Alaska and take her home. And she's going to live inside!"

Karen McCoy smiled at the child, then at the father. "My, my, that is exciting! I have a little kitty named Daisy living in my house. Well, if you need anything else, we'll help you find it. Oh, and your wood glue will be here Tuesday, Jonas. I'm afraid it was on back order."

He nodded, touched his hat, and held the door open for Abigail. As he loaded their haul into the boot of the buggy, he rolled his eyes, thinking he'd need to sell plenty of baskets if they were going to outfit a spoiled kitten. And wait until his friends found out about this. They'd say he was narrish.

But looking at his daughter, so excited about her new pet, he couldn't be annoyed. And thinking about how Ruth's Ginger Snap provided company for her, he thought maybe Alaska would provide company for his daughter, who, after all, had no brothers or sisters to play with.

"Let's go get Alaska, Dat!" Abigail bounced in her seat.

He smiled. "Let's go get her then, Abby. And remember, it's your job to scoop the litter pan!"

"I promise I won't forget," she vowed solemnly. He smiled to himself. He supposed she would do a gut job—with a little reminding. After all, she was only four.

"Gee-up, Samson," he called. "We've got a kitten to collect!"

CHAPTER THIRTEEN

Snow flurries drifted down from a gray sky as Ruth guided Buttercup down the road toward Jonas' farm a few days later. She hoped it wouldn't turn into real snow, as she hated driving in wintry conditions.

Ten minutes later she drove into Jonas' driveway and was surprised to see just how close to the road his house was.

"I'd forgotten this," she murmured to herself. It had been several years since she'd turned down this road. "I suppose it used to sit further back, but when they widened the road for the quarry, it took most of the front yard with it."

The house, a large white farmhouse with black shutters, was dusty from the road. Looking beyond, Ruth glimpsed the barn where Jonas had his basket business. It was considerably smaller than her own, and painted white.

"Hello, Ruth," Jonas called, walking over from the barn. He patted the horse's strong neck, then reached into his pocket and produced a small carrot, which he fed to her.

"She'll be your friend for life now. She's pretty easy." Ruth climbed down from the buggy.

"Never hurts to bribe the staff." Jonas stood looking down at her, and Ruth suddenly felt awkward. She'd never before noticed how tall he was, or how broad his shoulders, which, encased as they currently were in a dark blue work shirt tucked into denim pants, were impressive.

Ruth cleared her throat a bit and took a small step forward. Jonas seemed to snap out of a trance.

"Um, sorry. Well. It's gut you're here," he said. "Come inside and I'll show you my business." He turned and headed toward the barn, and with a small smile, she followed.

Opening the door, he gestured for her to precede him into a warm, drywalled space filled with activity.

"Hello, Ruth!" Sally called. "We wondered when you'd be stopping by!"

Rebecca Beachy, who was standing on a padded floor mat next to Sally, smiled and called a cheerful hello. Their skilled fingers were swiftly weaving maple shakes into baskets.

"It's sure gut to see you!" Rebecca said.

Looking around, Ruth saw Mary Yoder seated at another counter in a chair which offered her a secure perch while she created a miniature round basket decorated with an intricate pattern in slender blue shakes.

"That is really lovely, Mary," Ruth said.

"Denki. I like making pretty things, though you really couldn't say it'll be much use for anything other than decoration, I suppose."

"Well, you could keep small things in it," Ruth said, considering the basket. "Coins for example, or buttons."

"Or keys, maybe," Sally said.

"Hair ties," Rebecca offered. "Or paper clips!"

"Or you could put a little pillow inside and call it a pincushion," Mary suggested.

"That's a gut idea! I'll buy one of those and put a pincushion in it for my mudder's birthday in April. In fact, I'll buy two, because now I want one for myself," Ruth said. "I just love the color." She moved over to where Sally and Rebecca were working on larger baskets. Seeing the red shakes they were using, Ruth guessed they were currently working on the laundry hampers she had heard them discussing recently.

"Ja, that's right," Jonas said when she asked. "They're popular with tourists. We're filling a fairly large order for Dutch Valley Gifts in Sugarcreek right now."

Looking around, Ruth saw finished baskets standing by a wall, and many bins of material presumably used for weaving baskets of all sizes, shapes, and colors.

"It smells wunderbar in here," she said.

"That's the linden seed oil," Jonas remarked. He walked her around the room, showing her what various things were for, and had Sally talk her through weaving a basket.

"I'm impressed," Ruth said when they'd shown her everything. "So, do you think you could make a basket for Lydia's cats?"

"Come over here, and I'll show you what I have in mind." He led her to a stack of smallish baskets, oval, wider at the top than at the bottom.

"These are small laundry baskets," he explained. "They're open at the top, of course. But I thought if we altered the design a bit to create an opening on one side, and added a hinged, woven lid for cleaning, that would work. I even know a woman I thought I might ask to sew us cushions to put inside. I think this idea could work in a couple of sizes, for cats and small dogs. It's a gut idea, Ruth. I'm grateful to you for suggesting it. And so, the prototype basket, if it's any good, will be yours."

Ruth's eyes flew open wide. "Oh! No, I couldn't take it without paying, Jonas."

"The person who comes up with a design gets a basket. House rules, Ruth. Right, ladies?"

"That's right," Rebecca answered. "We all try to come up with interesting new designs, and our homes—and our families' homes!—are full of baskets of various types. I don't know why nobody here thought of this."

"Probably because we don't typically keep animals in the house," Mary chimed in.

"Ja, that's probably it," Sally agreed.

"I'm going to want one for Hope," Mary added with a grin.

He rolled his eyes. "I'll probably have to make one for Alaska. Speaking of which, come to the house and say hello to Abigail and

Alaska," he invited. "It's time for kaffi anyway."

Jonas held the door for Ruth to exit, and behind their backs, Sally's eyes met Rebecca's and Mary's, and the three women traded knowing smiles.

The two of them walked side by side up the stone path from the barn to the house. A huge truck rumbled past on the road.

"Oh! I didn't realize the big trucks came up this road!" Ruth said, surprised. "Although, I should have, since I know they widened it for the quarry."

"Ja," Jonas said grimly. "Since they reopened the stone quarry, there are big trucks up and down the road all day. It's how the cat got killed, and I worry for Abigail. She's still really too young to understand the danger, though I've hammered into her head that she is never to leave the yard. Plus, it's really dusty! The township doesn't always remember to oil the gravel regularly. Anyway, here we are!"

Before they could enter Jonas' home, a buggy turned into his lane. Turning, Jonas shaded his eyes against the morning sun. "It's Bishop Troyer!"

"And Evelyn," Ruth murmured.

The buggy pulled up in front of the house, and the bishop and his granddaughter climbed down.

"Hello! We're paying after-Christmas visits!" the bishop called cheerfully.

"Hello, Jonas. Hello, Ruth," Evelyn said, a bit too sweetly.

"Morning, Evelyn," Ruth said, trying not to resent the presence of the obnoxious girl and the man who was making her life tense and worry filled.

"Welcome, we were just going in for a cup of kaffi," Jonas said, opening the door and standing back for them to enter.

"Just the two of you?" Evelyn asked with an innocent air.

"Um, no, my daughter and her sitter are here," Jonas mumbled, opening the door and letting the others precede him into the house.

Inside, the kitchen was warm and cozy, though it could use a woman's touch, Ruth thought.

"It's a bit plain," Jonas said.

"So are we," Ruth reminded him. "It's nice. Those candlesticks are lovely."

He looked at them, a bit sadly, she thought. "Denki. I made those for Viola for our wedding. I couldn't bring myself to give them away."

"No! Of course not! And why would you? They should go to Abigail someday."

"Or to your next wife, should you remarry," Evelyn said with a pointed look at Jonas.

At that moment, Abigail ran into the kitchen, followed by an older woman.

"Hello, Selma, I hope it's okay that we all came in for kaffi?"

"Of course! I'll heat up the water."

"Dat! Are you done working for the day?" Abigail asked eagerly.

"No, Abby," he said. "I just brought Ruth and Bishop Troyer and his granddaughter in to say hello and to have a cup of kaffi with you. Have you already had some?"

"Dat! I'm only four! I drink milk!" Abigail said.

"Milk, then," he said with a smile.

"Hello, Ruth, Bishop, Miss. Sit, sit," Selma fussed. "The kaffi won't take long. Abigail, get some of the cookies we made this morning, child."

"Yes, Selma," Abigail said obediently, and she happily bounced over to a pie safe, opened it up, and took out a plate of chocolate chip cookies covered in plastic wrap. Abigail grinned at her father, and he ran a hand over her kapp before tweaking her nose. "My favorite!" he exclaimed.

"I'm known back home for my molasses crisps," Evelyn said. Her grandfather, looking helpless, shrugged and said, "She makes very gut molasses crisps. This is my granddaughter, Evelyn, Selma."

Selma nodded, and Ruth wondered why a grown woman would feel it necessary to compete with a little child over cookies.

"I'm looking forward to tasting your baking, Abby!" Jonas said.

"But first, let us thank Gott for his blessings."

Following grace, Ruth accepted a cup of coffee from Selma, along with two cookies. She tasted one and smiled in genuine pleasure. "Mmmm, this is a really gut coffee break. The cookies are excellent!"

"Yes, they are very gut," Bishop Troyer said. Evelyn nibbled on a cookie and sniffed disdainfully. Jonas frowned at her, but Abigail didn't seem to notice the young woman's rudeness.

"Denki!" Abigail said, pleased. Alaska wandered into the room just then. Abigail would have popped out of her chair and picked the animal up, but Jonas shook his head.

"No, Abigail, not while we're at table," he said. "We don't want to teach Alaska bad manners. She needs to understand when people are eating, we are not to be disturbed."

"Yes, Dat," Abigail said, looking sadly at the kitten, who was batting a wooden thread spool around the floor.

"Another house with a cat inside!" Bishop Troyer exclaimed, looking at the kitten. "This community is becoming decidedly odd."

"I still think it's odd too, but I'm getting used to her being in here," Selma said. "In fact, she's kind of nice company. I may decide to get one myself."

"You won't be sorry," Ruth said, finishing her snack and carrying her dishes to the sink. "Denki for the snack!" she told Abigail and Selma.

"Well, I think it's disgusting," Evelyn said. "Animals belong outside. I'm sure I can smell cat litter in here."

Selma stiffened, and Jonas hurried to smooth things before hostilities broke out. "I'm very sorry if my home isn't up to your standards, Evelyn," he murmured.

"Oh! Well, I didn't mean that," Evelyn stammered. "I'm just not used to a cat in the house, that's all. I'm sure I could learn to live with it. . . ."

"How lucky you don't have to," Ruth said with a bland smile.

Evelyn glared at her, but she didn't seem to feel any real remorse. Really, the young woman was over the top. Bishop Troyer stood, saying, "We need to get on to the next house, I'm afraid. Evelyn, where's the little gift you made the Hershbergers?"

"Oh, yes, *Grossdaddi*. Here it is." She picked up a small basket from the floor. "I made the jelly myself. It's sort of a specialty," she mumbled.

Jonas thanked her politely and then walked his guests to the door. When Abigail would have followed, Selma stopped her.

"I need your help folding the wash we did this morning, child," she said. "Say goodbye to Mrs. Helmuth and the Troyers."

Abigail skipped over and hugged Ruth hard, and Ruth closed her arms around the small, sweet shape of the little girl. She caught her breath. Moments like this always made her arms feel all the more empty later.

"Bye, Mrs. Helmuth!" Abigail called. "Bye, Bishop Troyer, bye, Miss Troyer!"

"What a well-behaved child," the bishop remarked, handing his granddaughter up into their buggy. "See you soon!" he called as they pulled away.

"Yikes," Jonas said when they were out of earshot.

"Ja."

He handed Ruth up into her buggy, and she leaned out to speak to him. "Lydia leaves for Florida in a couple weeks. Any chance I could have her basket before then?"

He nodded. "Ja, no problem."

"Denki!"

He smiled and stepped back, and she clucked to Buttercup, who was happy to head home. "Watch out for those trucks!" Jonas called. She waved as she turned her mare into the road.

As he watched Ruth drive away, Jonas chewed on his bottom lip. Lately he'd been finding himself woolgathering when he should be focused on work. He couldn't seem to stop thinking about Ruth, and about how Abigail had said she loved her and wished she were her maem. He shook his head. "You'd think I was a green boy," he muttered, turning to head back to the barn where plenty of work was waiting for him.

Inside, he picked up the drawings he'd roughed out of the remodel of Ruth's barn.

Staring at them, he found his mind wandering again. The last few days, a new idea had begun to form in the back of his mind. At first, he'd dismissed it as ridiculous. But now. . .

"I wonder if there's any chance. . ." he muttered to himself, the hand holding the drawings falling to his side.

"Jonas, what are you doing in here, talking to yourself?" Sally's voice snapped him out of his thoughts, and he slapped the drawings back onto his desk and turned toward his sister.

"Just looking at the barn drawings," he said. "I'd like to get started on this project now that Christmas is over. I'm thinking Monday will be a fine time."

"If you say so, bruder," Sally said with a knowing smile. Jonas frowned at her but kept silent and got to work. The last thing he needed right then was his sharp-eyed sister deducing that he had feelings growing for Ruth Helmuth. It still felt too new, too fragile, to share, even with his sister.

CHAPTER FOURTEEN

Ruth sang a happy morning song as she walked from the barn where she'd just done chores. The garden was asleep, with January well begun. The sound of a buggy turning into her driveway pulled her from her thoughts, and she turned to see who was coming. Shading her eyes against the morning sun, she saw a four-seat buggy pulled by two black horses she didn't recognize.

As it drew nearer, she could see that the driver was a stranger, but in the front passenger seat sat Bishop Troyer.

Suddenly nervous, Ruth turned and, planting a welcoming smile on her lips, slowly walked back to the gate to greet her guests.

"Guder mariye, Ruth. I brought some people for you to meet. Is this a convenient time for us to come in for a cup of coffee?"

Ruth was taken aback. This was very unusual. She glanced into the buggy and saw two women, one young and one older, in the back. "Of course. I've just finished in the barn and was about to have a cup myself." She smiled uncertainly at the strangers as they climbed from the buggy, and the man held out a hand. "Guder mariye, Mrs. Helmuth. I'm Amos Miller. This is my wife, Cynthia, and her mother, Ada Mazur."

Ruth shook each hand and offered each person a smile. "Please come inside. The kitchen is warm."

Mrs. Miller and Mrs. Mazur were looking around intently, and Ruth noticed Mr. Miller glancing toward the barn.

"That is a nice big barn you have, Mrs. Helmuth," he said.

"Ja, for sure and certain. I keep a herd of goats. Most are dairy, but I also have a number of fiber and meat animals."

"Really? How many goats do you have, if I may ask?"

"I have twenty dairy goats, twenty fiber goats and ten Boers. I milk twice a day in season and make cheese to sell in town. The does are all expecting, so I'll nearly double the herd in a few weeks." She held the door open and followed them into her warm kitchen.

"Goodness!" Mrs. Miller exclaimed, hanging her bonnet and cape on a peg. "That's a lot of work for one woman. No wonder you're—"

At that moment, the door opened again, and Bishop Troyer, who'd been tying up his horse, entered. He took off his coat and his warm felt hat and hung them on pegs by the door next to the Millers' and Mrs. Mazur's.

"Well then! What a fine morning! Ah, Ruth, that kaffi smells very gut!" He took a seat at the table. The others followed suit.

Ruth set mugs of kaffi in front of her guests, and rolls she'd baked the day before, along with containers of soft cheese flavored with rosemary and chives she'd made with the last of her goat's milk in December. Everyone spread cheese on their rolls and tucked in.

"Oh, this is very gut!" Mrs. Mazur said. "You make this yourself?"

"Ja, I do, denki." Ruth smiled at the woman, pleased that she liked her cheese.

"Would you share the recipe? It's the best I've ever had," Mrs. Miller said as she blotted her lips with a napkin.

"Sure, I'd be happy to. The quality of the goat milk makes a big difference in the taste of the cheese, ja? That's really my secret—excellent milk."

"Well, I had no idea," Mrs. Mazur said, while Mrs. Miller nodded her agreement.

"I wouldn't object if you learned to make this!" Mr. Miller said, helping himself to another roll.

"You should taste her cinnamon rolls!" the bishop said. "They remind me of my late wife's. So gut!"

Ruth bit her lip, hoping he wouldn't renew his proposal right then and there, and was relieved when talk turned to cheese making for a few minutes.

They finished their snack, and Ruth stood to clear up the dishes.

"May I please look around the house? I don't wish to impose, but I want to see if it will suit," Mrs. Miller said.

Ruth stared at her in confusion. "Suit? Suit what?"

Mrs. Miller looked at her husband, who tilted his head and looked at Ruth in puzzlement. "Why, suit *us*, of course, Mrs. Helmuth. I'd like to see the barn too. I'm not sure I'm interested in keeping the goats, but I'd like to learn more about the operation before I make up my mind on that. If I decide against them, I can always sell them, or we can simply leave them out of the deal for the property."

"As I started to say when we came inside, it sounds like a lot of work running a farm this size by yourself, and it's no wonder you've decided to sell out and move to Texas to be with your family," Mrs. Miller said sympathetically.

"Ja," Mrs. Mazur said. "A woman alone is no gut. We women need family around us. I'd like to see the dawdi haus, of course. That's where I'll be living if we decide to buy."

Ruth's mouth fell open in shock, and she turned to stare at Bishop Troyer, who had the grace to look sheepish.

"Well, now, I think we're getting ahead of ourselves," he said. "Ruth hasn't actually decided to sell her farm, not yet. I just thought you'd like to see it while you're in town so that, when she does, you'll know whether it's the property you'd like to purchase."

"But you said she had realized a woman alone couldn't manage a big farm by herself and would be willing to sell," Mr. Miller said, his cheeks turning red as he looked at the bishop, who squirmed a bit in his chair.

"Oh, goodness!" Mrs. Miller said, sinking back into her chair. "I am so sorry, Mrs. Helmuth. This is a misunderstanding. We are moving here from Pennsylvania, and this sounded like the kind of place we are hoping to find. But if you're not ready to sell, we are very sorry to have intruded."

"I'm sure Ruth will soon realize selling is what she needs to do— what is best for everyone," the bishop said, sending a steely-eyed look at Ruth. "She already missed out on one potential buyer by dragging her feet. And it isn't as if she isn't without options of her own," he added meaningfully.

"Well, it appears she is managing well here, Bishop," Mr. Miller said. "She has fifty goats she is caring for, and making a living from. The property is well cared for. It doesn't look to me like she's in over her head."

"Be that as it may, a childless widow has no need of a house this size, or a property this large. A family should be living here," the bishop said. "And Ruth should either remarry or go to live with her family. It's only right."

Ruth had had enough. Ignoring the shaft of pain she felt at the careless "childless widow" comment, she stood abruptly, facing the bishop.

"I am very sorry you've wasted your time," she said to the Millers. "I have no intention of selling my farm. I inherited it from my grossmudder and lived here for more than fifteen years with my husband. I make my living here, and I love it here."

She lifted her chin a bit and said firmly, "Bishop Troyer, I do not mean to be impertinent or willful, but I don't think it's right that you're trying to drive me off my land and deprive me of my living. What would I do anywhere else? I don't want to be dependent on the charity of others."

The Millers looked at each other, and Mr. Miller said, "Why don't we wait outside while Mrs. Helmuth and Bishop Troyer discuss this?" His wife and mother nodded, and they quickly went outside, leaving Ruth alone with the bishop in her kitchen.

The bishop frowned, as if he couldn't understand the problem. "But I thought you'd either take me up on my offer, in which case there would be no question of depending on the charity of others—you'd have an important role in this community! Or, if that doesn't suit, you are free to move to Texas with your family," he stuttered. "You could start over, maybe meet another man. You're young yet, Ruth."

Her eyes filled with tears. "Please, Bishop Troyer, I really just want to live my life as the Lord sees fit for me to do, using the resources He provided for me. Those resources are here, on my farm. I wish that, well meaning as I'm sure you are, you'd stop pressuring me. It makes me very uncomfortable."

Bishop Troyer looked at the floor for a few seconds, and Ruth became worried that she'd hurt the older man's feelings. She reached out and put a hand on the sleeve of his black coat.

"Bishop, I never meant to hurt you. I just don't have the kind of feelings for you I think a wife should have for a husband, and I can't marry again unless I find what I had with Levi. You had a wonderful relationship with your Amelia. . . . You must understand what I mean."

He swallowed and nodded. Then he looked up at her, and she saw regret in his eyes. "Ja, I do understand. I know if we married, it wouldn't be like what either of us had before. I just thought maybe we could be a comfort to one another. But I realize if I'm to remarry, I need to find a woman closer to my own age, not one who might still have a chance at a second young husband and a family of her own. Can you forgive me? I never meant to make you uncomfortable."

She smiled. "Of course I forgive you, Bishop. You made a kind offer. I'm only sorry I can't accept it. And as for my home, I need to stay here, for now at least."

"But this place must be too much for you, alone," the bishop said. "I only want what's best for you."

She took a deep breath and closed her eyes for a moment, gathering herself, looking for the right words to make him understand. Arguing with her church leader was not wise, nor was it what she intended. She just had to make him see she was where she needed to be. "Bishop Troyer, I know you're thinking of what's best for me, and for the community. But this farm is not too much for me. I love it. And I use it to make my living. My goats are in the barn. They graze in the pastures in the summer. I sell my cheese and grow my vegetables and herbs. I employ a neighbor girl part time to help with the milking."

The bishop was silent for a moment, and then he nodded. "I can see you are utilizing a good deal of the land—certainly more than I realized." He opened the door for her to precede him outside. The Millers were standing by the buggy talking. They looked up when Ruth and Bishop Troyer came outside.

"Ah! You've finished chatting?" Mr. Miller asked. "Gut! It's getting a bit chilly, and there is still that other farm you were going to show us, Bishop. . .although you said the house wasn't as large as this one, and there isn't a dawdi haus. But no matter. We can build on if we buy it."

"True, true," Bishop Troyer said, looking at Ruth's large house, then around at her land. "I understand your point, Ruth. But you can't blame me for thinking as I have been. This house is so big, and there's the dawdi haus. And the greenhouse. The tool shop. Others could make better use, more efficient use, at least of some parts."

She thought of the dawdi haus, filled with her grandmother's things, and couldn't stand the thought of losing it all. The farm had been in her family for a hundred years or more.

"But I'm planning on using the fields and greenhouse this winter and summer!" she blurted out. The Millers had wandered closer and stood listening.

Bishop Troyer stared at her. "How will you do that? Surely you don't think to plant crops? Plow the earth?"

"Although, to be fair, Bishop, women often do plow and plant," Mrs. Miller pointed out.

"Well, sure, if they're helping their husband. Mrs. Helmuth is talking about doing it all alone!" the bishop sputtered.

"No, no," Ruth interrupted. "I'm not planting crops. I'm going to grow flowers!"

When they stared at her, not understanding, she pressed on. "I'm going to raise chrysanthemums in the greenhouse from seed this winter, plant them in the two nearest fields, and let people dig them in the late summer. It'll be a new business for me."

"Well, that is ambitious, and it sounds like a wunderbar gut idea," Mrs. Miller said.

Then, deciding to take the plunge and mention another idea she'd been playing with, Ruth added, as if she hadn't just made up her mind, "I'm also going to grow sunflowers in the west field. They're valuable for their oil and seeds."

There was a moment's silence as they all considered what she had said.

"Will you plow the field for the sunflowers yourself?" Mr. Miller asked curiously.

"I could. I still have Levi's team and plow. I helped him plow in the early years. I remember how. But I'll probably hire the Byler boy down the road to do it. And the chrysanthemums will be planted one at a time, by hand. I'll have the Byler boy plow that field too, to prepare it. It's only three fields. I can do it myself if need be."

Bishop Troyer looked at her in amazement. "Well, nobody can say you're not a hard worker, Ruth Helmuth. But I wonder if you're really listening to Gott's voice as He whispers His plans for you. You may farm the land, but the fact remains you're a woman alone with two houses. . .enough room for a family of ten. It seems selfish to me. I want you to think on it, pray about it. We'll speak of it again."

"Wait! There is one more thing," Ruth said.

The bishop turned back. "Well? What is it?"

"I've been meaning to tell you, I'll be putting my barn to better use as well, Bishop Troyer."

"Really? How so?"

"Well, remember when you first came by a few weeks ago, and you said Samuel Mast was interested in finding a place where he could move his buggy business?"

"And a house to raise a family should he marry," the bishop said. "Ja, of course I remember. But now Samuel has purchased another place and is moving to Berlin. You've missed the chance to sell to him."

"Yes, I'd heard that. Well, as it happened, Jonas Hershberger came by that same day and asked if I'd rent the upstairs of my barn to him so he could move his basket business to bigger quarters. It seems he's outgrown his smaller barn. Your mention of Samuel Mast had got me thinking about how I could use more of my barn, and when Jonas asked to rent it, I thought, why not? It was going to waste, and this way, I get rental income from it. I. . .wanted you to know I really did listen to you, and now I'll be using more of my barn as well, Bishop Troyer."

"Huh," the bishop said, staring at Ruth. He turned to look at her barn, and his shoulders started shaking. Ruth was alarmed—what was wrong with the bishop? His shoulders shook harder, and then he started to laugh out loud.

"Oh, Ruth, you managed to get one over on me for sure and certain!" he chuckled, wiping tears from his eyes. The Millers stood looking at him, unsure what to do, but Ruth felt the corner of her mouth turn up in a smile.

"In truth, Bishop, I wasn't trying to get one over on you. The opportunity simply arose, and you'd paved the way for me to think favorably on it. So I took it," she explained.

He nodded, wiping at his streaming eyes with a large white handkerchief.

"Ja, ja, of course I know you aren't a conniving girl, Ruth. But you sure found a way to prove you're using your land, didn't you? Several ways, in fact. I'll wait to see how it all works out. Jonas Hershberger moving his basket business in here—my, my."

Then the bishop looked at Ruth keenly. "He's a gut-looking young man too, and he has that sweet little girl with no mudder. I guess you'll be seeing a lot of each other, won't you? Hmmm. Yes, yes. Perhaps you'll soon be using more of your house too!" He chuckled some more, looking rather pleased. "Well, let's go, then, Mr. Miller! We're burning daylight!"

Ruth felt her mouth drop open, and she stared at the bishop. "Well, I didn't mean. . ."

"Ja, ja, talk to you soon, Ruth. Off we go!" he said to the Millers, heading to his buggy.

"I'm sorry we intruded," Mrs. Miller said as their party walked toward their buggy. "Gut luck with your plans."

"Denki," Ruth said, rather shakily. "I do have some help. I'm not totally alone."

Mrs. Mazur smiled and patted her on the arm. "I think you'll do fine."

"It was nice meeting you all," Ruth called as they climbed into their buggy. "I hope you find a place you like!" They waved and smiled.

"Gott will lead us to the right place when it's time!" Mrs. Miller said. "If it's nearby, I'll hope to visit with you again and learn more of your cheesemaking!"

"Oh! Yes! I'll copy out my recipe and give it to the bishop to send to you!"

"Denki, denki!" Mrs. Miller and Mrs. Mazur said, waving from their buggy.

"I'll see you at services, Ruth," the bishop said. "Maybe you'll make that corn chowder Jonas and Abigail like so much again!"

She nodded, and he touched the brim of his hat and left, a grin still lighting up his face beneath his long gray beard.

Ruth walked inside and scooped up her kitten, who had come out from wherever he'd been hiding while Bishop Troyer and the Millers had been there. "Oh, Ginger Snap," she whispered, "what have I gotten myself into?"

The kitten purred in response, bumping his forehead against Ruth's chin affectionately.

Closing her eyes, she asked Gott for help and inspiration. Then, feeling a bit calmer, she took a deep breath.

"Well," she said, setting the kitten on the floor, "at least now the bishop will stop pestering me about selling out. And since I just scared off the second potential buyers he's brought me, it's a gut thing I don't want to sell!"

CHAPTER FIFTEEN

On the second Tuesday in January, Jonas tucked a few things into his buggy and then went into the house where Selma was watching Abigail.

"Where is she? I want to take her for a little drive to visit a friend," he said.

"A pretty young widow, by any chance?" the older woman asked.

He actually felt himself blushing—how long had it been since he'd felt that particular heat slide up his face?

"Well, yes," he mumbled.

"Gut! It's about time both you and Ruth Helmuth stopped mourning and got on with life! You need another *fraa*, and your child needs a mudder. I'm not getting any younger, you know! I think Ruth would be a very gut choice for both roles! I'll get Abigail," she said, hurrying out of the kitchen and up the stairs.

"But I'm just going to take her the basket I made for Lydia's cats," he muttered, knowing it wasn't the whole truth even as the words left his lips. "I'm just taking her the basket for Lydia's cats!" he called, more loudly.

"Ja, ja, but a little romance wouldn't hurt you any, I'm just saying!" she called back. Jonas stood where he was, wondering how his life had become public entertainment.

Selma returned a few minutes later, Abigail skipping in behind her, her prayer kapp trailing its strings down her back. "Where are we going, Dat?"

"Get Alaska, Abby," he answered, ignoring Selma's knowing grin. "Put her in her new basket and put on your warm cape. We're going to take the basket Mrs. Helmuth ordered for Mrs. Coblentz on over there, since it's finished and I'm done working for the morning."

"And we're taking Ruth the basket you made for Ginger Snap?" Abigail asked.

"Ja, that one too. Let's go. Samson is standing out in the cold."

"I'll see you both later!" Selma called from the door. Jonas shook his head. The woman was a bit of a gossip, even though he knew she'd never do anything to hurt him or Abby. But that wouldn't stop her from hurrying over to the basket shop as soon as he and Abby were out of the driveway to share the news that he was headed to Ruth's with the other women.

They climbed into the buggy, and Jonas steered them onto the road and headed for Ruth's.

"Dat," Abigail said, bouncing eagerly in her seat, "will she like the basket?"

He shrugged. "I suppose so."

"Alaska likes hers."

He smiled at her, then looked back at the road. "Is that so?"

"Ja, she does like it. It's warm and soft. But she still likes my bed better."

"Well, see if you can get her to sleep in the basket."

He hoped Ruth liked the one he'd made for Lydia—and the one he hadn't been able to resist making for Ruth's kitten as a late Christmas gift. After all, he'd promised her a prototype.

Ruth was returning to the house from the barn after caring for her animals when Jonas turned into the driveway. The buggy pulled up to the hitching post, and Jonas hopped out, then lifted his daughter down.

"Hi, Ruth, hi!" Abigail bubbled excitedly, practically jumping in place.

"Hello, Abigail! Hello, Jonas," she said, hoping she didn't have dirt on her nose.

"We brought Alaska to visit Ginger Snap," Abigail said.

"I hope that's all right?" Jonas asked, unsure.

"It's fine!" Ruth said. "What fun for the kittens! Bring her inside, and we'll see how well they remember each other."

"We also brought the basket I made for Lydia's cats. It's a lot like the one Alaska is riding in," Jonas said, pointing at the basket Abigail was hauling out of the buggy.

Ruth's eyes widened at the sight of the basket.

"Oh, that's wunderbar! Just what I hoped for!" she exclaimed, taking the basket from the child and looking it over. "How clever this opening is in front. It'll be a little ramp when it's open, and it closes tight to transport the cat, right? And the lid! Jonas, this is really nice. Lydia will love it!"

"Let me go get Lydia's," he said.

"It's finished? You have it here?" Ruth asked, her eyes lighting up. "That's great. She leaves for Florida in a few days."

"Ja, it's in the buggy," he said. "Why don't you two take Alaska inside, and I'll be right there?"

Ruth and Abigail went inside and hung their coats and warm bonnets on pegs. The little girl bounced on her toes, seemingly having a hard time containing her excitement about something, and asked, "Where's Ginger Snap?"

"You can look for him, maybe in the living room," Ruth said. "Let's release Alaska, and she can help search for her bruder, okay?" Abigail opened the clever latch holding the door of the basket closed, and Alaska slowly moved through the opening onto the little ramp created by the drop-down door. She sniffed the air and, finding no immediate threats, bounded down and scampered out of the room.

"Uh-oh, better follow her so she doesn't get up to mischief!" Ruth said.

Abigail scampered from the room calling, "Alaska, wait for me! Ginger Snap, your sister is here to play with you!"

Ruth moved to the kitchen door and opened it in time to see Jonas climbing the outside steps with not one but two baskets, which he carried into the kitchen.

"It took us a bit longer to perfect this one, so we had a few extra prototypes." He put them on the kitchen table, lining their edges up neatly. "Which do you think Lydia will prefer?"

Ruth smiled as she looked at the two baskets, which were very similar. One basket had green trim, the other red oak trim.

"Well, Lydia's favorite color is green, but I like this one better. Still, since it's for her, we'll go with the green," she decided with a regretful glance at the other.

"Well, gut," Jonas said. "We'll start production on these next month. The girls and I made quite a few to get them right. . . . You should see some of the rejected ones. . .all functional but some a bit weird looking. They all took one home for their own cats, and I have no room for this one, so you might as well keep it for Ginger Snap."

She looked at him narrowly. "Jonas Hershberger, do you think I'm so simple?"

He widened his eyes innocently and looked back at her. "What do you mean? I think you're very intelligent."

"Well then, you should know I see through this. I can't accept this. It's too valuable."

"But Ruth, remember, the one who comes up with an idea for a new basket always gets a prototype. It's tradition! And the girls want you to have it. You'll hurt their feelings if you refuse. They'll think you don't like it! Don't make me go back there and tell them you don't like the basket they made for your kitten."

He looked at her with puppy eyes, and she rolled her own eyes and laughed at him. "Well, I wouldn't want to risk hurting their feelings. Just stop looking at me that way!"

Jonas clapped his hands. "Gut! Think of it as a late Christmas gift and a thank you from all of us for giving us this gut new idea."

"Hmm, when you put it that way," she murmured, looking at the lovely basket. "I do love it, so denki for your kindness. I will accept it."

He smiled. "Gut! Where will you keep it?"

"Probably in the living room," she said, picking it up and carrying it into the room, where she found Abigail with the two kittens, tossing the little woolen mouse she'd made. They were obviously having a marvelous time.

Ruth set the basket in the corner by the hearth, and Abigail smiled and jumped up to go inspect the basket in its new home.

"You like it? Yay! I knew you would!" the little girl cried. "This is a gut place for it, next to the fireplace. Ginger Snap will stay warm all winter!"

"Ja," Ruth smiled. "That's what I thought."

"Dat let me help make it!" Abigail said.

"Really? Then I will cherish it all the more, Abigail." Ruth opened her arms, and the little girl ran straight into them for a big hug. Ruth felt her throat constricting as she hugged the little girl close, and she had to clear her throat.

"Abby," Jonas spoke, "I want to go look at Ruth's barn. Will you be all right here alone for a few minutes?"

"Sure, Dat. I'll play with the kittens."

"Stay away from the fire, Abigail," Ruth said. She placed the screen more securely in front of the hearth, and she and Jonas went into the kitchen where he picked up her cloak and settled it snugly over her shoulders. He glanced toward the living room and then dropped a kiss on top of Ruth's head.

She blinked. "What was that for?"

"I like you, Ruth. A lot. Thank you for accepting the basket. Abby would have been sad if you hadn't. And. . .so would I."

Ruth swallowed and nodded. "I like you too, Jonas. A lot."

Their eyes held, and the moment grew tense. Jonas reached out with his hand and tapped Ruth on the nose. "And besides," he whispered, "she got a hug when she gave you the basket. I felt left out, so I kissed you to make myself feel better. I hope you don't mind?"

Tension broken, Ruth laughed shakily. "I've never heard that logic before. I think you're reaching."

"But you don't mind?"

A warm feeling of happiness and belonging crept up from Ruth's toes to lodge in her heart. She wasn't sure she could trust the feeling, but she decided to embrace it, for the moment at least. Shyly, she shook her head. "I don't mind."

He laughed. "Gut! Or I'd have been crushed and embarrassed!" She found herself joining in with his infectious laughter, and she smiled up at him as they headed down the steps into the yard. "You're sure she'll be okay? She'll stay away from the fireplace and the hot stove?"

"Ja, she'll be fine for a few minutes," he said. "She's had to learn to be independent more quickly than other children her age. More quickly than I would have liked, perhaps."

"Ja, she's a gut girl," Ruth said. They walked through the brisk winter afternoon. Light flurries were drifting down from a sullen sky. Jonas squinted up at the clouds, and Ruth took deep breaths of the cold, clean air.

"I love this time of year," she said.

"Not me," he shivered. "I prefer to be warm. But at least it doesn't look like this is going to develop into anything serious. Just flurries for now."

"That's gut. I love snow, but I don't like trudging through it to the barn or driving my buggy through ice and slush. Yuck."

"I'm with you there," he said. "But I only like snow when it's powdery and perfect for sleigh riding."

"Sleigh riding!" Ruth exclaimed. "It's been years since I did that. I remember how fun it was, and the jingle of the sleigh bells."

"And a warm brick to keep your feet from freezing off," Jonas said with a sidelong look at Ruth.

"Oh, you're ruining the romantic image with your talk of freezing, Jonas," Ruth joked.

"Sorry. I'll try to remember not to mention frozen, dripping noses and chattering teeth."

"Next you'll tell me you don't like to go Christmas caroling because it's too cold."

"Um. . .time for a subject change! I just want to look at one or two more things in the barn to be sure I have everything right in my head. We're about ready to start the renovation. I've just been waiting on a couple men to be free to help."

"Really? That's exciting!" Ruth said as they entered the cavernous top floor of the structure. The space was mostly empty except for a wall stacked with hay and another with straw for the livestock. Over to one side were the supplies Ruth had let Jonas store in the barn. The big plow had been moved to another outbuilding in preparation for Jonas' crew's arrival. Down below, she could hear her goats talking to each other in their way.

Jonas looked around. He walked into the center of the large space and looked up, his hands on his hips, feet spread wide. A sunbeam snuck in through a crack between two boards and illuminated his winter hat. He squinted as it hit his eyes, then walked about a bit, testing the floor, which was solid, wide-plank oak. A trapdoor over by the hay and straw could be opened to toss down the bales for the animals.

"This is gut," he said to himself.

"You're the second man in a week to think so," she commented.

"What do you mean?" he asked, frowning.

"The other day Bishop Troyer showed up here with a family who thought I was ready to sell out—the Millers, from Pennsylvania. Mr. Miller wanted to see the barn too. Ach! It was very awkward."

"I'll bet!" He walked over to her. "Ruth, I know you don't want to leave here. Maybe if you tell the bishop you're renting the barn to me, it would help you convince him you're taking every measure to use the place wisely, and that you're fine here by yourself."

She smiled sheepishly. "Actually, I did. And you're right. It worked. He was surprised, but then he started laughing so hard he had tears coming from his eyes. He told me I'd got one over on him."

Jonas grinned. "Really? You have to give it to the old man, he still has a gut sense of humor. You bested him, but he didn't get mad—he laughed!"

"I guess you're right." She smiled. "I don't know why he can make me feel like a naughty child. But he can! I could never have married him. It would have been like marrying my grossdaddi!"

A loud whinny from downstairs forestalled any reply Jonas might have made. Ruth glanced at the stairs leading down to where her animals were housed. "One of the Shires, letting me know he hears me up here and would like an apple."

She turned to head downstairs, but Jonas caught her arm and turned her gently to face him. "Ruth, you did give the bishop a firm no, didn't you? He isn't holding out hope that you'll eventually decide to become Mrs. Troyer, is he?"

"No, Jonas, I made myself clear the day he came by with the Miller family from Pennsylvania—the family he brought here to look at my house. That was the day I told him I was renting you the barn. I think I cleared everything up for him. At least, I hope so."

"So do I," Jonas muttered. Another impatient whinny sounded from below.

"Hans wants that apple," Ruth laughed, reaching into her apron pocket to pull out a large red-and-green apple. "Gut! I have a nice big one. Come with me while I give him a treat?"

"Sure. I guess I didn't realize you still had Hans and Betty!" Jonas said, walking to the steps with her.

"I couldn't part with them. They're not young, and they graze outside most of the time. I just supplement with a bit of grain now and then. Levi loved those animals."

"They're fine beasts, that's a fact."

"They were outside the last time you were here, so you didn't get to say hello," she said as they entered the bottom floor of the big barn, where the animals were housed. The Shires were enormous black draft horses with pink-and-white noses and gentle brown eyes.

Wolke and Heftig bounded into the barn, barking. They ran up to

Ruth and sat at her command, panting and wagging their tails furiously.

"Gut dogs," she said, patting each and reaching into her apron pocket and pulling out a pair of large dog biscuits. Jonas raised his eyebrows as the dogs took them gently from her fingers.

"Those pockets are bigger than they look! Can I give the apple to the horses?"

She nodded and handed him the fruit. He reached into his pocket for a knife, which he opened and used to cut the apple in half. He put one half on his palm and let Hans lip it off before repeating the process with Betty, who nickered her appreciation. Jonas grinned and patted the big animals under their manes where their necks were warm.

"I also told the bishop about my idea for a flower business when he was here the other day," she said impulsively. "The mums, and I had an idea about growing sunflowers for the seeds and oil. He was surprised—but then I was surprised I told him. It was like I made up my mind to do it, really do it, right then!"

"Well, you'd already turned down his proposal and informed him you'd rented the barn. Better to make a clean breast of the whole thing. And I think it's a great idea, Ruth." he said. "You'd told me about the mums, but this is the first you've mentioned the sunflowers. That makes the plan even better."

"Actually, the idea came to me while I was talking to Bishop Troyer and the Millers, and I just blurted it out."

Jonas laughed. "Well, it's still a gut idea. They're commercially valuable for their seeds and oil, like you said, and for bird feeders. And they're simply pretty to look at too, especially a field full of them. Of course, the timing is tricky, I hear—letting them get to the point of readiness and harvesting them before the birds do."

"Oh, I hadn't thought of that. I'd better read up on this subject before spring!"

They walked back to the house and went inside, where they found Abigail rolling a small wooden spool for the kittens.

"You're back!" she cried, jumping to her feet. "I'm hungry again!"

"Perfect. How about a snack?" Ruth asked.

———————— ✲ ————————

As Ruth spread Amish peanut butter, a mixture of peanut butter and marshmallow fluff along with a few other things depending on the recipe, on bread, Jonas wondered what it would be like, being here every day. He thought he could get used to being cared for again by a special woman. He found himself imagining they really were a family, and he'd come in from work for lunch prepared by his wife. He smiled as Ruth said something that made Abigail laugh, and then she looked up and their eyes met, and she included him in the joke with a wide grin before going back to fixing the snack, her pretty hair where it had escaped from beneath her kapp gleaming in the sunlight coming in from the kitchen window, just like new copper.

He shook his head, feeling foolish. If she knew where his thoughts had gone, what would Ruth think?

He shrugged. Whatever she thought, she probably wouldn't be far off the truth. She was growing important to him, and to his daughter, and he wasn't exactly trying to hide the fact.

He suddenly noticed Ruth looking at him curiously and realized he'd been woolgathering, staring at her. He searched for a safe topic of conversation.

"This Amish peanut butter is really gut! Is it your recipe?" He stuffed a large bite into his mouth to keep from saying anything stupid and washed it down with cold milk.

Ruth smiled. "Ja, it's my secret recipe. It was my grossmammi's, and she passed it on to me along with her other recipes when I got married."

"It doesn't taste like my mudder's," Jonas said, taking another bite. "It's better, but I'd have to deny saying so if anyone asked, so mum's the word, okay?"

"I won't say anything," Ruth assured him. "It's the real maple syrup in the recipe that gives it its special flavor. I just love it."

"Huh. I think my mudder's recipe uses corn syrup, not maple syrup," Jonas said.

"Most people use corn syrup, and it gives the spread a lighter flavor," Ruth informed him. "But I prefer the maple syrup. I love the maple flavor it adds."

"You won't get any argument from me," he said. "Mind if I have another piece?" At Ruth's nod, he helped himself.

"I like it too," Abigail said. "It's fluffilicous!"

"Nice word! Did you make it up?" Ruth laughed.

Abigail grinned a peanut-buttery grin. "Nope. My Aunt Sally taught it to me. But she was talking about Grandma Hershberger's spread. Still, I think it works for yours too, Ruth. It's really yummy!"

Ruth was pleased. "Denki, Abigail," she smiled. "I'll give you the recipe, and you can make your own at home."

Abigail's eyes lit up. "Denki! I'll start a recipe book, just like Aunt Sally's!"

"And you can put both recipes for Amish peanut butter in the book," Ruth said.

"Gut idea," Jonas murmured, and Ruth smiled and nodded.

"So," Jonas said, using his napkin to wipe his face and hands, "I'll be coming soon to start on the barn if that's okay with you?"

"Ja, of course. I knew you would start after Christmas. I wasn't sure when."

"We had to wrap up a few things, but my crew is free and we're ready to begin. I was thinking we'd start Monday."

"That works for me."

"Perfect! Then I'll see you here with my crew on Monday."

"Can I come?" Abigail asked brightly. "I could hand you nails."

Jonas smiled. "That would be helpful. We'll see."

Ruth smiled, and Jonas thought, *Monday!* Starting Monday, he'd be able to see Ruth's smiles almost every day! The idea was both exciting and, oddly, anxiety provoking.

Get over it, man, you're acting like a kid, he thought as he wiped the peanut butter spread from his daughter's face. But he smiled a secret little smile at how fun it was to feel like a kid again.

He couldn't wait for Monday!

CHAPTER SIXTEEN

Come on, Tom!" Ruth urged, flicking the reins to motivate the gelding to pick up the pace a bit. "We're going to be late! Don't make me regret choosing you over Buttercup!"

As eager as Ruth was for Monday to arrive, first came Sunday, and that meant services this week. And she was running late—again!

Tom was unimpressed and continued trotting along at a nice steady pace.

"Why did Mimi have to choose today to cut her leg?" Ruth moaned. Glancing at her watch, she accepted the fact that not only was she going to be late, she already was late. Services—held this week at the Richard and Sarah Bontrager home in their large basement—had started nearly half an hour ago.

Ten minutes later she turned into the Bontragers' driveway, and a boy ran up and helped her out of the buggy.

"You're running late, Mrs. Helmuth."

"Yes, one of my goats got hurt, Zach," she said, handing him Tom's reins. "I had to care for her."

"I hope she feels better soon."

"Denki, Zach," she said, hurrying up the steps with the bowl of fruit salad she'd prepared last night. Inside, she found two women sitting at the table drinking coffee.

The older of the two looked rather disapprovingly at Ruth for being tardy, but the younger woman, Jane Bontrager, smiled. "Running a bit late today, Ruth?" she asked, getting up and taking the bowl from Ruth.

"Ja! One of my goats got hurt this morning, and I had to care for her before I could leave."

"Oh! What happened?" Jane asked. Since Ruth knew her friend, an animal lover, was truly interested, she told her how Mimi had cut her leg on a loose nail badly enough that she'd had to stitch it up.

"You're so clever, knowing how to do that," Jane said.

"The hard part is getting the animal to be still while you numb the area and then stitch it up," Ruth told her. "The pain and the smell of blood upset her. I had to calm her a bit before I could take care of the cut. It wasn't too bad, but it took time."

"I suppose animals must be doctored, even on the Lord's Day," said the older woman, a grumpy cousin of Jane's named Ethel Miller. "Services are well begun. You'd best go in quietly so as not to disturb the others. I suppose you washed your hands well after working with your goats this morning?"

"Oh, Cousin Ethel, of course she did!" Ruth heard Jane say as she tiptoed downstairs and peeked into the large basement room. She spied an empty place beside Mary Yoder. Bishop Troyer, looking up from his prayer book, frowned at her, but she pretended not to notice.

"What's kept you?" Mary whispered.

"Injured goat," Ruth whispered back.

She glanced over at the men's side and caught Jonas looking back. He grinned at her, then returned his attention to the front.

Mary caught the direction of her glance and nudged her with an elbow. "Now there's a gut catch!" she whispered. "Not only handsome, but a kind man. Not everyone would hire someone like me who has trouble walking. He's a very gut boss."

Evelyn Troyer leaned forward from Mary's other side—Ruth hadn't noticed her there—and in a loud whisper said, "It isn't very womanly to be kept from services by farm chores. I doubt you'll catch another husband behaving that way." She sniffed and leaned toward Ruth, over

Mary. "And you smell like a barn!"

Ruth's mouth dropped open, but before she could think of a response, Mrs. Stoltz, the self-appointed maintainer of church etiquette, glared over her shoulder at the younger women. Mary covered a giggle with her hand, Ruth nudged her gently, and they henceforth paid strict attention to the services. Afterward Evelyn hurried off to talk to some of the unmarried young men. Ruth and Mary helped themselves to lunch. They took their plates into the living room, where tables and benches had been set up, Ruth carrying her friend's plate.

"May we join you ladies?"

Ruth looked up to see Jonas and Abigail standing by their table.

"Of course!" Mary said. "There are two empty places. Sit! Sit!"

"When you were late, Abigail was worried," Jonas said.

"Dat, you were worried too, remember? You were wondering where she could be, just like last time, only that time she didn't come at all."

"Um, that's true," he mumbled. "So, what happened?"

"My goat Mimi was slightly hurt this morning. I had to doctor her before I came."

"That's part of animal husbandry," Mary said. "Will she be okay?"

"I hope so. She's one of my favorite goats."

Mary finished her plate and, glancing at Ruth, said, "Well, I'm going to take a turn in the kitchen. I'll see you all later."

"Leave your things, and I'll clear them for you in a bit," Ruth said.

Mary smiled her thanks, picked up her crutches, and pushed to her feet. "I guess Jonas is starting on your barn tomorrow. I'm so excited about moving the business to your farm! I'll get to see you every day!"

"I can't wait," Ruth grinned. "I've been looking forward to seeing you get started, Jonas."

"Me too. I'll come by a bit before the crew and make sure everything is ready."

"Well, why don't you bring Abigail, and we'll have breakfast together to celebrate?" Suddenly worried she was being too forward, and confused about her feelings, she backtracked quickly. "That is, if you want to."

"We'll be there, won't we, Abby?"

"Ja! I'll bring Alaska to play with Ginger Snap!"

"We'll see," Jonas said. Abigail happily ate her lunch, while Ruth and Jonas sat quietly. Jonas broke the silence, though not in a way likely to settle Ruth's nerves.

"Well, we're about to become the subject of speculation, because we're sitting together and unmarried."

"I'm not married, Dat," Abigail said. "I'm marrying you when I'm all grown up."

Ruth and Jonas laughed, and it broke the ice. They smiled at each other.

"I wanted to ask you something," she said at the same time as he said, "I need to talk to you about something."

They laughed again and both said, simultaneously, "You first."

Abigail laughed and pointed at Ruth. "Ladies first, Dat."

Jonas smiled and nodded. "Okay, then."

Ruth took a deep breath. But before she could speak, a petulant voice broke in. "This is not fair. You sat with Jonas after the services two weeks ago, Ruth. It's time to let someone else have a turn. After all, you've already had a husband and I, for one, have not!"

"And you won't, being that forward, young woman," a stern voice said. Ruth glanced to the right, and grimaced to see Evelyn's grandfather, Bishop Troyer, standing with his hat in his hands and a grim look on his face. "I have heard of your unguarded tongue, miss, but this is the first time I've had the opportunity to hear it for myself. Come. We are leaving." To Ruth and Jonas he said, "Please excuse us. I am sorry for the rude interruption to your meal." He took his granddaughter's hand and pushed her in front of him. By the mulish look on her face, she was unrepentant. But the bishop couldn't see her face, and he propelled her before him through the kitchen and out of the house.

Ruth and Jonas stared at each other. "Whoa, I didn't see that coming," Jonas said.

Ruth shook her head. "Okay, she was pretty rude, but I still feel kind of sorry for her."

"Don't waste your energy," Jonas advised. "She isn't sending any kind thoughts your way, you can be sure."

"No doubt," Ruth said. "It's probably been hard on her, not having a mother while she's grown into a young woman."

"Bah. I doubt three mothers could have instilled good manners into her." But Ruth saw him throw a worried look Abigail's way, and she put her hand over his. "Jonas, Abigail is nothing like Evelyn Troyer. She is a well-behaved, mannerly child, and you and your family are doing an excellent job with her. So don't go there."

"Hmm," was Jonas' only response. Ruth wondered what was going through his stubborn head.

———————— ⚓ ————————

Later, as Jonas drove Samson quietly along the road toward home, he thought about Evelyn Troyer not having had a mother's influence while she grew up. In spite of Ruth's reassurances about Abby, he worried that she too might suffer from the lack of a mother's example.

Viola was gone forever, but was it within his power to secure another gut mother for his child? Another gut wife for himself? Maybe even someone who might grow to love him?

Someone for whom he may already be developing feelings?

"Father," he prayed silently, "I need Your guidance. Please help me to know what is the right thing to do, which is the right way to turn. If it is your will that Ruth become part of this family, that she becomes a mudder to Abigail, please let me know. Your will be done."

He stared ahead, hands loosely holding the reins. Samson didn't need much guidance, but he surely did! His feelings were all tangled up, like Abigail's hair if he didn't spray detangler on it right after a bath and carefully comb it out.

On the one hand, there was Viola. His feelings for her had softened, gone a bit out of focus. Now he was filled with a huge love for Abigail and a soft, fond remembering of Viola. And sometimes he felt disloyal to her memory because of this.

Then there was Ruth, for whom he was definitely developing feelings. But were they true? Or did he simply find her attractive, his lonely heart urging him to grasp at available straws?

"Ach!" he softly exclaimed, "How can I know the difference?"

"Know what difference, Dat?" Abigail asked in a sleepy voice.

Jonas started. He hadn't meant to speak aloud and wake Abigail. "The difference between something that's real and something imagined," he finally answered.

"That's easy, Dat," she answered. "Just ask Gott."

"Of course, Abby," he murmured. "I'll ask Gott."

"Then you'll know soon." She patted his knee in a way that made his heart stutter with love. What had he ever done to be so blessed?

Silently, he prayed, "Father, show me the way and the truth. Show me your will. Would Ruth be a gut mother to Abigail? Is she the right wife for me? Am I being greedy, wanting to find another love now? I don't mean to be greedy, but I'm still a young man. I'm lonely. And Abigail needs a mudder. I sure don't want to risk her turning out wild like Evelyn Troyer. Please lead me to make the right choice."

Samson nickered and was answered by another horse nearby. Jonas peered through the darkness. They'd arrived home. So, now all he had to do was wait for Gott's answer.

Of course, he thought with a grimace as he carried Abigail into the house, Gott's time wasn't always the same as a man's time—especially an impatient man's time!

Tomorrow, he'd get started on the barn, and he'd see Ruth. The thought lightened his heart, and he smiled.

CHAPTER SEVENTEEN

❧

Ruth hurried through her chores the next morning. She checked on Mimi, who seemed better, though her leg was a bit warm and red. But she didn't look as miserable, Ruth thought as she applied a poultice. "You'll be fine soon." She stood and put away her supplies. "I'll see you in a few hours, girl. If you get an infection, we'll deal with it, don't you worry."

She washed a load of laundry and hung it out to dry in the crisp January air.

She was just pulling a pan of cinnamon rolls from the oven when she heard a buggy turn into the drive. "Ah! Perfect timing!"

She took a pitcher of milk from the propane-powered fridge, set it on the table, and placed three cups, plates, and napkins at the places. Wiping off her hands, she threw open the door and waved at Jonas and Abigail as they climbed down from their buggy.

"Where's Alaska?"

"She didn't want to come this morning," Abigail said.

"She was hiding under the bed upstairs, and I didn't want this scamp bellying under there in her nice white apron to try to get her. There are dangerous dust bunnies under the beds in our house."

"Dat! There's no such thing as dust bunnies," Abigail said, rolling her eyes and looking more like a teenager than a four-year-old.

"If you say so," he smiled. "But I saw one eat a sock last month, so

I'm not sure you're right."

Ruth smiled at him. "Well then, Abigail, I guess you'll have to play with Ginger Snap so he won't feel left out, if you don't mind?"

Abigail jumped up and down excitedly. "I'd like to do that!"

"Then, when you've worked up an appetite, we'll have breakfast together."

"The men are coming soon to work on the barn. Can I see the goats?"

Ruth laughed. "After breakfast, if it's okay with your dat, you can pet my goats, okay?"

"Ach, ja!" the child said, clapping.

After sharing breakfast, all bundled up against the cold day, the three set out to check on the goats.

Jonas, holding Abigail's tiny hand, followed Ruth outside. At the gate leading out of her garden into the larger farmyard, Ruth paused and looked at the greenhouse.

"What are you thinking?" Jonas asked.

Ruth took a breath. "Just that so much has changed, and that change is hard. But I have to change even more. They say Gott doesn't ask more of us than He knows we can handle, but sometimes, doesn't it seem as though He has too much faith in us, Jonas?"

He looked at her seriously. "I know what you mean. I've faced challenges in the last few years I never would have believed myself capable of, and I'm very glad I found the courage." He glanced meaningfully down at his daughter, who was looking over at the Shires grazing in a field of dry, brown grass.

Ruth nodded fervently. "Ja. Think what you would have missed if you hadn't."

He smiled at her. "And think what may await you if you have the courage to keep moving forward into the unknown. Gott knows what He is doing."

She nodded. "I know He does. Thanks, Jonas. Okay, let's go meet some goats."

She opened the gate, and they went through. Abigail tugged on her father's hand, and he released her. They were not close to the road here, and the road that went past the farm was a quiet one with little traffic. He didn't have to worry here about Abigail in the same way he did at his home. Looking around, he thought how nice it would be to raise Abby here, away from the road.

He shook his head. It was too soon for such thoughts. Wasn't it? Besides, avoiding traffic was no good reason for considering such a big step.

They followed the little girl toward the barn, walking along a set of stepping stones Ruth's grandfather had laid there decades before. The three of them entered the lower level of the big structure.

"It's so warm in here! But it's cold outside. Why is it warm in here?" Abigail asked.

"It's all the animals, Abby," Jonas said. "They warm the place up with their body heat."

"Ohhhhh, just like the barn where baby Jesus kept warm in a manger! Are there any baby goats?"

"Not yet, but it won't be too long. Around Easter we'll have baby goats," Ruth told her.

"I can't wait to see them! They're so cute! If any need to be fed with a bottle, can I help?"

Ruth shrugged. "I don't see why not, if it's all right with your father."

He nodded. "Babies are a lot of work, Abby. They eat all the time!"

"Hello, there," Ruth said, reaching in to scratch a goat between her horns. "It's not time to eat. I'm giving a tour."

Abigail tentatively reached between the slats to pet a goat on the nose. She giggled when it tickled her fingers with its soft lips.

"Why do some goats look different?" Abigail asked, standing by a pen of fiber goats.

"Those are Angoras. I raise them for the soft hair they grow, rather than for their milk. Over there are goats that make milk and fiber," she said, pointing at a row of pens where she housed her Nigora crossbreeds.

Abigail walked over to a pen containing a large Nigerian buck.

She wrinkled her nose. "Ugh! This goat smells bad!" she said. As if in protest, the goat let out a loud bleat. Abigail laughed and looked at him and made a pretty good approximation of the sound back at him. "He has really pretty blue eyes!" she said.

Ruth laughed. "The does actually like the way he smells. But I agree, he's pretty stinky to us humans."

She showed Abigail around the rest of the animal stalls. The horses were all outside. "I'm going to let the goats out in the sunlight for a few hours, Abigail," she said. "Do you want to help?"

The little girl nodded enthusiastically. Ruth walked to the end of the barn opposite where they'd entered and threw open the double doors. Outside was a large fenced-in pasture. Her dogs came running, and she gave them each a quick pat. "Hey, guys! Gut timing. I'm letting the goats out for a couple of hours, so you're on duty."

Abigail's eyes grew huge and round at the sight of the two enormous white dogs.

"Will they bite?" she squeaked, hiding behind Jonas.

"No, *liebchen*, they're here to protect the goats. They're very friendly to little girls. Come here if you'd like to feel how soft their fur is."

Jonas held her hand, and Abigail tentatively stepped forward.

"Down," Ruth commanded, and both dogs dropped down to lie expectantly, their tongues lolling, eyes on Abigail, who approached a bit closer before cautiously reaching out toward one of the dogs. She touched the closer dog, Wolke, who wiggled with pleasure and the desire to jump up and play. "Stay, Wolke," Ruth softly said, and the dog obeyed.

"He's so soft!" Abigail said. She buried her face in his fur, and he reached around and licked her on the cheek.

"Yuck!" she laughed.

Jonas laughed too, and Ruth asked, "Okay? I'm going to let them up, now. Be ready, they may kiss you again."

At her signal, the dogs leaped up and danced around. Ruth reached into the pocket of her apron and took out a couple of treats, which she gave the dogs.

"Okay, time for them to get to work. Protect," she commanded, and the dogs barked and ran outside, doing a quick run around the perimeter of the fence.

"Impressive," Jonas said.

"Abigail, step to the side of the door so you don't get run over by eager goats," Ruth instructed. Jonas took her hand, and they stood to the side as the goats started running, leaping, and gamboling out of their pens and out the door into the field.

"Oh, look at them! They dance!" Abigail said, jumping up and down, her hand in Jonas'.

When the last goats hurried out into the sun, Ruth closed the doors. "The dogs will keep an eye on them. I'll let them back in later."

They walked back to the small door on the opposite side of the barn. "Your crew should be here soon. While you're working in the barn, I'm going to caulk some of the windows in the greenhouse I noticed were loose, get my soil sample ready to mail off to be analyzed, and order seeds. We'll be very productive around here! The goats and horses won't know what to think."

"And Ginger Snap! He'll wonder what's going on too!" Abigail piped in.

"Ja," Ruth smiled. "Ginger Snap will probably think it's very strange. He can watch from the living room window."

"Ruth, again, denki. I think this will be gut...for all of us," Jonas said.

Ruth considered the way Jonas and his small daughter were starting to sneak into her heart. She hoped it would be gut for them, and not end up hurting her.

Abigail had run over to the fence and was talking to the goats and dogs. Ruth smiled at her wistfully.

"Ruth," Jonas said. She turned to look at him questioningly. He studied her face, an earnest expression on his. "At church yesterday, I wanted to say something to you. I've been thinking," he said. "That is, I've noticed how you look at Abigail, and it got me thinking." He reached out and took her hands in his.

"Jonas!" she said, smiling at him and squeezing his hands. "You're being so serious. What are you trying to say?"

He took a deep breath and glanced at Abby to make sure she was still occupied. "Ruth, it's been years since I lost my Viola, and your Levi has been gone a year. Abigail needs a mudder, and I think you'd make a fine one. I can tell you care for her, maybe even love her a little. And it makes sense, you see, with me moving my business here, and then you'd have a family in the house, and it would be gut for us all! What do you think?"

She blinked and stared at him. "Are you. . .asking me to marry you, Jonas?"

Frowning, he took off his hat and pushed one hand through his hair. "Well, ja, but I'm making a mess of it," he muttered. "Or you wouldn't have to ask for clarification."

"But why do you want to marry me? To have a mudder for Abigail? To have a house farther from the road? To be closer to your basket business after you move?" She stared at him, waiting for an answer she could live with, hardly daring to breathe.

He looked relieved and grinned at her. "Ja! All those things! I wish I'd have put it all so clearly." He smiled expectantly at her.

She swallowed, looking at his hopeful face. That face had become rather dear to her lately. But his impromptu speech didn't make it sound as though he cared for her. It made it sound as if he wanted a marriage of convenience. And after the loving relationship she'd shared with Levi, how could she settle for less than that with another man? Especially one she had feelings for. She was afraid that if he didn't return those feelings, in time hers would turn to bitterness. And both he and Abigail deserved a content wife and mother, not a disillusioned, angry one.

In fact, she felt herself becoming angry as she thought about it. And when she got angry, she couldn't control her emotions, or her mouth. How could he have acted like such a callous clod? She'd thought he had feelings for her! Hadn't he kissed her?

She felt tears come to her eyes and turned from him, impatiently brushing them away.

"Ruth?" he asked, alarm in his voice. "Are you crying?"

"Oh!" she dashed tears from her cheeks. "You're so clueless, Jonas! Ja, I have come to love Abigail, and I'd love to be her mudder. But I can't marry you for that reason and because living here would be handy for you! I want what I had before! I want a marriage where my husband cares for me, and I care for him. Not some cold marriage of convenience! I can't believe you even suggested such a thing!"

Turning, she strode for the house, blinded by her tears of fury and disappointment. He followed, falling into step with her. "Wait. What?" he stammered. "Ruth! I'm sorry! I didn't mean it the way it sounded!" He desperately tried to fix his blunder, but she was too hurt to listen.

"No! You've said your piece, Jonas Hershberger," she said between gritted teeth. "Please leave me alone."

"But please let me try to explain again what I meant!" He caught her arm, drawing her to a halt. She wouldn't look at him. "Please, Ruth! I didn't say it right."

She shook her head. "No. You said it honestly, Jonas. Now you're trying to turn it around so I'll believe you care for me. But it's too late. You just want another employee, but one you don't have to pay!"

He released her, looking shocked by her words.

"And while we're being honest, has it occurred to you that there is every possibility that I can't have children? Levi and I never did. In marrying me, you might have to settle for having only one child. No sons to help on the farm or to take over your business! You deserve better! And so do I."

She hurried up the steps into her house and closed the door firmly behind herself.

Jonas stood staring at the door Ruth had just closed, wondering how he'd messed things up so badly and whether it was possible to fix the situation. Later, he'd reflect on how he simply lost his head and completely forgot his plan for a cautious approach to the possibility of him and Ruth and Abigail someday forming a family. The thing was, he really did care for Ruth. Why hadn't he said so? Why had he started with the part about needing a mother for Abigail? And as for other children, did that matter to him? He hadn't thought about it. Why hadn't he grabbed her and kissed her until she saw reason?

"Stupid!" he said, kicking the fence.

"Dat?" a small voice said from behind him. "You're not supposed to say that word. Did you say it to Ruth? Is that why she's crying?"

Ah. That's why he hadn't grabbed her and kissed her senseless. His four-year-old daughter had witnessed his idiocy.

Jonas closed his eyes and prayed for patience. Taking a deep breath, he turned and looked at his small daughter, who looked worried. He reached for her, and she came into his arms. Picking her up, he patted her back and said, "No, liebchen. I was talking to myself. I hurt Ruth's feelings by mistake, and now I don't know how to fix it."

"You should say you're sorry, Dat." Abigail cupped a small hand on his cheek. "That's the best thing."

He smiled at her. "Ja, I expect you're right," he said. "But not today. I don't think Ruth will talk to me today. Maybe tomorrow." He carried Abigail to their buggy and tucked her inside before climbing into the driver's seat and taking up the reins.

"Aren't the men coming to work in the barn?" Abigail asked.

"Ja, but I've decided to take you home, Abby. I'll be back soon, and they know what to do."

He'd talk to his sister. She'd call him a simpleton, but maybe she could help him fix this.

Driving home, he sent up a silent prayer. "Father, I really messed up. Please, if it is your will that Ruth and I make a family, help me to find a way to make amends for hurting her, and to show her I really do care for her. And Father, help me to know my own heart. Do I care if Ruth can't have bopplin? Help me to know. Amen."

He sighed. As much as he loved his child and being a father, he now realized it wasn't enough. He needed someone to relate to on an adult level. Someone smart, who understood his humor, and who liked him for himself. And not just someone. . .Ruth.

"I sure hope Sally has some gut ideas, or I'm sunk."

CHAPTER EIGHTEEN

About an hour after she'd shut the door in Jonas' face, Ruth was addressing the envelope for a letter she'd written to her mother when she heard a wagon turn into her driveway. Peeking out the window, she saw Jonas along with two other men from the community. She drew back before they saw her, then shook her head in disgust.

"Ach, I'm behaving like a boppli." She opened the door and stepped out onto her stoop. A young man she recognized from a neighboring Amish community paused in unloading lumber, looked up, and tipped his hat to her.

"Gut morning, Ruth!"

She smiled and waved good morning, as Jonas and the other young man climbed out. "Hello, Simon!" she called.

"Morning, Ruth," Jonas called, looking a bit uncertain. "I've brought helpers."

If he could act as if nothing had happened, well, that would make it all the easier for her to do the same. He must have realized he'd made a foolish mistake in proposing to her. He didn't want a wife. He wanted a nanny. And for that, he already had Selma. Pasting on a smile she hoped looked natural on her face, Ruth said, "I've got a fresh pot of kaffi on. You can take it out to the barn with you to keep you warm while you work."

"Denki." Jonas said. "There are a few more men coming with the drywall sheets."

"I'll make another pot of coffee. Come get yours now, and I'll refill it."

They all trooped up the stairs into the kitchen, where Ruth supplied them with large mugs of coffee and a plate of fragrant rolls, dripping with sticky icing.

"Ach, Ruth, you make such gut cinnamon rolls!" a young, beardless man—signifying his single state—said as he savored the treat.

"Denki." Ruth smiled at the young man.

"Ja, she does," Jonas said. "This must be our lucky day, hey? Ruth, this is Zeke Yoder, and he's visiting from the Sugarcreek area. He's passing the time today helping us out." Turning to Ruth, Jonas looked at her for a moment, as if searching for some sign that she was still upset. Ruth regarded him with a politely detached look, and he frowned a bit before saying, "We'll be here tomorrow morning as well. Just in case you have a hankering to bake more rolls."

The other men laughed, and Ruth smiled sweetly and said, "We'll see tomorrow, Jonas. Now get out of my kitchen, all of you! I have work to do." She shooed them out the door, promising to bring more coffee out to the barn later. After they'd left, she sank into a chair and rested her head in her hands.

"Things were so easy between us, Father! Why did he have to ask me to marry him in that way!"

When silence greeted her query, she lifted her head and looked out the door to where the men were still unloading the wagon.

"Maybe he didn't mean it the way it sounded? He tried to say so, but I was angry. Ach! When my temper gets away, I can't listen!" She remembered her mother telling her she was her own worst enemy at such times.

"Please, Father, if it is Your will that Jonas, Abigail, and I should make a family, let him have the courage to speak again, for I don't think I have the courage to bring it up. I'd feel like a fool!"

A while later, Ruth carried a fresh pot of coffee out to the barn, along with a large platter of cinnamon rolls and several more mugs.

Placing the refreshments on a board sitting across two sawhorses, she sought Jonas with her eyes. There he was, climbing a stepladder. Once he reached the top, he turned and reached to where another man handed him some lengths of wood, which he used to begin building a wood frame for the ceiling which would go over the work area, lessening the area they would need to heat. He glanced over and, catching her eye, nodded and sent her a small smile. His eyes seemed to ask her for understanding, and possibly for forgiveness. After a moment, she smiled back, and then turned and headed for the door.

As she walked back toward the house through the barnyard, Ruth thought about how Jonas made her feel things she hadn't felt since she and Levi were courting. And to tell the truth, she'd never expected to experience it again. She'd thought the symptoms were reserved for the very young.

"Guess I was wrong about that," she murmured as she opened the gate to her garden. "Jonas makes me feel just as I did back then. The only question is, do I want to feel like this? With him? Now?" She laughed at herself. "Who am I kidding? Of course I do! The real question is, do I want him to propose again? Do I want to be his wife?" Shaking her head at her own uncertainty, she climbed her porch steps and entered her house.

She pulled out the ingredients for a hearty stew. "Those men will be hungry. And dithering about Jonas isn't going to solve anything."

Ginger Snap, napping in a pool of sunlight on the window seat, meowed softly in agreement.

In the barn, Jonas held several nails in his teeth and skillfully hammered each one into position with two strikes of his hammer. His mind, free to wander while he did such familiar work, drifted across the yard to Ruth.

Should he try to talk to her again? Would she welcome his explanation, after his clumsy proposal? Ach! He was mortified to think of how he'd flubbed that.

"I couldn't blame her for never wanting to see me again," he muttered around the nails.

"What's that, Jonas?" Elam Miller, working nearby, asked.

"Oh, sorry, Elam. Nothing. I'm just talking to myself."

"It's a sign of living alone for too long, man," Elam said, wiggling his bushy eyebrows. "That pretty lady over in the house looked at you a lot while we were over there. Maybe you should think about finding a solution to that talking-to-yourself thing."

A couple men working nearby laughed, and Jonas smiled gamely. Gut thing they didn't know about his botched proposal, he thought, bringing his hammer down carelessly and yelping as he struck his thumb.

"You okay there, boss?"

Jonas nodded glumly, sucking on his injured thumb. "Ja, just distracted."

He didn't see the other men exchange knowing looks and smiles.

Elam was right. He was lonely, and he did want to find a solution— and the solution's name was Ruth! Not because he needed a nanny or a cook or anything else except her specific company!

Now he just had to find a way to make her believe it.

CHAPTER NINETEEN

The next day, Ruth got up a little early and finished her chores before the sun was up. Her breath puffed out before her as she hurried back to the house through the winter dawn after feeding all her critters. Inside, she preheated the oven for the cinnamon rolls she'd promised the men this morning. She was just pulling the first batch from the oven when she heard the wagons turning into the driveway.

Opening the door, she leaned out and called, "Come get some kaffi and fresh cinnamon rolls before you start work."

They didn't need to be asked twice, and Ruth heard the squeak of her garden gate as they filed in and up the steps into her kitchen. They stomped their feet before coming inside.

"Denki, Ruth," they said, helping themselves to mugs of coffee and hot rolls.

Jonas came up the steps and pushed the door open, sending a blast of icy air into the kitchen. He slapped his arms as he closed the door against the wind.

"Ach! I think we may have a winter blast on the way." His face was rosy below his wool hat. He glanced at Ruth to see whether she was going to toss him out the door, and when that didn't seem likely, he breathed a sigh of relief. Maybe she would give him another chance. He smiled tentatively at her and sniffed the air. "Do I smell rolls?"

"You'd better hurry, Jonas, or they'll be gone," Elam said, helping himself to seconds.

Jonas hurried over to the table and took the last roll. "Just in time!" he said with a mock frown at his friends. "Don't your wives feed you breakfast before you leave the house in the morning?"

The men laughed, and Ruth poured Jonas a mug of coffee and handed it to him. He accepted gratefully, allowing his fingers to briefly touch hers as he took the mug. She inhaled sharply at the contact, then bustled away to the oven.

"Where is Abigail today?" She pulled another pan of rolls out and set them on the stovetop to cool.

"More rolls! I guess I won't starve after all," Jonas said. "She's with my sister, playing with her cousins," he said, sipping the hot brew.

"I'll bet Sally fed you when you dropped Abigail off! Tell the truth, now!" Elam teased.

Jonas smiled and wiggled his eyebrows, taking another bite of his roll. "Maybe, but I'm a big man, and I need a lot of fuel if I'm going to work hard all day in the cold!"

The men laughed some more and poked fun at him good naturedly, but he ignored them. "Ruth, you make gut coffee. Just right for an icy winter's day."

"Will you finish putting up the walls and ceiling today?" she asked. "Or should I plan to feed you all again tomorrow?"

The men looked at one another, some grinning mischievously. "Well, that depends on what's on the menu," Zeke, the young man from Sugarcreek, said.

"I was thinking sausage, biscuits, and gravy tomorrow. It's supposed to be very cold, and possibly snow," she said with a straight face. "I wouldn't want you to go hungry. Even though I know your wives feed you before you leave home!"

Zeke's face lit up. "I'm not married yet, ma'am. Jonas, I think we need to slow down. We wouldn't want to make any mistakes because we're rushing the job, you know."

Jonas smiled. "I think it's safe to say we'll be here one more day, Zeke."

Zeke laughed and patted his belly. "Gut. For sausage, biscuits, and gravy, I might have to propose!" He winked at Ruth. "I'll wait and see if yours is as gut as my maem's!"

Ruth blushed, and blushed again, because she was embarrassed at such a girlish reaction to a young man's joking. He was nearly ten years younger than she!

She looked up and caught Jonas' eye. He smiled slightly at her, and she knew he'd seen, and she blushed a third time.

Disgusted with herself, she rolled her eyes and placed the rolls on the table. "They need to cool a bit, and then I'll ice them and bring them to the barn along with some more kaffi. Then lunch at noon. Now scat!"

"That's our hint, boys," Jonas said. "Everyone out of Ruth's kitchen before she puts us to work scrubbing something." He was last out the door, and he glanced back at Ruth, touching the brim of his hat in respect before closing the door behind him.

———————————— ✿ ————————————

When Ruth walked over to the barn to call the men for lunch, she couldn't believe her eyes. The walls were up, and the men were applying drywall mud to the seams. Kerosene heaters were working hard to keep the space warm enough for the work. Jonas showed her the two rooms they'd made, complete with ceilings. One space was large and open, and the other was smaller and would house a small bathroom.

"Tomorrow we'll sand and paint," Zeke said.

Ruth nodded.

"Come see the storage area." Jonas led Ruth through a door into the larger barn area, where she was surprised to see they had already built racks and shelves to hold stocks of wood and completed baskets. In this area they hadn't framed in a ceiling, as the supplies wouldn't mind temperature changes.

"My! You have been busy!" she exclaimed. Turning, she looked at the enclosed area, which looked a bit odd sitting inside the big barn.

"It's funny looking, ja?" Jonas asked, looking at it with her. "But more useful. And we can expand if the business grows."

"Ja," she nodded. "It's gut."

"Tomorrow the outdoor woodstove is coming."

She nodded. "Gut. I really don't like having the kerosene heaters going in here, with the straw and all. Though I'm sure you're being very careful."

He nodded. "Of course. And they'll be fully off before we leave tonight."

"I've made progress on my project too. I sent away for seeds yesterday and mailed off my soil samples to OSU to see what supplements I may need to get my greenhouse business started," she said. "I want to go to Berlin to Orme Hardware soon to purchase a few things I'll need. The seeds should come next week, and the results of the soil testing. I should be able to start planting seeds in a week or two. And none too soon! It's nearly February!"

"You have been busy," he said. "After we sand and paint tomorrow, I'll be able to help you get the greenhouse in order, if you like."

"I wouldn't want you to feel obligated."

"I want to help, Ruth."

She nodded, unsure of how to respond. "Well, I'll be back out later with lunch." She turned and hurried away.

Jonas watched her go and silently sent up a simple prayer. "Father, please help me to know what to say next time," he asked. "I really botched it the other night. And, although I sense that Ruth is part of Your plan for my future, I confess part of me is a little afraid to love again. What if I lose another wife? I don't know how I'd stand it."

He had just returned to the unfinished shop space when the out-side door opened, and a female voice called out, "Hello? Are you men working hard?"

"Oh boy," Jonas mumbled under his breath as Evelyn Troyer sashayed inside, carrying a covered picnic basket and looking very pretty in a light green dress and black wool cape.

"There you are, Jonas!" she called gaily. "I heard you were all hard at work fixing up Ruth's old barn, and I thought to myself, Evelyn, you can't let those poor men go hungry. So I made a picnic!"

"Evelyn, I'm afraid we don't have time to stop work for a break right now," Jonas started, but Zeke had spotted a pretty girl carrying food, and he clambered down from the ladder he'd been working on and hurried over to take the heavy basket from her.

"Here, Miss, let me take that!" Zeke placed the basket on a board balanced on two sawhorses. When Evelyn saw the remains of Ruth's cinnamon rolls, her eyes narrowed. "Oh, I see you already had a snack."

"That doesn't mean we wouldn't welcome another!" Zeke said, opening the picnic basket to peek inside.

Evelyn looked at him consideringly. Zeke was a good-looking, well-built young man, and although only twenty-one, he was still a couple years older than she, and he was obviously a hard worker.

Jonas thought the lad had better watch out or he'd find himself lassoed in by the bishop's granddaughter.

"Why, thank you. I'm afraid we haven't been introduced. I'm Evelyn Troyer, Bishop Troyer's granddaughter, visiting from New York."

Zeke snatched his hands back from the basket and regarded the young woman. "Oh, the bishop's granddaughter, are you?" His Adam's apple bobbed up and down nervously. "I'm actually not from here. I live in Sugarcreek, but I'm visiting my aunt and uncle, and they told me Jonas needed help this week, so here I am."

"Meet Zeke Yoder, Evelyn," George helpfully said.

"No need to be shy, Zeke," Evelyn cooed, peeking at him through her eyelashes. "Here, have a sandwich. They're ham and cheese, with my special secret sauce." She handed him a sandwich, and he unwrapped it and took a large bite. His eyes widened. "That's gut!" he exclaimed around a mouthful of bread, ham, cheese, and secret sauce.

Evelyn glowed with pleasure. "Denki! Let's sit down, and I'll tell you about New York."

Jonas moved forward. "Evelyn, Zeke has a job to do here. Thank you for the sandwiches, but I'm afraid we can't stop now. We've barely gotten started for the day. Perhaps you and Zeke can visit Saturday at the social."

Zeke jumped up, stuffing the last of the sandwich in his mouth and nodding at Evelyn while hurrying back to his ladder. "Right, boss, sorry! Pleasure meeting you, Evelyn! Denki for the delicious sandwich! I hope to see you Saturday!"

Evelyn looked a bit vexed, but she recovered and smiled sweetly at Jonas. "Sorry to interrupt. I'll leave the basket here, and you can return it to me later, Jonas." She gave him a smoldering look from under her lashes and walked out the door, leaving her basket behind.

Elam gave a low whistle. "I'd heard she was a handful. I don't envy the bishop!"

Zeke looked down from the ladder. "I thought she was very nice. And she makes a gut sandwich!"

Elam snorted. "You're thinking with your stomach and other illogical parts, boy. I'd think twice about that one. She'd be a handful for sure. Now get back to your job. They're calling for snow tomorrow, and we may not be able to work."

"I dunno," Zeke said. "If that sandwich is any indication of her cooking, it might be worth it. She's mighty pretty too."

"It's what's inside that matters, boy," Elam reminded him.

"Of course! But the pretty face is a nice bonus, wouldn't you say? And the inside of that sandwich made my stomach mighty happy." Whistling, he got back to the job at hand. Elam gave Jonas a wry smile, and Jonas returned it, thinking that it wouldn't hurt his feelings if Evelyn Troyer turned her attention to Zeke, and that was a fact. He had enough female trouble as it was.

Shaking his head, he picked up his hammer and turned back to the drywall, careful to keep his thumb out of harm's way this time.

CHAPTER TWENTY

With morning came a stillness, which could only mean one thing. Ruth jumped out of bed, slipped her feet into warm, fuzzy pink slippers, and hurried to peer out her bedroom window. "Ohhhhh, beautiful," she breathed reverently. The world was covered in a glittering blanket of white. At least six inches of snow lay on the ground. "Well, I guess Jonas won't be showing up here today." She tied her fuzzy pink robe as she headed downstairs. In the kitchen she turned up the gaslight on the wall and put several new logs into the stove before brewing herself a pot of strong coffee in her speckled blue-and-white stoneware pot.

She sat with her legs curled beneath her in the window seat in her living room, enjoying her coffee as the sun came up, its radiance almost too much to look at as it crept across the farmyard, banishing shadows as it climbed above the rooftop of the barn and danced on millions of individual ice crystals, revealing all the colors of the rainbow in the blanket of pristine snow.

"Gott's creation is stunning!" she whispered in awe.

Then she dressed warmly, pulled on knee-high muck boots, and headed outside to take care of her livestock. There was an eerie stillness, almost an expectation, in the air. Opening the small door, she entered, turned on the generator, and flipped the light switch, and the bottom floor of the barn was illuminated by hanging lights dangling from the ceiling. The goats called to her, and she smiled. It was warmer in the barn than outside, thanks to all the bodies creating heat. Ruth took off her long cloak and hung it on a hook, putting on an old wool cardigan she kept in the barn for use in the winter.

"Gut morning!" she called to the goats, the horses, and her milk cow. "It snowed! So you might not want to go outside today."

She trudged through the snow to her chicken house after leaving the barn. Inside, she spoke softly to the sleepy hens as she prepared to clean up their little home.

"It's cold and snowy, girls. You'll probably want to stay hunkered down in here today, where it's nice and warm."

The rooster was scratching around on the floor of the building, looking for something interesting to eat. He scooted out of Ruth's way when she went over to pick up the broom to give the floor a good sweeping.

"Look out, George." She swept bits of dirt and molted feathers into a pile in the center of the floor for disposal. She opened up a bin and dug into the feed with a scoop before turning and scattering it around the clean floor of the building. George dug right in and was quickly joined by the hens, who roused themselves from their sleepy state and fluttered down to get their share. She left the chickens gobbling up their morning ration and headed back out into the cold, carrying the basket of eggs she'd gathered while the hens were busy eating. They'd be slowing down in the laying soon, she knew. But for now, she could still enjoy fresh eggs each day.

"Brrrrrr!" She shivered, setting the basket on the kitchen counter. She grabbed a sage-green cardigan she'd knitted the winter before off a hook and pulled it on over her dark green work dress. She added more logs to the fire and sat down with another cup of coffee. "I'm going to need to bring in more wood. I'm getting low."

Ginger Snap strolled into the room, stretching mightily before looking at Ruth and giving a sleepy "Mrrp!" He sauntered over to his dishes and checked out the kibble and the water.

"Good morning, lazybones. Are you just getting up? I've already completed most of my chores while you slept the morning away."

Ginger Snap flicked his tail and settled down to some serious munching.

Ruth stood and stretched and wondered what to do next. It wasn't a good day for laundry, so she decided to do some mending instead. "That way I can sit in front of the fire with you and keep warm," she told the kitten, who was now diligently bathing in front of the warm stove.

She had just finished sewing a button back onto one of her work dresses when she heard a sound that made her sit up and listen hard. "That sounds like sleigh bells. But who could it be?" She heard the sound again, more clearly this time. The silvery peal of bells rang out through the still air.

"Definitely sleigh bells!" Ruth jumped up and placed her mending on the chair behind her and hurried to the window. Pushing back the curtain, she squinted against the brightness of the snow and saw a black sleigh pulled by a prancing team of horses. Bundled up in the sleigh were two people—one big and one small.

"Jonas and Abigail!" Ruth grinned delightedly. How she loved sleigh riding! She threw open the kitchen door and called out, "You must be freezing! Come inside, and I'll make some hot chocolate!"

"We're not cold!" Abigail cried.

Ruth could barely see the child's face, all wrapped up in a warm muffler, with a colorful knitted stocking cap covering her hair.

"We came to kidnap you for the afternoon!" Jonas' eyes smiled above his blue woolen scarf. "Bundle up and come sleighing with us!"

Ruth considered. Things were still a bit awkward between them. But. . .maybe she should give him another chance? Her chores were done, and it was hours before she'd need to care for her livestock again. Why not go have a little fun? It had been so long since she did something that didn't involve some kind of productivity.

And the fact that he was here was a gut sign, right? She made up her mind. "All right! I will! Give me a few minutes to get ready."

———————— ❦ ————————

Jonas felt a huge wave of relief. Was he forgiven? Or did Ruth just really want to go on a sleigh ride? He puffed a breath out from his cheeks and shook his head. Women were complicated, and so was courting. But having decided to go ahead, even though he still felt fearful at the thought of risking his heart again, he had decided to do things right. This time, he wouldn't act like a dumb kid.

When Ruth came out her door bundled up for the cold ride, Jonas jumped out of the sleigh and hurried around to help her climb in. Abigail scooted over to the middle of the seat and lifted up the lap rug for Ruth to slide underneath. On the floor there were warm bricks wrapped in towels to help keep their feet from getting too cold. Jonas hopped back into the driver's seat, made sure the rug was settled securely over all their laps and legs, and took up the whip. Clucking to the team, he called, "Giddyap, boys!" and they were off. "We'll stick to the back roads. They haven't been plowed, and there's not much traffic out today."

The sleigh moved swiftly over the snowy lanes, and soon the three of them were singing merrily, their breath puffing about them as the sleigh sped along behind the matched team of bays.

"What pretty horses," Ruth said. "I don't remember seeing them before."

"I got them this summer. They were a bit wild, fresh from the racetrack. So I worked with them for a few months before trusting them to pull people."

"Well, they're beautiful, and perfect for pulling the sleigh," she said. "Hard to believe they're not brothers! They look so much alike."

The team was spirited, but they responded well to Jonas' directions and never tried to bolt. They drove past Lydia's house at one point, and Ruth glanced back, seeing that everything looked to be in order. "I miss Lydia. She won't be back for months yet."

As they drove merrily past farms, people who were outside stopped what they were doing to wave. Jonas, Ruth, and Abigail waved gaily back as they whisked by.

"This is so much fun! I'm so glad you came by to kidnap me!"

Jonas felt glad too. He sort of wished Abigail was snug at home with Selma instead of squeezed between them. That way, he might let their shoulders and legs "accidentally" touch during the drive. *Ach! Don't be selfish!* he chided himself. *Abby is loving this!* And she obviously was, if the way she constantly chattered about things they passed and everything she saw was any indication.

After an hour or so, Jonas turned the team toward Ruth's house, and by the time they turned into her drive, the bricks had cooled and so had their feet. "Brrr!" he said. "That hot chocolate sounds gut now!"

Ruth lifted the blanket and started to climb out of the sleigh. Before she could, Jonas appeared beside her and lifted her down. He then set Abigail on the ground, saying, "You two go inside and get warm. I'll tie up the team. We won't stay too long, so I won't unhitch them."

"Ach! It feels gut to be inside!" he said a few minutes later as he hung his coat on the peg inside Ruth's warm kitchen. "Where's Abigail?"

"She's looking for Ginger Snap." Ruth stood at the stove, stirring milk over the gas flame. Jonas found himself just staring at her. She made such a pretty picture, her cheeks rosy from the cold and a few tendrils of hair escaping from her prayer kapp.

Catching himself staring, he nodded. "That should keep her occupied for a bit."

"Pull the rocker up by the stove and get comfortable. The milk has to warm up for a few more minutes."

Jonas sank down onto the maple rocker, basking in warmth. "I could get used to this." He sighed, closing his eyes.

"Better add a couple logs to the fire, or you won't stay toasty long." Ruth took the milk off the stove and poured it into mugs containing cocoa. She added little marshmallows to each mug.

Jonas looked into the stove's firebox and then added a few logs. "You need more wood, Ruth," he commented. "You're about out. Where is your woodpile? I'll bring some logs in before we leave."

"Oh! You don't need to do that. I can get them."

"You could just say thank you and let me do this for you," he said quietly. "Remember? I want to be a gut nochber."

Blushing a bit, she nodded. "Ja, you're right. Denki, Jonas! The woodpile is just to the right of the house."

He smiled. It felt like a tiny victory, getting her to let him do a neighborly little chore for her. "That wasn't so hard, was it?"

"Not so hard," she agreed. They stood looking at each other, silly smiles on their faces, before Ruth looked away, picking up the poker to stir the fire.

"Ruth," Jonas began hesitantly, "I want to apologize for my clumsy words the other night. I didn't say what I meant at all, and I hope you'll forgive me. And, maybe, give me another chance?"

She looked at him searchingly, and he felt hope. He wasn't offering pretty words, but maybe she didn't really need them. Maybe she just needed honesty and caring.

"Are you asking to court me, Jonas?"

His heart pounded and he nodded slowly. "Ja. That's what I want. I've prayed about this, and I'm trying to overcome some fears about caring for someone again, like I cared for Viola. I...I'm not sure I could stand such a crushing loss again."

"I understand, Jonas," she said, compassion shining in her eyes. "But life is full of risks. If you risk nothing, you gain nothing. I've been praying too. I worried that if I allowed myself to care for you, I'd be betraying Levi. But now I don't think so. I think both he and Viola would be okay with us getting to know each other and maybe finding happiness. Anyway, I'm willing to explore the possibility."

He smiled and reached for her, but before his hands could capture hers, Abigail ran into the room, trailed by the kitten, and asked whether the hot chocolate was ready yet. Ruth shot him an amused look and gestured for father and daughter to sit down. She served them, and they sat nibbling cookies and blowing on the tops of their mugs before sipping carefully.

"Mmm, I love hot chocolate! Denki!" Abigail said. "This has been the absolutely most perfect day ever!"

Jonas reached over to tug on Abigail's braid. "It has, hasn't it?"

"I don't know when I've enjoyed a day more," Ruth confessed.

"May I please have more marshmallows?" Abigail asked politely.

Ruth tipped a few more into the little girl's cup.

"Denki, Ruth! Look! It's snowing again!" Abigail pointed at the kitchen window, where sure enough, fat flakes drifted lazily down from a sky that had clouded over since they'd come inside.

They sat there together while the snow fell outside, just enjoying each other's company.

When their cups were empty and the cookies gone, Jonas stood up. "I'll fill your woodbox, and then I'd better get Abby home before dark falls. The team has been standing long enough in the cold."

"Denki." Ruth smiled, and Jonas smiled back.

"There you go." He grinned before bundling up and heading outside. It took several trips to fill the wood rack on her porch. How was she managing all of this by herself? The farm, the stock, the house. He had help and couldn't imagine doing it all alone. He opened the door and called to Abby, "Come take these logs and fill the woodbox, child." He handed two small logs to Abigail.

Ruth and Abby carried logs to the box by the stove until it was full. Then Jonas said it was time to go, and Ruth dressed the child in her winter cloak and pulled her stocking cap over her prayer kapp.

As he drove away, with the sleigh bells ringing merrily, he looked back and saw Ruth standing at her door watching them.

And he realized it was too late for caution. He'd already fallen for the sweet widow. He could only hope he wasn't falling alone.

CHAPTER TWENTY-ONE

The snow fell on and off for two days, leaving around a foot of the white stuff on the ground. On the afternoon of the second day, Ruth was hanging clean, wet clothes in the kitchen when she heard an engine outside. Looking out the window, she saw her English neighbor, Paul Chesler, plowing her driveway. She stepped out on the porch, waving at him in thanks. He tipped his hat to her and continued working until he had her entire driveway and the area between the house and barn cleared out.

She put on her boots and carried a mug of coffee out to him.

"You didn't have to come out here in the cold, Ruth."

He was a shy man, around forty, and a bachelor. He had always been kind and was always very proper in his dealings with her. He was a farmer, and to make extra money he drove a fifteen-seat van which he hired out to Amish folk going on trips too long to make in their buggies. Ruth had ridden with him and a group of young people on a church mission trip to Illinois one summer. It had been great fun, and she'd been amused to learn that he'd nicknamed his van the Big Green Pickle. It *was* about the color of a gherkin.

"Well, you didn't have to plow out my driveway, Paul."

"Aw, it wasn't any trouble." He drank the coffee with evident enjoyment. "I've seen Jonas Hershberger and that pretty daughter of his around here quite a bit, lately," he remarked with a sly gleam in his eye.

Ruth was surprised. Generally, Paul did not pry. But he lived right next door, and he was no doubt curious about the people around him, especially as he had no family of his own to occupy his time.

"Jonas is going to move his basket business into my barn," she replied rather more primly than she'd intended. "He's been getting the space ready."

His eyes twinkled. "That sleigh ride you took with him and young Abby didn't look like business to me."

She was stumped. "He was just being friendly. His daughter and I have kittens from Lydia Coblentz's last litter. That's all."

"Kittens from the same litter? Ma'am, that don't generally cause a man to come around with sleigh bells ringing. That's courting!" He laughed and handed her the mug. "Thank you kindly for the coffee. I have to get on now. Lucy Nichols on down the road will need her driveway plowed out too. And she makes the best chocolate chip cookies I've ever tasted. Makes me hope for snow in the winter!"

He winked at her and drove away.

"He winked at me!" she said in astonishment. But wasn't it interesting that he was driving on down to Lucy Nichol's house to plow her driveway? She was a single English woman in her late thirties. Maybe he was seeing romance everywhere because he was interested in a romance of his own.

And who was being nibby now?

Feeling better, she finished hanging her wash, made a cup of tea, and went into the living room to read for an hour.

After a while she put down her book—she was reading *Little Women* by Louisa May Alcott for maybe the sixth time—and bundled up to walk out and get the mail.

It certainly was nice being able to walk right down the driveway without having to lift her knees practically up to her chin while wading through snowdrifts.

She opened the mailbox and found the *Budget*, the Amish newspaper printed in Sugarcreek and sent all over the country, and a letter in a green envelope addressed to her.

"It's from Lydia!" she exclaimed.

Hurrying back inside, she stomped off her boots, hung up her cloak, and then sat at the kitchen table and opened the letter.

> *My dearest Ruth,*
>
> *I do hope you are well. I hear it has snowed quite a bit up in Ohio. Here in Florida the weather is fine. It is 75 degrees out right now, and sunny. Later we will take a bus to the beach, and I will walk along the shore in my bare feet. I'll look for a smooth stone for you, or maybe a piece of sea glass!*
>
> *I miss everyone, but I must confess that I do not miss Ohio winters. My sister has asked me to stay here in Florida with her, and I am tempted. What do I have at home but an empty house with only a pair of old cats for company? And they are doing very well here in Florida, by the way, and love their comfy basket. They like sitting in the window watching the odd birds strut around outside. We have a wood stork that visits daily, begging for scraps! We've named him Roy, after that tall, skinny farmer who used to have the place along the Mill Creek bend years back. Remember him? His nose sort of reminds me of Roy the stork's nose too.*
>
> *Anyway, I'm digressing because I don't really want to write about leaving you and all my other friends. But I am considering my sister's offer, even though the thought of Florida heat in the summer, and us without air conditioning, gives me pause! Anyway, I just wanted you to know.*
>
> *I'll pray about this and see what Gott has in mind for this old woman.*
>
> *Yours in friendship,*
> *Lydia*

Ruth stared at the words on the page and felt bereft. What would she do without her old friend down the road?

She would be so much lonelier if Lydia stayed in Florida!

But why should Lydia stay in Ohio just so she would be available on the occasions Ruth had time for a visit? What was that, maybe twice a week?

She folded the letter and carefully placed it back in the envelope. She would also pray about it, so that if Lydia did decide to remain in Florida, Gott might help her get used to the idea.

———————— ⚓ ————————

Jonas pulled his buggy into Ruth's driveway and looked around in surprise. "Looks like someone beat me to the job," he told Samson. He scratched his chin. He'd planned on offering to plow Ruth's driveway as a way to get to see her today. "Well, I'm here, so I might as well say hello, ja, Samson?"

The horse nickered and was answered by Ruth's horses in the barn. A moment later, the small door in the barn opened, and Ruth poked her head outside. Jonas tied Samson and walked over to the barn.

"Jonas! What a nice surprise. I'm just doing a few chores."

"I'll join you. Who plowed your driveway?"

"Oh! Paul Chesler, my English neighbor. He just left a little while ago. He has a plow on his old truck, and I think he enjoys visiting and helping his neighbors, especially Lucy Nichols down the lane, who, he says, bakes a fine cookie."

"Ja, I know her. She's pretty too." Jonas' eyes twinkled as he looked at Ruth from beneath his warm wool hat. Today he had a red woolen scarf dangling from his neck. With so many women working for him, plus his sister and mother, he had lots of hand-knit and crocheted scarves, hats, and mittens.

"Hmmm, ja. So what brings you by?"

Jonas was pleased to detect a note of jealousy in her voice at his mention of how pretty Lucy Nichols was. He smiled as he followed her into the barn. That was a gut sign, he thought.

"I was going to offer to plow for you. I noticed the old snowplow against the barn a few days ago. I figured Hans and Betty could handle it. But I was too late! Next time, I'll get here sooner. Can't let Paul beat my time."

"Oh, Jonas," she chided, grabbing a broom and beginning an energetic sweeping of what seemed to Jonas like an already-clean barn floor. "He's not interested in me, and you know it."

"Only because he knows it wouldn't do him any good. You're not likely to leave the church, and I can't see him giving up his nice truck and electric service." He backed up to give her room, and she glanced up, her eyes widening in alarm.

"Jonas! Look out!" she cried. But she was too late. The billy goat, not liking someone using the wall of his stall as a resting spot, had lowered his head and, with a great bleating, rushed at Jonas and, through the space between rails, butted him hard in the rear, sending him stumbling several feet across the barn to land on his face on the flagstone floor.

With a cry of dismay, Ruth rushed to help him up. "Jonas! Are you hurt?"

Jonas rolled over onto his back and stayed still a minute, taking stock of his situation. The old goat had knocked the wind out of him, good and proper, and he wasn't sure he could talk yet. He held up a finger and concentrated on getting his breath. Ruth reached over and picked his hat up from the floor and dusted it off as she knelt beside him. After a couple of minutes, during which Jonas felt like an idiot, he sat up and looked over at the goat, who was munching hay and looking back with mocking blue eyes. "I think I'm still in one piece," he said, reaching for his hat.

Ruth handed it over and then reached into her sweater pocket for a clean white hanky, which she offered him. "You have a little blood, just there," she said, pointing to his chin. He blotted at it.

"And there," she said, pointing to his nose, which felt painfully swollen from its meeting with the flagstones. He blotted at that too. She impulsively placed a kiss on her finger and touched it to his scrapes. "Poor thing," she crooned.

He felt warmth spread through his body as he struggled to stand. "I'm okay," he said, dusting off his pants and jacket. "Nothing really hurt but my dignity."

"That can be bad enough," she said. "I'm so sorry. He can be a nuisance."

"I see that." He held the hanky out to her, but then pulled it back. "I'll, uh, wash this first," he mumbled, sticking it in his pocket.

"Other than the scrapes, you're not hurt?" she asked anxiously.

"I'm fine. He just took me by surprise." Jonas felt embarrassed that she'd seen him taken out by an old goat. She bit her lip, and his eyes dropped to stare at her even white teeth clamped on her plump lower lip. His eyes rose to meet hers. The corner of his mouth quirked up.

"That kiss made me feel better, though," he said, feeling a bit wicked. "Maybe another would make me gut as new."

Her eyebrows rose, but she made no comment. Merely stared at him, before lifting a finger to her lips and placing a kiss on it, then tentatively reaching out to touch his scraped chin. "Did that help?"

"Ja," he said, feeling a bit breathless. He raised his hand and touched his nose. "It hurts here too," he murmured. She placed another kiss on her finger and touched his nose gently.

"Better?"

"Mm-hmm." He swallowed and slowly lifted his hand to touch his lips. "It hurts here too. . ." he whispered.

Her breath shallow, she raised her fingers to her lips. He watched as she placed a kiss on her finger and then lifted it to softly touch his lips. He captured her hand and, still looking into her eyes, turned it over and placed a kiss on her palm. She gasped, and he felt heat coursing through his body.

"Jonas," she whispered, and he lifted a hand to brush the hair from her eyes before cupping her cheek in his palm. What would she do if he kissed her properly? He felt himself leaning toward her, and her eyes drifted closed. Time to find out. He lowered his face toward hers. . .and a horn blared outside, sending them reeling away from each other in alarm.

"What on earth?" she gasped, staring at the door.

"Are you expecting someone?" he asked, seriously irritated.

"No!" She hurried to the barn door and, opening it, looked outside. A UPS truck sat idling in her driveway, and the driver hopped out, a package in his hand. He waved cheerily at her. "'lo, Mrs. Helmuth. I've got a delivery for you. Sign here."

She signed and took the box. "Oh! My new candlewicks! I've been waiting for these. Now I can get to work on some new scents I've been wanting to try."

The UPS driver touched his cap, hopped into his truck, and backed into the road. Ruth glanced shyly at Jonas. "Um, well, I should go inside and get to work."

If he were a cursing man, he'd curse the timing of that driver, but he smiled wryly at Ruth. "Ja, I have some chores waiting at home. I'll see you tomorrow. We'll be here early to finish the job."

As he drove home, Jonas took comfort in the fact that Ruth had invited his kiss. . .even if it didn't happen. Tomorrow was another day!

CHAPTER TWENTY-TWO

A week later the snow was gone, and Jonas and his crew had finished transforming the barn. This morning several wagons full of baskets and materials had pulled into the drive, and the men were busy moving the items inside. Jonas' sister had just pulled her buggy into the driveway, and she drove up to the hitching post near the barn.

Ruth helped Sally unhitch her Morgan gelding and turned him into the paddock, where he was greeted by several other horses.

"What a lovely day it is!" Sally said, reaching into her buggy for a lunch basket.

"It is," Ruth agreed. "Maybe I'll do some laundry. It would dry fast today."

"How's the greenhouse project coming along?"

"Gut! My soil sample analysis came back the other day, and yesterday I went to Berlin and bought the amendments I need. Jonas helped me cart it all into the greenhouse, so now I'm going to go in and prepare my soil. My seeds came too, so I can plant them as soon as the soil is ready. I'm excited!"

"Oooo, I would be too! I can't wait to see it," Sally said. "But now I'd better get inside or Jonas will wonder what happened to me. I'm running late today. Abby has a little cold, and I wanted to help Selma get her settled before heading over here. She's a bit cranky."

"Selma or Abby?"

"Ha! Both."

"Nothing serious, I hope?"

"No, just a run-of-the-mill head cold. She's sturdy, and she'll be fine in a day or two." She gave a little wave and turned to hurry toward the barn.

Ruth headed to the greenhouse, saying a little prayer for Abigail as she walked.

Inside the greenhouse, she looked around in satisfaction. A lot had changed in there in the last couple of weeks. Jonas, who had been spending a bit of each day with her, sometimes bringing Abigail along and sometimes alone, had helped her caulk the panes of glass, and he and a few of his work crew had hauled the old woodstove away and connected the new outside wood burner to the greenhouse. Now, in addition to being sunny inside, it was toasty warm. The two of them had dropped the bags containing what Ruth needed for soil amendment in the trays up and down the aisles. Today Ruth would cut the bags open and spread the contents in the trays, creating the perfect growing medium for chrysanthemums. There hadn't been a repeat of the near kiss, and Ruth was okay with that for now. She didn't mind taking things slowly. But she had to admit to herself that she was curious.

"Well, the work won't do itself," she said, reaching into her pocket for her knife and grabbing the first bag.

Two hours later, Ruth was filthy, dusted from head to toe in fine particles of potting soil, vermiculite, manure, and sphagnum moss.

"I look like some sort of woodland creature," she laughed, attempting to brush the stuff off her skirts and sweater.

The door to the greenhouse opened, and Jonas came inside. When he saw her, he laughed.

"What?" she demanded. "So I'm a little dirty—that's good, honest dirt!"

"A little?" he asked, coming closer. "Ruth, you're covered in four or five kinds of dirt. You give dirty a new meaning. . .and this coming from a farmer! In fact, you have a smudge right on your nose."

Without thinking, he licked his thumb and then used it to wipe at the smudge of dirt on Ruth's nose. Her mouth dropped open in surprise, and his eyes dropped to stare at her lips.

They stood very close together, and she stared at him, wide eyed. Realizing her mouth was hanging open like a landed trout, she snapped it shut. He raised his eyes to hers and slowly smiled. "Here we are again," he said softly. "I'm sorry," he said, looking anything but. "I guess I'm used to cleaning Abigail up all the time, so I forgot myself."

Ruth, a bit breathless, shook her head and smiled at him crookedly. "Aside from preferring not to have spit rubbed on my nose, I don't really mind."

He stared at her, not sure what to make of that. He stepped back, suddenly a bit self-conscious, and looked around. "Well, you've gotten a lot done in here. You've earned your dirt, that's for sure."

She looked around, pleased. "Ja. All the bags are mixed together in the trays. Now all that's left to do is plant the seeds. Then I water them and hope for the best."

"It's almost February," he said. "Are you in time?"

She nodded. "I can move the plants outside into the fields at the end of May, around Memorial Day, after the danger of frost is past. That gives them four months to grow. They'll be nice little plants by then."

She looked around at her grandmother's greenhouse, now fixed up, with glass gleaming clean and trays prepared to receive new life. And she was pleased.

"Jonas, denki for your help. I'm not sure I could have gotten this all done in time—or maybe not at all—without you."

"I didn't do much."

"Say 'you're welcome,' Jonas."

"You're welcome, Ruth. You've been a help to me too, organizing my basket supplies."

She waved her hand. "Nonsense. You knew right where you wanted everything. I just did what I was told by you and the girls."

"Say 'you're welcome,' Ruth!" he shot back at her, a teasing gleam in his eyes.

"All right then. You're welcome! Now, I have to get inside. The sky was looking pretty angry when I checked a while ago. I think we're in for another storm tonight."

He cocked his head, listening to the wind. "Ja, I think so."

"You can tell by the sound of the wind?"

"Sure," he said, his eyes laughing at her. "That, and I heard it on the radio at the hardware store this morning."

She swatted his arm. "Jonas Hershberger! Out of my way, I have things to do." She walked past him out of the greenhouse. He followed, careful to latch the door firmly behind him, and they both had to brace against the wind when they were outside.

"Goodness! This is blowing hard!" she called over the wind. "I need to go take care of my stock now, before it gets worse."

"We're under a blizzard watch," he said, looking uneasily at the sky.

"Really? I hadn't heard that. I hope it doesn't get too bad."

"You just never know." He looked at her barn, then at her house, nodded once, and said, "Before I head home, I'll help you get your stock in, and then there's something I need to do." He walked purposefully off toward the barn, and Ruth hurried after him, entering the bottom portion to care for her goats and other stock. A few minutes later Jonas opened the big doors and led the Shires in. "I'll get your buggy team next!" he called over the growing howl of the wind, putting the big black horses into their stalls. Ruth had already filled their feed bins and water buckets, and they nickered in satisfaction and tucked into their dinner.

"Ho, Hans, ho, Betty," she said, rubbing each enormous horse on its soft pink nose. "What's a little storm to you as long as you have your snug stalls and plenty to eat, right?"

The door opened again, and Jonas led Tom Sawyer and Buttercup into their stalls before heading back outside again.

"Denki!" she called, hurrying to feed and water them. She finished her chores about half an hour later and was hanging her sweater on the hook, preparing to go care for the chickens, when Jonas opened the small door.

"Jonas! I thought you'd left! Now I'm going to worry about you getting home safely," she said, peering past him at rapidly scudding clouds in the angry-looking sky.

"I'll be fine. I took care of your chickens. Come, I want to show you something, and then I do have to go home. Abigail wasn't feeling well this morning. I hope she isn't getting sick with a possible blizzard coming."

"Sally mentioned that. I've got a nice herbal tea that's gut for colds and fevers. I'll get you some before you go, if you'll wait a minute."

"Ja, denki. Let's hurry, though."

She followed him outside, and he pointed to where he'd fastened a stout rope to the barn just outside the small door. It led to the chicken shed and then to the house and then back to the barn again, in a triangle.

"In case of a blizzard, you hold on to this rope," he said. "You're all alone out here, and though I don't like the idea of it, I know you'll need to go out, whatever the weather, and do chores. So follow this rope. Don't let go of it! People get lost in blizzards and wander into the snow and freeze to death, sometimes just a few yards from safety."

"Goodness! Denki, Jonas, but I doubt it'll get that bad." They looked up at the sky. An odd, almost-greenish light filled the heavens. "It does look weird, though. If it were summer, I'd worry about twisters." She frowned.

"Just promise me if it's bad, you'll follow this rope to the barn and chicken shed, then back to the house, all right?"

He looked so serious, she nodded. "Of course. I promise. Now wait just a minute while I grab that tea." She hurried into the house and put the medicinal tea, along with some honey lozenges she'd made to soothe the throat, into a small bag. She quickly filled another bag with half a dozen cinnamon rolls, then gave it all to Jonas, who was waiting just inside the door. "The directions for the tea are printed on the label," she said. "I hope she feels better soon."

He took the bag and nodded. "I have to go. The storm is coming fast, and I need to get home and tend my stock. I'll talk to you soon."

She watched as Jonas hurried to his buggy and drove toward home.

The wind moaned through the bare tree branches and blew debris around the farmyard. "It is definitely a day to be inside!" She noted that Jonas had securely attached the rope to a ring beside the door. "Hopefully I won't need that!" Ruth hurried inside and shut her kitchen door securely against the coming storm.

———————— ⚓ ————————

Getting Abigail to bed had taken Jonas longer than usual. She felt terrible with red, achy eyes, a runny nose, a headache, a sore throat, and a cough. She had taken a cup of the tea Ruth had sent and even pronounced it tasty. Jonas had given her a honey lozenge to suck on after she finished the tea, while he carried her up to her room and read her favorite book by the light of her battery lamp. He'd kissed her good night and gone downstairs to read for a while. But the sound of the restless wind kept pulling him from his book, and he finally decided to call it a night. He turned off the lamp in his kitchen and headed upstairs, Alaska following at his heels. At the stair landing, he paused and looked out at the night. The moon was hidden behind clouds, but if he craned his neck, he could see the streetlamp out on the road. By its light, he saw the snow had started. It was falling in tiny pellets, driven by the wind, which was blowing stronger than ever, causing the snow to sail past horizontally rather than fall straight down. But he could still see a good distance, so it wasn't a blizzard—yet.

In bed, Jonas thought about Ruth, a couple miles away, snug in her tidy home.

She's probably letting that cat sleep in her bed, he thought, smiling a bit in the dark. He knew perfectly well that Alaska waited until he was in bed to climb the quilt up the side of Abby's bed and curl up next to her. "Well, he'll keep her warm in this weather."

As he drifted off to sleep, he listened to the sound of howling wind and was glad he'd thought to put up that rope for Ruth. He'd done the same between his own barn and house when he got home, and he knew Sally's husband would have done so as well. *I hope Ruth remembers to use it*, was his last conscious thought before sleep took him under.

Ruth awoke to the sound of the wind howling just before dawn. She climbed out of bed and crept to the window.

Outside, the world was still black. She wrapped an afghan around herself to keep warm and sat on her window seat staring out at nothing. The world began gradually to lighten, and Ruth realized that she was looking out at a blank gray wall of blowing snow.

"Goodness!" Ruth gasped. "This is a blizzard!"

She dressed warmly, knowing that, snow or no snow, she must care for her animals.

Ruth fed Ginger Snap and made herself a pot of coffee. She put on her warmest cloak, pulled one of Levi's old woolen hats on over her hair, leaving her prayer kapp on the kitchen table, wrapped a scarf around her face, and pulled on her boots and mittens.

"Here I go, Ginger Snap," she said through the scarf. "If I'm not back in an hour, send out the Mounties."

The cat, unimpressed, yawned and crunched more kibbles.

Not knowing what to expect, as she hadn't seen weather conditions like this since she was a young child, Ruth opened the kitchen door. It was nearly snatched from her hand by the wind, and she squinted her eyes against the tiny ice pellets passing for snow, pushed the door firmly closed behind her, and stepped out onto her porch.

"Ach! I wish I had sunglasses or goggles!" she gasped, standing on the porch and squinting into the yard.

Looking out into the storm, she was amazed at the vast blankness. She couldn't see three feet in front of her. She couldn't see her garden, her gazing ball, her gate, or the big barn she knew to be across the farmyard.

Remembering the rope Jonas had strung, she grasped it and held on. "I didn't really believe it could be this bad. Thank Gott Jonas thought to string this rope." Firmly grasping the sturdy rope, she followed it down the steps, then waded through snow up to her knees. At one point, she pulled her foot right out of her boot and had to stuff it back on with snow falling in from the top. Fortunately, her thick woolen stockings and socks kept her legs and feet warm, in spite of the snow sneaking into her boots. She had a hard time opening the gate far enough to squeeze through. *If I didn't have this rope, I'd never find my way*, she thought, looking around. All she could see was unrelieved whiteness. Occasionally a gust of wind would blow a swirl of snow close to her face, but mostly, the hard little pellets flew horizontally past her in an endless stream of white. It was disorienting, dizzying.

Tightly holding onto the rope, she squeezed her eyes closed against the stinging pellets. She couldn't see anyway. Going on faith, she fought her way to the barn and fumbled with the latch, pushing the door open and stumbling in, then pulling the door closed behind her. Inside, all was warm and calm. The animals greeted her with their calls, and she turned on the electric lights, glad they were run by a generator and not dependent on the English power lines she figured were probably not faring well under all the ice and snow. Most of her English neighbors also had generators, but she knew there were some who did not. At times like this, it was easier not to be dependent on the public infrastructure for light and warmth.

She reached into the nearest pen and scratched Mildred, now very pregnant, between her little horns. "Let's get you girls fed and mucked out, and you can spend the day warm and safe inside."

About an hour later, she reluctantly left the warmth and safety of the barn and went back out into the teeth of the storm, which didn't seem to have let up at all. She made her way to the chicken shed, again thanking Gott for Jonas' thoughtful placement of the rope. She cared for the chickens and collected their eggs and then braved the storm again to get back to her house.

"Goodness!" she gasped, slamming the kitchen door closed behind her. "I hope this doesn't go on for long."

She placed the egg basket on the counter before tossing a couple more logs into the woodstove, again thankful to Jonas for filling her woodbox.

Taking her mending over to the rocking chair and gently dislodging the cat from his comfy bed, Ruth said, "Sorry, Ginger Snap. I need to sit here." He flipped his tail at her, stalked off to his basket, and resumed his nap without really opening his eyes.

Meaning to mend a tear in her apron, Ruth instead found herself staring out the kitchen window at the swirling whiteness outside, now eerily illuminated by the weak sunshine filtering through the clouds and snow.

"I'm lonely," she whispered to herself, only now admitting what she'd been keeping at bay for over a year.

Outside, the wind howled, and the snow fell. Ruth realized that it was Jonas and Abigail, not so very far away through the storm, for whom she was lonely. "This can't last long, can it?" she whispered to herself before giving up on the mending and sitting down to pass the time with the March sisters.

CHAPTER TWENTY-THREE

Two days passed, and the snow didn't stop. The wind didn't let up. At one point, Ruth was sure she heard thunder rumbling ominously through the wind.

She followed the rope from house to barn to chicken shed to house twice a day, wearing a pair of sunglasses to keep most of the flying snow out of her eyes.

Aside from the excitement of making her way through the growing snowdrifts morning and evening, Ruth was getting pretty tired of snow and isolation. There was nothing to see outside except an unremitting wall of swirling white. The sun came up; the sun went down. That was the only difference.

She used the time to experiment with new scents for the candles she made to sell in town. She didn't enjoy overly sweet scents, preferring the ones based on herbs and flowers. A new scent based on honey and sage seemed promising as a good seller. She jotted down the recipe in the notebook she kept for such things and felt that the day had been a productive one.

On the third morning, Ruth opened the door to the barn and heard the unmistakable, high-pitched bleating of a baby goat. She hurried over to the pens where the Angora does were housed and found three tiny newborn kids.

"Oh, Clementine! You had triplets!" she cried, delighted. Clementine looked less enthusiastic as the babies vied for space at her udder, which had only two teats.

"We'll let you try to care for them all for a day, and if you can't handle three, I'll take one to the house," Ruth promised.

"Maaaaaaa," the goat replied, looking skeptical.

"Well, you're the first, but you won't be the last," Ruth said. She checked the new babies, and they all looked fine. She gave the new mama a going over to make sure she'd come to no harm delivering her babies alone in the barn, and she found the doe to be sound, her milk coming in well.

Then she checked the rest of her pregnant does, thirty-one in all.

She spent more time than usual with her animals that morning and was fairly certain that two other does were in labor. The expectant mamas were all in individual stalls and had all they needed—food, water, and clean straw for bedding.

"You'll be fine," she said, and opened the door to return to the house.

At first, she didn't understand what she was seeing. Then she realized, "It's stopped snowing!" She did an undignified little dance. She hurried to take care of the chickens and gathered their eggs, and she was nearly back to the gate when, without warning, the snow hit again, with full force, the wind possibly stronger than before.

"Where's the rope?" Ruth cried, panicking. She took a few steps one way, then another, quickly becoming disoriented. Then she stopped.

"Ruth. You were almost at the gate. Stop and think." She realized that in her panic, she had taken an unknown number of steps in several directions. She could be in the driveway, pointed toward the road, possibly. If so, she could quickly become hopelessly lost and freeze to death.

"I must pray," she whispered. Tucking her hands under her armpits, the basket of eggs hanging from the crook of an elbow, she closed her eyes.

"Gott, please, if it is Your will, let me find the gate so I can get back inside safely. I confess I am not ready yet to die. If You say it is my time, I accept. And if so, I pray to enter Your kingdom. But Gott, if it is not yet my time, please, help me find my way."

Opening her eyes, she strained to see where she was. She looked at the ground, and there were her footprints. She gasped. "I can see where I was!" Knowing it wouldn't last long with the wind blowing and new snow falling, Ruth fell to her knees and examined the footprints. "I think I came from that way," she whispered and, standing, took a few, tentative steps in what seemed to be a straight line. Suddenly, she crashed into the large oak tree next to the gate. "Oh, thank You, Gott!" she cried, rubbing her forehead, which she'd hit rather hard on the tree. She felt her way along the trunk of the tree, found the fence, and followed it to the gate. There was the rope! She followed it to the steps and up to the house.

Entering the kitchen, she sank into a chair and thanked God for His mercy.

"Thy will be done, Lord, but thank You for sparing me today!"

Ginger Snap circled her and rubbed against her as she sat there, getting used to the idea that she wasn't going to die right now.

After a few minutes she stood and was surprised to discover the egg basket still hanging from her arm. She put it on the counter and removed her outer clothing. She was a bit shaky, which seemed reasonable to her, considering. There was a pot of coffee staying warm on the stove. She poured herself a cup and warmed up as she drank it in front of the fire.

Feeling tired, she decided that, in the circumstances, and with no pressing chores, it would be understandable if she was to go up and take a nap.

Ginger Snap followed her up, and they curled up together on her bed, toasty under a spare quilt made by her own mother, listening to the wind.

"Ginger Snap, this wind is driving me crazy. I hope it stops soon."

Some time later, Ruth opened her eyes to bright sunlight coming through her bedroom window. Accompanying the sunlight was…silence.

She sat up and looked out the window. The storm had, again,

stopped. But she knew better now than to trust it completely.

Going to the window, Ruth saw blue skies to the northeast. . .the direction from which the unusual storm had come.

"Maybe it's over. I hope so!" she said. She straightened her hair and put her prayer kapp back on and went downstairs.

"I want to check on the girls," she told Ginger Snap. "We probably have more kids."

She bundled up and was careful to keep a hand on the rope all the way to the barn, where she found three more baby goats—a set of twins and a singleton.

"Oh, you're doing so well!" she told the mamas. Nobody else seemed to be showing signs of being in labor, and the triplets were doing fine, so Ruth left all three babies with their mama for the time being.

Heading back to the house after finishing her chores, she noted that the sky looked clearer toward the north and south. The storm was truly moving on.

"Still, I'm leaving this rope up for a few days in case it comes back!" she said as she went back into her kitchen.

She was just putting a chicken pot pie into the oven when she heard sleigh bells.

Hurrying to the door, she looked out and saw Jonas and another man driving into her driveway.

She opened the door. "Hello! It's so gut to see someone! I was starting to feel as though I were the last person on Earth! Please, come in for coffee and cake."

A look of relief passed swiftly over Jonas' face as the sleigh passed the kitchen door on the way to the hitching rail, and he waved at Ruth. The men tied up the horse and came inside, wading through the deep snow and stomping their boots on the mat outside the door.

"Ach, you're well snowed in, Ruth Helmuth!" said the second man, who Ruth saw was Henry Miller.

"We were worried about you," Jonas said, looking at her intently.

"Well, thanks to your rope, I'm fine. It was a lifesaver, I'll tell you!"

"Gut! I was so glad, when the storm hit, that I'd put it up for you," Jonas said. "And you had no trouble following it?"

"Mostly, no," she said. "But I almost got lost coming back to the house the first time the storm stopped this morning. I wasn't holding the rope, because I thought it was over, and suddenly, it was just there again, full force. I stumbled, and at first I couldn't find the rope. It was really scary."

Jonas took a step toward Ruth but, glancing at Henry, didn't touch her. "What did you do?"

"I prayed. Gott led me back to the rope and to safety," she said simply.

Jonas stared at her, dumbstruck. "Ruth, you humble me," he finally said.

Henry scratched his beard. "Must have been right scary!"

"Yes, it was! But then I came inside, warmed up, and took a little nap, and when I woke up, it was really over! And Jonas, the goats have started having their kids! You'll have to bring Abigail to see. There's one mama with triplets!"

"Can she handle three?" Jonas asked.

"We'll see," Ruth said. "She's had babies before, but three is a lot. I'll know by morning if I need to bottle-feed one."

She poured them each large mugs of fresh coffee and cut a chocolate cake she'd baked the day before to kill time.

When she placed the cake and coffee in front of Jonas, he reached out and gripped her wrist, peering intently up at her forehead. "Ruth, you have a nasty bruise on your forehead. What happened?"

She brushed a hand self-consciously over the painful lump. "Well, Gott did guide me back to the rope, as I said. But he took me by way of the big oak tree first," she said, making light now of the incident.

"If you'd been knocked out…" Jonas began, his face suddenly pale.

"But she wasn't, man. Gott was watching out for her." Henry punched Jonas in the shoulder. "And your rope got her home safe."

Ruth smiled, and Jonas took a sip of his coffee, while Henry tucked into his cake.

"Mmm, you are a gut baker!" Henry said, eyeing Ruth appreciatively. "Maybe I should marry you so I can eat cake like this every day!"

Ruth laughed and topped off their coffee before sitting down to her own place.

"I think Agnes might object," she said, speaking of Henry's wife of thirty-five years.

"Then don't tell her I said so," Henry said, taking another large bite of rich cake.

Her eyes twinkled at him. "Mum's the word. So what brought you men around today?"

"Well, we wanted to see if you were all right," Jonas said, suddenly serious. "Not everyone came through the storm as well as you did, I'm afraid."

"Oh no!" Ruth said, alarmed. "What happened? Is there anything I can do?"

Jonas shook his head sadly. "An old English man to the north got lost when his car went in a ditch. He tried to walk to safety. He didn't make it, Ruth."

Ruth's eyes filled with tears. "The poor man! And his family! How awful!"

"Ja."

"And then there was the fire over at Lydia Coblentz's place," Henry added, washing down the last of his cake with a swallow of coffee.

"What?" Ruth asked, looking to Jonas for elaboration.

He bit his lip. "Ja, Ruth, it's true. That's one of the things I needed to tell you. But I got distracted by hearing of your adventure. Lydia's house burned down some time in the last couple of days. We can't be sure when it happened. The fire department wasn't even called. Nobody knew there was a fire, and even if they had, the trucks couldn't have gotten there. The house is a total loss, I'm afraid."

"They say it was probably lightning that started it," Henry said. "Did you hear the thunderstorm in the blizzard?"

"Ja, I thought I did, but the wind was so strong, I wasn't sure. Oh, poor Lydia! All her things, gone! And how will she rebuild? She's all alone!"

"Well, as to that, if she wants to rebuild, of course the community will help her," Jonas said. "But when I spoke with her this morning on the phone, she said she might not come back. That this might just make her decision easier."

"Her house was so cheerful, so welcoming. I can't believe it's gone. And all her things. Her quilts!" Ruth felt close to tears.

"It was Gott's will, Ruth," Jonas said, reaching across the table to take her hand.

She nodded stiffly. "Ja, of course. But it's so hard to understand sometimes, isn't it?"

He looked back at her, understanding that it wasn't only Lydia's house to which she referred.

Henry cleared his throat, and Ruth realized Jonas was holding her hand. She pulled away, not wanting to become fodder for gossip, not that the good man was likely to spread tales.

"At least she'll have many of her clothes with her in Florida, and the cats are safe with her there. I'll call her from town tomorrow," she said, "and see if there's anything I can do."

"Henry and I drove past the place on our way here. There's nothing left. The place burned right to the ground, and what's left is buried under four feet of snow. Darndest thing I ever saw," he said. "Even the chimney is down, probably pushed over by the wind."

"Ja, where there was a house and barn last week, now it appears there's an empty field," Henry said, shaking his head.

"The barn too?" Ruth asked.

Jonas nodded. "The wind must have spread the flames. But her horse and cow were both at a neighbor's, so they're fine."

"Right, right." Ruth pulled out her hankie and blew her nose. "I need to think on this. It seems there must be something I can do!"

The men stood to go. "We'd best get on. A number of us are driving around, making sure nobody needs help. We still have a ways to go to check on a few families down this road, and on a couple roads heading back."

"Oh, make sure Paul Chesler is okay. He plowed out my driveway a while back."

"He's fine. We saw him driving into town. He stopped and said he'd checked on Mr. and Mrs. Green, your English neighbors down the way. He said the Muellers are fine too, past there, and Lucy Nichols. We'll drive out and check on the three families past them, then turn and head back on the township road that intersects up about two miles from here."

Ruth nodded. "Gut. And tomorrow let me know if anyone needs any help. I can do whatever needs to be done."

"Ja, and the Red Cross is helping too," Jonas said, putting on his coat and hat and opening the door.

"Denki for stopping and checking on me," Ruth said. "Bring Abigail by soon to see the babies! Oh! How's her cold?"

"She's much better. Your tea really helped. Denki for sending it."

"No problem. I'm glad I was able to do something."

Jonas paused and sniffed the air. "What's that gut smell?"

Ruth glanced around the kitchen. "Oh, maybe you're smelling the new candles I made while I was stuck inside. They're scented with honey and sage." She walked over and picked up one of the jars containing a candle and handed it to him. He sniffed deeply and smiled.

"Ja, that's it. I like it, Ruth. This should sell well in town."

She smiled. "Denki. That's what I thought."

Jonas handed the jar to Henry, who sniffed and said, "I know my wife will like this. Can I order some now? Her birthday is coming up."

Ruth nodded. "Sure, I can have them ready next week. I'm glad you both like the new scent. Sometimes I develop something I think will be popular, and nobody else likes it. So it's gut to have someone confirm my own feelings."

The men left, and Ruth sat down at the kitchen table with her leftover coffee, and she started thinking about what Jonas and Henry had said about the storm and the people who hadn't been as fortunate as she had. She cried a bit for Lydia's loss and for the English man lost in the blizzard.

"Why did You spare me, Gott, and not him?" she wondered.

Only silence answered her.

In the sleigh, Jonas snapped the reins. "Gee-up, boys!" he bit off, mouth set in a grim line, and thought about what might have happened to Ruth, alone in the storm.

After a few minutes, Henry said, "Well then, Jonas, she's fine."

Jonas started at Henry's voice and looked at the older man, fear in his eyes. "But it could so easily have been different, Henry. We might have pulled in there this afternoon to find her lying there, frozen in the snow." He shuddered at the thought.

Henry took a moment to reply. "Ja, we might have. I won't sugarcoat it. But Jonas, she kept her head and found her way back to that rope you put there for her safety. She prayed, and Gott heard her. There's no use playing the what-if game."

Jonas chewed the inside of his cheek as he drove his team toward the next house on their list. He hadn't expected the tidal wave of emotion that had washed over him when Ruth said she'd lost her grip on the rope and then hit her head on the tree. He'd felt powerful surges of protectiveness, fear, and tenderness. He realized his feelings for Ruth were deep. His eyes widened. *I love her*, he thought, astonished both at the realization and at his obtuseness in taking so long to come to it.

He glanced at Henry, who was smiling at him. "Your face is like a book, Jonas."

"I need to find a way to make her realize she needs me. She's so independent, and capable, Henry."

Henry shrugged. "Gott will help her see that taking you on wouldn't be such a bad bargain. It probably doesn't hurt that you come with Abigail, since she's such a cute child. But just to be sure, you'd better pray about it."

Jonas laughed. "Not such a bad bargain, huh? You're so smooth."

"Just don't wait too long. Someone else might see her and convince her he's a better bargain than you are, Jonas. Of course, the fact that she's already letting you rent her barn for your business probably gives you an edge."

"Because it shows she likes me?"

"Nah. Because it would be too much trouble to move you out and move some other man's business in at this point."

"Right, thanks, Henry. I feel much better now." The sound of Henry's deep laughter followed them down the road. And Jonas realized he did feel better. Now he just had to find the courage to ask Ruth to marry him—again. And hope she didn't laugh in his face.

Gott, I'm going to need Your help! he prayed silently, as the next house came into view. A sunbeam broke through the clouds to the east, and Jonas smiled. He'd take whatever positive signs he could find.

CHAPTER TWENTY-FOUR

Several days later, Ruth was working in her greenhouse, planting flower seeds. It was taking plenty of time to plant 2,500 seeds. The blizzard had set her back several days, but she didn't think that would matter much in the long run.

After planting, Ruth thoroughly watered the seeds using a fine mist on her hose.

"That's all I can do here today." She cleaned up, then let herself out of the greenhouse. Glancing over at the barn, she couldn't resist heading over to see what Jonas and his crew were working on. She poked her head in and called, "Mind if I come in?"

"Come on in!" Mary cheerfully replied. "You can give us your opinion on this new design."

Ruth walked over to where Mary sat on a stool, working on a round basket with smaller shakes at the bottom and wider shakes at the top. There were red shakes interspersed with the stained-wood ones.

"Pretty," she commented, sitting on the stool next to Mary. "What's it for?"

"Oh, just about anything," Mary answered. Ruth watched her guide a red shake through the guide shakes and then press it down uniformly with a stick so that it was even all around.

"I could see using it to hold sewing supplies, or apples, or tea bags," Ruth said.

"I especially think this red one would look great holding green apples on a kitchen table," Mary agreed.

The door to the storage area opened, and Jonas came in carrying an armload of red and green shakes.

"Look who stopped by, boss," Mary called.

Jonas glanced over, and his face lit up with welcome. "Gut morning, Ruth!" he called. "How's the planting coming along?"

"All finished!" she said with a grin. "Twenty-five hundred chrysanthemum seeds planted and watered. Now I just have to hope they'll come up in a week or so."

"Gut! I have to move some inventory. I'll talk to you later." He headed back into the storage area.

"How are all your baby goats?" Sally asked from her workstation.

"We can sometimes hear them down there," Mary said. "They sound so cute!"

"I'll take you down to see them, if you like," Ruth offered.

"Oh, I'd love that!" Sally said. "I've been considering getting a few milk goats, just for our use. I'd like to see what kind you have and what it takes to care for them."

"I'd be pleased to show you."

"After work I'll come knock on the door at the house, and if you're not busy maybe we could go then?"

"Ja," Ruth nodded. "That would be gut. That's about feeding time anyway." She brushed her hands on her apron and said, "Well, I'd better get back to the house. I'm going to try out another new scent for my candles. I'll see you all later!"

She glanced once more at the door to the storage area, but Jonas didn't reappear, so she headed back across the farmyard to her cozy house. As she walked, her eyes passed over the wintry landscape, the land she used to share with Levi. How things had changed!

The big house, formerly home to the two of them, was now home to her alone, and a cat Levi probably would have never wanted in the house.

The big barn now housed Jonas' business, and the greenhouse was being put back into operation. Her grandmother would have been pleased.

Thinking of her grandmother, Ruth turned her gaze to the small dawdi haus which was connected to the big house by a breezeway.

"It's a lonely place now," she mused, standing and staring at the little white house. "I wish Grossmammi were still in there, baking my favorite cookies. It would sure have helped this last year."

"Penny for your thoughts?"

Startled, she spun around. "Jonas! I was just looking at the dawdi haus and thinking about when Grossmammi lived there, after Maem and Dat moved to Texas and Grossdaddi was gone. Grossmammi offered the big house to Levi and me and said she'd welcome our company."

He looked at the little house. "Did your folks build it for her?"

"No, she and Grossdaddi moved here after they married. It was Grossmammi's grandmother's farm, and their situation was similar. They were both ready to retire and wanted Grossmammi and Grossdaddi to move to the farm and help take care of it, and so they built the dawdi haus. It must be around sixty years old. I hate to see it standing empty."

He looked thoughtful for a moment, his eyes narrowed.

"What?" she asked.

"I was just thinking," he said slowly. She waited, raising an eyebrow questioningly.

"Ja? Thinking about what?"

"Well, it's none of my business, absolutely. But if you won't be offended, I just had this crazy idea pop into my head."

"Jonas, we're friends. I won't be offended."

"Friends? Is that what we are?" he asked, looking at her intently.

She felt a lifting of her spirits, a newborn hope too fragile for words. "What's your idea?"

He looked puzzled for just a second, which amused Ruth a bit, and then he said, "Ach, ja! My idea. Well, you have that nice little house, just right for an older lady. And Lydia. . ."

"Lydia has nowhere to live!" Ruth exclaimed. "At least, not in Ohio. Oh, Jonas! What a wunderbar idea!" Overcome with joy at the prospect of her friend living so close, Ruth threw her arms around Jonas in an impulsive hug. He stood stiffly for a moment, and then his arms came up slowly to circle her back, and he gave her a squeeze.

Suddenly awkward, Ruth drew back in the circle of Jonas' arms, and he smiled down at her. He reached a hand up, smoothed the stray lock that was always escaping her prayer kapp, and softly said, "I like holding you, Ruth. I'd like to kiss you, except it's broad daylight and we're standing in your barnyard with people just in the barn. But I'd like to. I need you to know that."

She smiled tremulously up at him and whispered, "I think I'd like that too."

He groaned and put her away from him. "A man can only take so much. A kiss will wait. We were talking about. . .something."

Ruth grinned. "About how Lydia could come here and live in my dawdi haus! And then neither of us would be alone anymore!" She blushed a bit, embarrassed to have revealed so much to him. But he acted as though he hadn't heard.

"Ja, it would be gut for both of you. Although it is possible—that is, I'm hoping that you may not be alone for long anyway." He cast her a sidelong glance, the corner of his mouth tipped up in a little smile.

Unsure what to say to that, she plowed on. "And Bishop Troyer would have one less reason to try and get me to sell out! The dawdi haus, the barn, the greenhouse. . .all being used. That would be so gut!"

He smiled at her. "Well then, are you going to invite her to come live with you?"

"Do you think she'll want to?"

"You won't know unless you ask," Jonas reasonably pointed out.

"Ja, but she said she was considering living with her sister. . .and that was before her house burned down!"

He shrugged. "Let her know her options. She can't decide if she doesn't know what all her choices are. She'll say yes or no. What have you got to lose?"

She considered. *Don't ask, and she certainly won't come. Ask, and she might not, but she might.* "I'm going to do it."

He reached out and squeezed her hand. "I hope she says yes."

She smiled at him and nodded. "Well, I'd better get inside. Sally is coming over later, and I'll show her the baby goats. And anyone else who wants to meet them. And I'll call Lydia tomorrow and invite her. Or maybe I should write her instead? Calling her may be awkward and put her on the spot. Ja," she decided with a nod. "I'll write. In fact, I'll do it right now!"

"Okay, do it!" He waved and headed back to the barn.

Hurrying inside, she was filled with buoyancy and hope. And a little leftover tingle at Jonas' words about wanting to kiss her. She sat down to write her letter with a secret little smile on her face. It seemed she was not at all the staid widow she'd tried to convince herself she must be.

CHAPTER TWENTY-FIVE

"Ruth! Gut morning!" Jonas called. She turned and saw him hurrying toward her from the barn. "Are you going to see if your mums have sprouted?"

"Ja. It's been a week, and it says seven to ten days on the packages, so I'm hopeful." She didn't mention that she'd checked daily. She had to water, didn't she?

"Well, let's hope together." He held out his hand to her, and she took it without thinking. They turned toward the greenhouse, walking together. Her hand felt small and warm in his large, work-roughened one. She'd forgotten the simple pleasure of holding hands with a man.

"Have you heard from Lydia?"

"Not yet. Maybe that means no." She frowned.

"Maybe it means her letter isn't here yet."

"Ja, maybe." Their steps matched. She'd forgotten the pleasure of that as well. She sighed, and he looked at her.

"What is it?" he asked.

She shook her head and looked at their joined hands.

He glanced down too. "Do you want me to let go?"

"No, Jonas, I like holding hands and walking with you. I'd just forgotten how nice it is."

He looked ahead, toward the greenhouse. "Ja, me too," he said quietly. Suddenly, he stopped walking and turned toward her.

"Ruth, I want to talk to you, here, outside, where we are not alone."

She looked around at the deserted yard. "We are alone, actually."

"Ja, I know we are alone," he said, exasperation evident in his voice. "But we are not alone, if you understand me. If anyone were to look outside, they would see us here, in plain sight. I want to be careful of your reputation."

"Don't be ridiculous. I was married for fifteen years. I'm thirty-three years old. No one will think about my reputation."

"You're wrong," he said. "If we are alone too often in private places, there are those in our community who would gossip."

"Not kind people," she said. "Not people whose opinions I care about."

"Maybe, but talk spreads, and no one remembers who started it. Soon, people believe it. So I am talking to you here, in public. Just humor me, okay?"

"Okay, I'm listening, right now, in public." She couldn't help the tiny smile that quirked one corner of her mouth.

He rolled his eyes. "Will you please be serious? I'm trying to pour out my feelings. Women are always saying men won't share their feelings—well here I am, trying to, and you're making jokes." He waited a moment, and when she just looked at him, he continued. "The truth is, I care for you, Ruth. I really enjoy your company. The fact that Abigail already loves you is just a bonus."

"Did she say that? That she loves me?"

"Ja, and that she wishes you were her maem. But Ruth, if I didn't care for you myself, that wouldn't motivate me to court you."

Ruth's heart swelled at his revelation. "Jonas, I've come to care for you both too. And the idea of having a family of my own—a daughter! It's overwhelming."

"Overwhelming? Ja, I could see that. Abigail and I, we come as a set." He frowned. "Not everyone would be interested in getting a little girl and a husband all at once. Maybe you're not interested in having children?"

"Not interested!" she said, genuinely shocked at the idea. "I mean, yes! I am. It's just that Gott never blessed Levi and me with any bopplin. I do so very much want children. And Abigail is wonderful! I love her already."

He smiled softly at her. "Ja, I thought you did."

She took a deep breath and broached the source of many of her fears. "Jonas, the thing is, I don't know why Levi and I had no children in fifteen years. I may not be able to have any children at all. You need sons to help you on the land. I may not be able to give you any. If you want more children, maybe you should consider someone else, someone younger, maybe."

He shook his head, his eyes holding hers. "Ruth, it's you I want. I've known for a while now, but the first time I tried to tell you, well, you know how badly I messed up. If we can't have children, and we decide we really want them, we can look into fostering or adoption."

Ruth paused at that. She hadn't considered it before, but why not? "That's an interesting idea. I hadn't thought about it. Maybe we should look into that eventually."

"Maybe we should," he said. "But right now, the important thing is for you to know how I feel about you, Ruth."

Before he could say more, a cheerful voice calling a greeting cut into their conversation, and Ruth spun around, hardly believing the timing. Evelyn Troyer was making her way toward them from the direction of the barn.

"Yoo-hoo!" she called, waving. "Well, don't you two look cozy," the girl cooed, inserting herself between Ruth and Jonas and taking his arm. She smiled up at Jonas and giggled a bit. "Gut thing I came along! Wouldn't want people thinking you were having an. . .intimate . . .meeting, ja?"

Ruth's mouth dropped open. "Evelyn! Why do you say things like that? It's as if you don't want people to like you. Jonas, I'll be in the house if you want to talk further." She turned to leave, but Jonas grabbed her by the arm.

"No, wait! Don't go. Our business isn't finished," he explained politely to Evelyn. "Why don't you wait in the barn with Sally and the others? I'll just be a minute."

"I can't believe you just said people don't like me, Ruth," Evelyn said, big crocodile tears filling her eyes.

Ruth rolled her eyes. "I didn't say people don't like you, Evelyn. I said it seems you're determined to make people dislike you by always saying something rude or provocative! Now, I don't have time for this nonsense. I have ironing to finish. I'm going inside."

"Wait for me, Ruth," Jonas said, moving to join her.

Evelyn's pretty lips pursed in an adorable pout. "Oh, but, I need your advice, Jonas." She glanced quickly at Ruth before returning her melting gaze to him. "I mean, if you aren't too busy? I want to discuss something. . .private." She blushed prettily.

Ruth's eyes narrowed. She looked at Jonas, waiting for him to send the girl packing, but he gazed back helplessly. So Ruth nodded firmly. "Well then, as I said, I have mending to do." She turned and marched away, feeling angrier than she could ever remember having felt. She just wasn't sure whether it was Jonas or that little schemer she was angrier at.

"You said ironing," Jonas called weakly.

Evelyn tittered. "She obviously wanted to get away. You're probably too much man for her, Jonas," she cooed, taking his arm again and gazing up at him soulfully. "But not for me."

Jonas looked down at the young woman currently clutching his arm in a death grip and wondered how this had happened. A minute ago, things had been going exactly as he'd planned. And now, everything was a mess!

"Um, right, well, I have work to do. What was it you needed?"

She pouted a little but then smiled at him and reached up to tuck a strand of hair behind his ear. Jonas jerked as if scalded. "Evelyn, I have to ask you not to touch me like that."

She blinked innocently. "What do you mean?"

"You know what I mean. I'm nearly old enough to be your dat!"

"I like mature men," she whispered. "I feel safe around you."

He knew he should pull away, but he hated to be rude and didn't want to hurt the kid's feelings. But enough was enough. He tried to withdraw his arm from her death grip, but she resisted. "Oh, Jonas, I know you're the man for me!" she cried, reaching up on tiptoes and brushing a kiss over his lips.

Shocked by her forward manner, Jonas took her upper arms in his hands and put her away from him and was just opening his mouth to deliver a lecture when the sound of a throat clearing loudly snapped his attention to the path from the barn.

"Well, Jonas," Bishop Troyer said, frowning mightily at the two of them frozen in what Jonas suddenly realized could be misconstrued as a mutual embrace.

The bishop continued, "I assume you're proposing marriage to my granddaughter? Otherwise, I can't imagine what would possess you to be holding her in that familiar manner. I'd thought your interests were turned in another direction, but I suppose one never can tell what you young people are thinking."

Jonas looked at the bishop and then down at the young woman whose arms he held in his hands, and he felt a noose tightening around his neck. How could this have happened? He shook his head, unable to speak. But Evelyn didn't have that problem.

"Oh, Jonas!" Evelyn cried, her eyes bright with joy. "I can't believe it! Ja, ja, of course I'll marry you!"

She threw her arms around him and hugged him tightly. Jonas' eyes met Bishop Troyer's, and he swallowed, hard. He just had to explain that there had been a misunderstanding, and all would be well. But as he tried to find the words to diplomatically tell his bishop that his granddaughter was something of a hussy, to use an old-fashioned word, he heard a small, distressed sound, and turned to look at the path.

He closed his eyes in disbelief when he saw Ruth standing there, a look of dismay on her face.

"Ruth! This isn't what it seems!" he gasped, desperate to make her understand.

"Really?" she said, her voice rough with emotion. "It looks to me as if I've arrived just in time to offer you congratulations. I hope you'll both be very happy. But be careful, Evelyn. Jonas seems to change his mind rather quickly. You could find yourself thrown over for someone else!" She turned and stalked back down the path toward her house. Jonas looked at Evelyn, who was smiling smugly back up at him, her arms wound tightly around his waist. He looked at the bishop, who had a puzzled expression on his face. And he took a deep breath. He had to find a way to extricate himself without insulting Bishop Troyer's granddaughter, or finding himself engaged to her. But how?

CHAPTER TWENTY-SIX

Ruth sat in her rocking chair, Ginger Snap in her lap. His eyes were squeezed shut and a loud purring filled the air as she stroked him absently while she rocked, staring into the embers in her living room fireplace. Above the fireplace hung the colorful quilted wall hanging of cats that Lydia had given her for Christmas. She stared at it, moving her eye from calico cat to plaid cat to gingham cat while her mind went over and over the scene from that afternoon. She still couldn't quite believe what she'd seen and heard when she'd come upon the strange tableau in her barnyard. Bishop Troyer had been asking Jonas whether he intended to marry Evelyn, and that young woman's arms had been wound around Jonas' waist. And then, meeting Ruth's eye for a moment first, Evelyn had loudly accepted a proposal Ruth still couldn't believe Jonas had actually made. So if she knew in her heart Jonas wouldn't have done such a thing, why had she taken Evelyn's bait and swallowed it like a trout? Why hadn't she stayed and fought for her man? Or at least to find out what had actually happened, for crying out loud?

"Sure, I was upset, and why wouldn't I be?" she asked Ginger Snap. "It was a perfectly understandable reaction. That little schemer had her arms around Jonas! And they were talking marriage!"

But. . .had they been? Looking back, she wasn't sure. The bishop had looked surprised and upset, and Jonas had looked like a drowning man. Come to think of it, only Evelyn had looked happy.

"Ja, and she looked like the cat who'd stolen the cream," she told the kitten. "No offense."

Ruth had been very angry and very hurt. And as usual, that hadn't left much room in her brain for thought. "Maybe I should have stuck around, Ginger Snap," she muttered. "At least I'd know the worst, instead of fearing it!"

She leaned her head back to rest her eyes and was just drifting off when a loud knocking on her kitchen door jolted her awake. "Ja! I'm coming!" she called, standing up abruptly and dumping the protesting kitten onto the floor. When she saw who was at the door, she stopped and stared, unsure what to do.

"Are you going to let me in? It's cold out here!" Jonas called through the door. Ruth bit her bottom lip. Should she let him in? If he was engaged to Evelyn Troyer, she didn't want to hear about it.

Before she could decide, he opened the door himself. "Never mind. I'll get it myself," he said, closing it behind him and stepping into the kitchen.

He rubbed his face with his hands. "Ruth, give me a minute here to explain what happened. In fact, I can't believe you bought that act. It's kind of insulting, to be honest."

She waited for him to say something, and when he didn't, she lost her patience again. "Well?"

He took off his hat and held it in his hands. "Gathering my thoughts."

She stared at him, eyes narrowed, and nodded once before turning and stalking back into the living room where she sat in the rocking chair again. And waited.

Jonas sighed and walked around her to sit in the other rocking chair, the one that had belonged to Levi.

Ruth tried to wait him out, but she had to know. "Are you engaged to her?"

"What? No!" Jonas said. Then, grimacing a bit, admitted, "But it was a close thing."

"How did that happen? Have you secretly been courting both of us all this time, hedging your bets until you decided who you wanted?"

"Of course not!"

"So you're saying it was all in her imagination? You didn't do anything to make her think you wanted to marry her?"

"Ruth, you've known her as long as I have. Does she seem like the kind of girl who needs much encouragement?"

Considering, Ruth slowly shook her head. "No. I guess not."

"Thank you. I don't know why, but she's been fixated on me from the beginning."

"Well, you are a gut catch, I suppose," Ruth conceded. "A settled, older businessman. Sort of a father figure, probably."

"Hey, I'm not old enough to be her father," Jonas said. "Or, just barely. Look, Ruth," he said, reaching for her hand, "it's you I've come to care for, not someone else, whether you can have bopplin or not. I'm not looking for cheap farmhands. I want to get to know you better and see if maybe you, Abigail, and I are meant to be a family. And if we are, and if it's in Gott's plan for us to have other children, then I am open to that."

Ruth sat thinking for a moment. Then she looked up and met his eyes. "You care for me, as a person. As a woman. Not just as a mother for Abigail. Not just as a cook or a companion in the evenings? Not just as someone to. . .to warm your bed?" she whispered, blushing at her forwardness, but she felt it had to be asked.

He met her gaze squarely. "I've said so, Ruth. I care for you, as a person." He grinned a little wickedly. "As a woman. Should we decide we suit and marry, I admit I'd love the idea of you in my bed, but it wouldn't be enough if I didn't care for you and respect you. Please, put me out of my misery. Do I have a chance with you? Or have I blown it with one too many clumsy mistakes?"

Her cheeks tinged pink from his remark about having her in his marriage bed, and she answered a touch snippily at first. "They *were* clumsy. But. . .I would very much like to get to know you better and see if it is Gott's plan for us to make a family."

"Just that simple?"

She sighed and nodded, tossing embarrassment to the wind and embracing happiness. "Ja. Just that simple."

"All right then." He closed the distance between them and framed her dear face in his strong, work-roughened hands, oh so gently. "We must seal this new relationship with a kiss, I think."

She gazed up at his familiar, beloved face and smiled a tiny smile. "I believe that would be right."

Smiling, he lowered his lips to hers, brushing them gently against her mouth once, twice, then allowing himself to sink into her comforting embrace. Their arms went around each other, and they shared what would hopefully be the first of many such embraces. After a few moments, he sighed and pulled away from her. He stood looking down at her in wonder. Her eyes slowly opened, and she looked back at him, a bit dazed.

"All right then," he breathed again.

"All right then!" she echoed. "So, we're dating. Which sounds really weird, like we're teenagers."

He grinned, his dimples popping out. "I don't care what you call it. Dating. Courting. Just spending time together. I'm glad we are."

She smiled and reached up a finger to trace one of those beguiling dimples. "Ja. I am too. Do you think we're right for each other?"

He caught her hand, brought it to his lips, and planted a kiss on the palm. "If I didn't, I wouldn't be here. Gott's plans unfold as they will. We just have to go along for the ride."

"The funny thing is, sometimes the ride is slow and calm, like a wagon pulled by an old horse. But sometimes, it feels like one of those fast English sports cars zooming down the road, and you don't know how anyone could possibly keep it all under control!"

"That's the fun of it. And besides, it's not up to us humans to keep it under control. That's what we have Gott for."

Ruth bit her lip and looked up at Jonas and laughed. "Well, if nothing else, I'll get to look at your adorable dimples while we decide if we're right for each other."

"My what? Dimples?" He touched his cheek and rolled his eyes. "Ach, silliness."

"That's the fun of it, Jonas!" she parroted.

Suddenly she walked to the door, put on her cloak and bonnet, and said, "Come on. I want to see if there's a letter from Lydia!"

Jonas walked along with her as she crossed the road and opened the door on the front of the mailbox. There were several items inside. One was a garden seed catalog. One a letter from her mother, and the third, the anticipated letter from Lydia.

"Oh my goodness, it's here!" She looked at Jonas, her eyes wide.

"Well, are you going to open it, or are you just going to stand there in the road wondering what she says?"

"I'm going to stand in the road and read it. You watch for cars." She puffed air out of her cheeks, nodded, and tore open the white envelope, pulling out several pieces of paper.

She looked at Jonas, took a deep breath, and turned her eyes to the paper. Glancing back up at Jonas, she read aloud.

> *Dear Ruth,*
>
> *I received your offer of a home with you in your dawdi haus with pleasure. I had thought I'd probably just stay here in Florida with my sister and her husband, but I've been here in the summer, and honestly, it's just too hot here for me.*
>
> *If you really think you'd like having an old woman living next door to you, then I gratefully accept your offer. I can always visit down here in the winter, as usual.*

"Oh, Jonas! She's coming!" Ruth cried excitedly.

"That's wonderful! What else does she say?"

Ruth read on:

> *I plan to remain here until Easter, at which time I will take a bus back to Ohio and join you there. I have nothing to contribute to*

the household—no furniture, no quilts, no kitchen items. I do have my clothes, of course, because I brought them here with me. And I have Hephzibah and Zed, of course, and the lovely basket you gave me. So I will come to you without much in the way of baggage. Of course, I'm aware the house is furnished, so I guess you really don't need much from me. In fact, if I still had my things, I'd be faced with the pesky decision of what to keep and what to give away or sell. So this is probably a blessing in disguise, ja? Anyway, it's all as Gott wills it. No use crying over burned-up quilts and such. (Though I may have, just a little. My wedding quilt and a couple made by my mother and grandmother were in the house. Thankfully, I had already passed a few family quilts down to the kids.) So I will see you late next month, and I thank you very much, my dear, for welcoming me into your home. I'm excited to see how your venture with the greenhouse is coming, and I can't imagine how lovely a field of sunflowers will be. Gott bless you, child.

With love,
Lydia

Ruth looked at Jonas, her eyes shining with happiness. "Well! I'm to have someone in the dawdi haus again, and a close neighbor. I'm so happy she said yes. I guess I hadn't let myself realize until just now how much I dreaded her saying no."

"I am glad she said yes. She's a gut friend, and as she's getting on in years, it'll be gut for her to be close to you here. Abigail and I are also very fond of her, as you know," he said, smiling at her meaningfully.

"How could you not be? And she's like a grossmammi to Abigail, I know."

He nodded and looked at his watch, then said, reluctantly, "I suppose I've been here as long as is proper, and I should probably go now."

She nodded.

"May I pick you up for church Sunday in my buggy?"

"Yes, that would be nice," she said. They both understood that this, more than anything they could do, would proclaim to their church community that they were seriously courting.

He smiled and, before she knew what he intended, leaned toward her and kissed her swiftly on the mouth. Then he touched the crown of his hat, climbed into his buggy, and headed home to Abigail.

Ruth went inside, closed the door, and leaned back against it. Ginger Snap came into the kitchen, looked at her, and then scampered over to check out his food bowl, which was empty. She scooped a serving of cat food and poured it into the bowl.

"There you go, cat," she said. "If things work out, you'll soon be living next door to your mama and papa. And maybe, eventually, your sister will be moving in here with you."

Ruth hugged herself, still feeling a bit giddy at the fact that Jonas truly wanted to court her for herself! Then a thought occurred to her. In all the excitement, Jonas hadn't told her how he'd nearly become engaged to Evelyn Troyer—and more importantly, how he didn't!

"I can't believe I forgot to get that out of him," she told her kitten. "At times like this, I almost envy the English and their cell phones! We'll get to the bottom of that tomorrow, Ginger Snap."

CHAPTER TWENTY-SEVEN

The next morning Ruth watched for Jonas to arrive at work. She was determined to find out what had happened with Evelyn first thing.

When she heard Jonas' buggy she hurried outside. "Guder mariye!" he called. "Couldn't wait to see me?"

Ruth rolled her eyes. "You got away last night without telling me something rather important!"

"If you give me kaffi and whatever baked goods you have on hand, I'll tell you anything," he promised with a grin.

"Fine!" She did an about face and marched into the kitchen and plunked a mug of coffee onto the table. He helped himself to a fresh cinnamon roll from a plate on the counter.

"Make yourself at home!" she said sweetly, sitting at the table with her own roll and coffee.

"Denki. I will," he said around a mouthful of sweet pastry. He swallowed. "So, what did I forget?"

"Merely the details about what happened with Evelyn Troyer!"

"Oh, yeah. That would account for your unusual snippiness this morning." He grinned to show he was kidding.

She just raised her eyebrows and waited.

"Okay, okay. I did forget to tell you about that. But be fair, Ruth. We were discussing more important things."

"That depends, Jonas. If I'm not satisfied with your answers on this subject, those 'more important things' might be moot points."

"Ah." He took a cautious sip of the hot coffee, then put the cup down and looked at Ruth. "Well, she basically set me up."

"What? How?"

"She and her grandfather had come to check out my new operation in your barn, and she saw us walking toward the greenhouse. She thought fast—you can't accuse her of being dim—and told her grandfather that she wanted to show him something by your greenhouse. She asked him to give her a couple minutes and hurried after us. You can guess the rest."

"Go on," she prodded.

"After she drove you away—and can I just say you gave up way too easily?—she told me I was the man for her, and she kissed me!"

"No!"

"Yes! Right in front of her grandfather, who walked into her trap as easily as I did and demanded that we marry."

"Then how is it you aren't engaged to her?"

"Please. I'd have gotten myself out of the mess, but it turns out I had help."

"Help?"

"Before I could set Bishop Troyer straight, young Zeke Yoder came along. He saw us standing there, looking very awkward, I'm sure, and he walked right up, looked me in the eye, and said he was there to find out what my intentions were toward Evelyn!"

Ruth could hardly believe what she was hearing. "Right in front of the bishop?"

Josh grinned. "Ja, it was very bold. Evelyn was impressed, I could tell."

"So what happened next?"

Jonas shrugged. "Not much. Bishop Troyer told Zeke that Evelyn and I were going to marry, and he should leave. Zeke turned to face the bishop, and his face got bright red. He told the bishop he would say his piece first, if it was all the same to the bishop. I'll tell you, the bishop didn't know what to do. So Zeke turned and looked at Evelyn and blurted out that he loved her and wanted to marry her. Something about her being the most beautiful woman he'd ever seen, yada yada. And then, to prove the depths of his feelings, he punched me in the face."

"What?! Oh, Jonas, are you hurt?" She moved forward and examined his face, moving her fingers gently over his skin, probing for injury.

When she pressed his jaw, he grimaced. "Yep, that's the spot."

"Sorry! I can't see anything. Your beard must cover the bruise."

"Well, I guarantee it's tender. Anyway, the bishop was scandalized, Evelyn was thrilled, Zeke is facing a disciplinary meeting with the elders for his violent, un-Christian behavior, and he and Evelyn are engaged. That's it."

She was stunned. "That's it? He punched you, and she tossed you over for him?"

"Yep. Lucky for me he's so handsome."

Ruth shook her head. "Lucky for you she's such a fickle ninny."

"Ja. A fickle ninny who packs a mean picnic hamper. I think that's what won him over."

She giggled. "Thank Gott! And from now on, I expect to be the only woman packing picnic hampers for you!"

"Works for me. Your Chow Chow is much better than hers."

"Huh. My grossmammi was right."

Jonas finished chewing the last bite of his cinnamon roll, wiped off his mouth with his napkin, and asked, "How so?"

"She said to stick to the fundamentals if I wanted to succeed! Nothing more fundamental than Chow Chow!"

Jonas laughed in appreciation. "You should always listen to your elders."

"Yep. I always listened to her! If I'd thought about it sooner, I might have opened up her greenhouse years ago."

Jonas shrugged and stood up to get back to work. "Better late than never." He grabbed his hat from the peg by the door, and Ruth walked over to brush a couple crumbs off his shirt. He captured her chin in his hand and leaned in to give her a kiss.

"Mmmm," she said, pressing her lips together in appreciation. "You taste gut! Like fresh cinnamon rolls!"

He laughed. "See why the bishop proposed? Your cinnamon rolls are very romantic."

She rolled her eyes. "But really, Jonas, I hate to think Zeke is in serious trouble. Violence is never our way. What could he have been thinking?"

His face lost its look of amusement. "No, it isn't the answer, that's for sure and certain. He could have talked to me and saved everyone a lot of trouble and embarrassment. I suppose our elders and his back in Sugarcreek will discuss the situation and decide what to do."

"You don't think he'll be expelled?"

"Ach, nee. But I expect he'll have to confess his sins before at least our congregation, maybe both. The fact that he's going to marry the bishop's granddaughter won't hurt his cause," he said, a tiny twinkle appearing in his eyes again.

"No, I don't suppose it will. But he should apologize to you, as you're the one he injured."

"He already did that, and I forgave him straightaway. I understand how being hung up on a gut woman can make a man forget himself."

"Hung up. Hmpf."

He laughed. "See you later, Ruth," he said, and went out the door toward his shop in the barn. She watched him walk away, and when he was halfway there, he turned around. "Will you be around for lunch?"

"Ja," she said, smiling and leaning against the doorjamb. "Maybe I'll have Chow Chow."

He touched his hat. "I'll be here! I may have Abigail with me. Is that okay?"

"Even better!" Ruth grinned. "Maybe she'd like to spend the afternoon here after lunch?"

Jonas paused, then nodded. "Ja, I'm sure she would. And Selma can get the shopping done without the help of a four-year-old. I'll tell her when they stop by later." He waved and went to work, and Ruth went inside, humming happily at the prospect of company for lunch.

Sunday morning, ready for church, Ruth found herself gazing at her bed with its pretty blue log cabin quilt.

She stared for a few moments at the quilt, then moved decisively to the hope chest at the foot of the bed and opened it. Inside, carefully stored in a plastic bag, was her wedding quilt. She looked at it for a few moments, remembering how carefully she'd pieced it before her wedding to Levi, and how she had removed and stored it following his death, as if she didn't feel right sleeping under it without him.

"I am ready to let you go, Levi," she whispered. "I think Jonas is the right man for me to spend the rest of my life with. But even if he turns out not to be the one, I'm ready to move on. But Levi, I will always honor your memory and cherish the years we had together."

She removed the quilt carefully from the plastic bag and gently shook it out. Thinking it was getting a bit colder and she could use another quilt on the bed, she didn't remove the log cabin quilt but rather smoothed the wedding quilt over it.

Ginger Snap scampered into the room and, with his sharp kitten claws, climbed the quilt.

"Oh no you don't, mister," Ruth said, catching the frisky kitten and holding him against her chest, stroking him as she wandered over to the window and stared out at the wintry scene.

"Life can be such a surprise, can't it, Ginger Snap? Just look how much has happened in the last couple of months in our lives! You came here to live, and Jonas and Abby came into our lives, and soon Lydia will join us here. Of course, Gott knew it was all going to happen, but it was all a surprise to me!" She snuggled him under her chin, smiling dreamily at how well everything was turning out. "And now Jonas and Abby are picking me up for services, and everyone will know we're courting. I'm praying we're going to be a family!"

She twirled around, holding the cat close to her chest, heart filled with happiness and love. He purred, undisturbed by her odd behavior.

Outside, snow still lay on the ground, though the roads were all clear. The *clip-clop* of approaching hooves reminded her that Jonas and Abigail were picking her up for church. Looking at the quilt on her bed, she felt lighthearted and ready to move on.

"Goodbye, Levi. I won't forget you," she whispered, giving the quilt one last smoothing with her hand.

Setting Ginger Snap on the bed, she grabbed her cardigan and pulled it over her dress as she skipped down the stairs, feeling just like a young woman who was being picked up by her beau.

Jonas stood inside the kitchen when she came in, and he smiled at her. "Guder mariye, Ruth. You look fine today. Are you ready?"

She felt strong and sure, and said, "Ja, Jonas. I am ready."

———————— ⚜ ————————

At the Millers', Ruth and Abigail carried the food inside while Jonas helped set up the benches.

Mrs. Harriet Mueller, a widow known for her avid interest in other people's business, approached them, bright eyed, before they reached the house. "Ruth, did I see you drive in with Jonas Hershberger?" Then, looking at Abigail, the older woman nodded sagely. "Well, I must be right, for this little girl is Jonas' daughter, Abigail, ain't so?"

"Yes, ma'am, you're right," Abigail said, smiling at the woman.

"Well, isn't that nice? I'd heard that he'd moved his basket business to your big barn, Ruth. And now, here you are, coming to church together, just like a family."

Ruth smiled and supposed it was bound to be big news that the widow Helmuth and the widower Hershberger, along with his motherless child, were "keeping company" together.

Inside, Mrs. Miller hurried up and took the basket of cookies from Ruth. "Oh! And here's Ruth Helmuth with little Abigail Hershberger!"

"May I go into the living room and see what the other little girls are doing?" Abigail asked, tugging on Ruth's hand.

"Ja, Abigail, I'll come get you when it is time for services."

"Well, it is so nice to see her with you!" Mrs. Miller said. "The poor baby has been without a mother so long!"

"She has a very attentive father, though," Ruth pointed out.

The women smiled at each other and nodded.

"Ja!" giggled Elizabeth, who had come into the room and stood listening to her mother and Mrs. Mueller speak to Ruth. "And a handsome one!"

"And you rode here together?" asked Mrs. Miller, with a meaningful glance at Mrs. Mueller, who smiled smugly back.

Ruth nodded. "Ja. Jonas was kind enough to pick me up for church today."

More nods. "Well, that is very nice," said Mrs. Miller.

And that was all that was said. Following services, Ruth, Jonas, and Abigail shared lunch and then stayed for the singing. Ruth found that she didn't mind the good-natured teasing and speculative glances of her friends. After all, these people had known her and Jonas all their lives and truly cared about their happiness.

And it didn't hurt that Evelyn and Zeke, while not officially engaged, as no announcement had been made, were clearly courting. Their arrival together in his buggy drew quite a bit of attention away from Ruth and Jonas.

At the end of the evening, following a full day of services, delicious food shared with neighbors, and rousing singing, Jonas and Ruth walked to Jonas' buggy, a sleepy Abigail carried in her father's arms.

"Be careful on that dark road, everyone! Make sure your lanterns are lit!" Elizabeth called from the kitchen doorway.

"We will! Denki for a gut day!" Ruth called back to her friend.

Bishop Troyer's buggy was parked next to Jonas'. "I see you have the new battery-operated lights on your buggy," the older man said. "They really show up in the dark. The elders and I considered hard before deciding they were all right for us to use, and now I'm glad we did. I have them myself. Feel much safer. Well, I see you two came together. How's the basket business in the new location?"

"Very gut, Bishop, we really appreciate the added space," Jonas said respectfully.

The older man nodded. "Ja, ja, I expect so. And you, Ruth, how are those chrysanthemum seeds coming? Are they up yet?"

She nodded. "Ja, they are several inches tall already."

"I expect your grandmother would be pleased. Good woman, your grossmammi. Pity about Lydia Coblentz's house," he said. "I hear she may stay in Florida with her sister. Pity, pity. She'll be missed here in the parish."

"Actually, Bishop," Ruth said, "as to that, I've invited her to move into my dawdi haus. She and my grossmammi were gut friends, as you know, and she has agreed. I am very happy she'll be so close."

"Ja, and when we were getting it ready for her, we found a quilt she made for Ruth's grossmammi, didn't we, Ruth?" Jonas reminded her.

"Ja! But it's going to be a surprise, Bishop. She lost so many beautiful quilts she and her own mudder and grossmammi made when her house burned, we're hoping that this one will really help welcome her home."

"Ah! Is that so?" he asked, rocking on his heels and stroking his long gray beard as he considered this news. "Well then, that's gut for all of you. Gott works in mysterious ways, and He's brought you a good deal recently, hasn't He, young woman?" Looking at Jonas, he smiled. "Sorry about that business the other day, Jonas. But it all turned out fine, so enough said. Well, time for me to get home. I'll see you soon, I expect. I'm of a mind to see these chrysanthemum seedlings for myself," he said, before turning and wandering toward the house.

Ruth looked at Jonas and raised her hand to her lips to stifle a giggle.

He winked and said, "Well, come on then, let's get you home. It isn't getting any warmer out here."

Jonas drove Ruth home under a starry sky, the child asleep on the seat between them. "Thank you for riding to services with us today, Ruth. I'll see you tomorrow morning, then," he said as he walked her to her door. He reached out to nudge a stray tendril of hair back under her kapp, then leaned in and gave her a brief kiss. "I'll come a bit early, and we can have a cup of coffee together?" She nodded, and he smiled at her and then turned and headed back to his buggy.

As he drove off, Ruth hugged herself and thought it couldn't have been a more perfect day. Everyone knew that they were courting and seemed happy for them. She could hardly wait to see what the next weeks would bring.

CHAPTER TWENTY-EIGHT

As Ruth brewed coffee the next morning, she thought about the turns her life had recently taken. From a lonely existence in an empty house, with no one around to keep her company but her farm animals and an occasional visit with a friend to look forward to, she now had a kitten living in the house, a greenhouse full of young flowers, plans for planting her fields, her dear friend planning to move into her dawdi haus, and best of all, Jonas was courting her. And Jonas came with beautiful, delightful Abigail!

"Gott has blessed me mightily lately!"

Yet one worry was tugging at her mind, marring her newfound happiness—would she make a gut mudder? Was it too late for her to learn how?

"Gott," she whispered, "I care for Jonas very much, and I already love his little daughter. I think we could make a gut family. Is that what You intend? Because I think I would like that. And please, help me to be a gut mudder to Abigail if it is what You want for us all." She thought a minute before adding, "And let Abigail be patient with me while I learn! Amen."

"Let me tie Samson before you get out, Abby," Jonas cautioned as they pulled up to Ruth's hitching post. As soon as she was free, Abigail ran to the house.

"Ruth! Ruth! I brought Alaska for a visit with Ginger Snap! Don't you think they'll be glad to see each other?" she called as Ruth opened the kitchen door.

Abigail had already taken off her boots and set them by the door and was running through the house looking for Ruth's cat when Jonas came inside.

"Abby!" Jonas called sternly. "It isn't polite to run through someone's home uninvited. Come back to the kitchen now."

"It's all right. I don't mind," Ruth said.

"Denki, but she needs to learn her manners," Jonas said.

Ruth could tell he wasn't really cross, and she reflected on how much there was to teach a child. This was what she'd been worried about. She had no experience with this. If she and Jonas were to become a couple, would she really be qualified to be a mother to Abigail? She shook her head. "With Gott's help, I can do it," she whispered to herself as she listened to Jonas instruct his small daughter, gently but firmly, on the manners of visiting.

"I'm sorry for being rude, Ruth," Abigail said, and Ruth was afraid the child might cry and had a hard time not brushing it off.

"Thank you for your apology, Abigail," Ruth said instead, glancing at Jonas. "You are welcome to go look for Ginger Snap now, if your father says you might."

Jonas nodded. "You may, since Ruth says you may, as it is her house. Remember your manners next time, though."

The child's face transformed with a sunny smile, and she spontaneously hugged Ruth. "Denki! I'll find Ginger Snap, and he can play with Alaska!"

She ran out, hauling the carrier, from which issued the sound of a plaintive "Meow!"

"I think Ginger Snap is hiding," Jonas said with a twinkle in his eye.

"Ja, probably under my bed," Ruth said. "I'll bet she finds him pretty quick. There aren't that many places."

"Um, I didn't mean to contradict you there, about Abby," Jonas said, looking carefully at Ruth.

She looked at the ceiling a moment, considering what to say. "I actually understand. You might not think I would, since I have no bopplin. But I get how hard it must be to raise a child right. In fact, I've been a little worried about whether or not I'll be able to pick up on it this late in the game."

"I think you'd be an excellent mudder," Jonas said seriously. "And I only have four years' head start on you, after all. It's not like I've raised a brood of kids and can tell you how it's done. I'm totally guessing most of the time myself. I really watch Sally and Joseph to see how they handle things a lot of the time, since their kids are older than Abigail—and they have three of them."

"You really think I'd do all right at being a mudder?"

"If I didn't, as much as I care for you, I wouldn't have asked to court you. Abigail is too important to me."

"Oddly, that makes me feel better," Ruth laughed.

A triumphant cry sounded from upstairs, followed by the sound of Abigail chattering away to the two cats.

"Well, she'll be occupied for a bit," Jonas said. "Got any of your tasty rolls?"

"Have a seat, they're ready to eat!" Ruth said, and then giggled at her silly, unintentional rhyme.

"You're a poet, Ruth!" Jonas smiled, accepting a plate and a cup of kaffi.

"In two languages!" she joked in return.

She took a roll and coffee for herself and then joined him. They smiled at each other and ate in companionable silence, listening to Abigail playing with the cats upstairs.

"I enjoyed going to church services with you yesterday," Jonas said, regarding her steadily.

"Ja, so did I," she smiled at him mischievously. "And Mrs. Mueller was very interested to see us arrive together," she added with a twinkle in her eye.

He laughed. "I'll bet she was. And even more interested to see Evelyn and Zeke arrive together." He cleared his throat. "I have been thinking about—"

But whatever he'd been thinking about would have to wait, as a knock sounded on the door.

Ruth started and stared at the door. "I didn't hear a buggy, did you?" she asked Jonas.

"No, but we were talking and might have missed it," he said.

She stood and walked to the door. Jonas remained seated.

"Bishop Troyer!" Ruth said in surprise as she opened the door. "We didn't hear your buggy pulling up." She moved aside and gestured the older man in. "Come in from the cold and have a cup of kaffi and a cinnamon roll. They're still warm."

Bishop Troyer stomped his feet on the mat and hung his coat and hat on the pegs by the door.

"Denki, I will. It's mighty cold out there! Gut morning, Jonas. You've beat me to the rolls, I see." He took a seat at the table and accepted a plate and cup from Ruth.

"They're mighty gut, Bishop," Jonas said. Ruth freshened Jonas' coffee and poured another cup for herself.

"Oh, don't I know it! I told Ruth her rolls remind me of my late wife Amelia's."

"A high compliment," Jonas said, and Ruth smiled at Bishop Troyer's wistful look.

"Ja, she was the best cook and an excellent wife." He looked at Ruth. "I know now I really couldn't replace her. I guess I just wanted to pretend I could."

Her eyes suddenly moist, Ruth nodded at the older man. "Denki, Bishop. I do understand."

"I imagine you do. I imagine you both do," he said, looking from one to the other of them.

"But you know," Ruth said. "It's not like finding someone else you can have feelings for and make a life with is exactly replacing someone you lost. Those we've loved who have gone to be with Gott can't be replaced. But I think if we are very blessed, we can find someone else to move forward with, and they're just as special in another way entirely."

Jonas nodded. "Ja, I agree."

"Hmmm," the bishop said. "I will consider that. You're saying I don't have to be alone the rest of my life but that finding someone who could be my equal partner—no offense, Ruth, but someone my own age—wouldn't be betraying what I had with Amelia."

"Exactly," Ruth said, smiling gently at the bishop. "And no offense taken."

Abigail came running into the kitchen holding a cat under each arm. "Dat! Look, I found Ginger Snap, and I'm taking the cats to play in the living room, okay?" She stopped short and stared at Bishop Troyer.

"What do you say to the bishop, Abigail?" Jonas prompted her.

"Gut morning, Bishop Troyer," Abigail said politely, and Ruth smiled. Surely that would make any parent proud.

The cats squirmed in her arms, and Ginger Snap let out a low warning growl.

"Abigail, perhaps you're squeezing the cats a bit too tightly," Ruth said, standing to take Ginger Snap out of the child's arms so she could adjust her grip on Alaska. Ruth stroked Ginger Snap and set him down. He went to see if anything interesting had appeared in his food bowl since the last time he'd been in the room.

Bishop Troyer's eyebrows rose. "It seems Lydia's odd habit of keeping cats in the house is spreading throughout the community."

"They are from Hephzibah's last litter, and Lydia gave them away only after extracting promises from each recipient that they would be indoor cats. Abigail and I were each lucky enough to get one."

"And now their mama and papa will be living right next door in the dawdi haus," the bishop said. "Well, it's your house, but I wouldn't want them inside."

"I haven't seen a mouse since he moved in," Ruth commented with a small smile. It was well known that Bishop Troyer had a bit of a phobia about mice, though he wouldn't admit it.

"No mice in the house, you say?" he asked, his brow furrowing. "Hmmm. Shouldn't be a surprise. They keep them out of the barn well enough, but I hadn't thought about it." He sniffed. "I don't smell litter. Can't abide smelling cat litter."

Ruth nodded. "You have to scoop it out regularly, and then there is no odor. But I keep the litter in the basement. He uses a little door to get downstairs," she said, pointing to the basement door and the little cat door Jonas had installed there a few weeks ago.

"Well, that's clever, though a shame to harm a nice door," the bishop said. "Who put it in for you, Ruth?"

"I did, Bishop," Jonas said.

"Ah, you're quite the handyman around here these days."

Jonas looked at Ruth as if for permission before turning to the bishop and saying, "The fact is, Ruth and I are courting."

Bishop Troyer looked relieved. "Ah. Gut. I had thought…but then, the other day… Well, that was awkward. The least said about that the better. Of course, when you arrived at services together yesterday, I hoped you'd gotten past that… Well, no harm done, then. Gut, gut, it would suit you both, and the child. Pray about it, of course, and see what Gott's will may be. Ja. Ja."

He stood suddenly. "Now! How about showing me your flowers, Ruth? And Jonas, I'd like to see the basket shop, as well, if you don't mind. Never got around to it the other day, what with the, ahem, excitement."

"Oh!" Ruth said. "Yes, I'd be happy to show you, Bishop. Just let me clear these plates and cups away."

He sniffed the air again and shook his head. "Can't smell cat litter. Dirty job, keeping it clean though."

Jonas shrugged. "No more objectionable than mucking out stalls, and we're all farmers here, ja?"

The bishop raised his bushy gray eyebrows at that. "Well, that's true. I hadn't thought of it in that way. Mucking out the cat stall. Heh

heh." He put his warm hat back on and shrugged into his coat.

Jonas called Abigail downstairs. "The cats will be fine here for a bit while we show Bishop Troyer the greenhouse and the basket barn," he said, bundling the child into her coat.

"The greenhouse first, if you don't mind," Bishop Troyer said, raising an inquiring eyebrow at Ruth.

She smiled nervously, hoping he would approve of all she'd accomplished there.

Bishop Troyer entered the warm, fragrant greenhouse and drew a deep breath, evidently savoring the rich scents of soil and greenery. He turned and smiled at Ruth.

"Well, I haven't been in here since your grandmother used it." He looked around nostalgically. "She grew the strongest vegetables in the area. You always knew Eliza Weaver's cucumbers and tomatoes would stand up to drought and pests, yes indeed."

He turned and looked at Ruth. "And now you're growing flowers here. I think that's fine," he said, bending over to inspect a row of young chrysanthemum seedlings about three inches high. "When will you move these out into the field, young woman?"

"After the danger of frost has passed, so around the end of May," she answered, looking around at the thousands of small mums thriving in the warm, humid environment of the greenhouse. It was odd to stand inside where it was almost uncomfortably warm and humid, while outside snow pressed up against the lower windows of the structure.

The bishop turned to face her. "You've proven me wrong, haven't you, Ruth?"

She stared at him. "I. . .I never meant any disrespect, Bishop. I only wanted to stay here on my family farm, where I'd been happy with my grandmother and my husband."

"Ja. I realize that now. I am sorry for trying to force you to sell. I didn't believe, in truth, that you could manage the place alone. But even without Jonas' help, I think you would have done fine. You've brought this greenhouse back. You have your herd of goats doing very well, I understand, and your cheese business in spring and summer. You do make *appenditlich* cheese! Delicious! And you'll have Lydia's company in the dawdi haus. I could only wish there were more people in the big house."

Then he looked at Jonas and smiled. "But perhaps in time there will be. We'll see."

Before Ruth could think how to respond to that, much less take in the fact that Bishop Troyer thought her cheese was delicious, he said, "Well! Now I'd like to see your new operation, Jonas. I hear it is very efficient." He smiled at Ruth and walked out of the greenhouse. Jonas, holding Abigail's hand, shrugged and then, with a wink at Ruth, followed.

Ruth took a deep breath, let it out slowly, and took a look around her greenhouse. "It's gut."

She smiled and followed the men and the child toward the barn, where they were getting ready to go in and look over Jonas' basket business.

"I've got to go in and check on my roast!" she called to the men, who hadn't yet disappeared inside the barn. They looked back and waved to let her know they'd heard.

Soon enough they'd be back. Ruth would invite them all to lunch. Used to being alone for so long, she found that she was enjoying having company around the place.

Later that evening, as Jonas drove himself and Abigail back home, he thought what a remarkable day it had been. Bishop Troyer had been impressed with his shop and Ruth's growing operation.

He wished the bishop's timing had been better, though, as he'd been about to readdress his proposal to Ruth—although less clumsily, he hoped.

"That's okay, right, Samson? That discussion can wait for another opportunity—maybe when a child and two kittens are not nearby."

Samson didn't answer. He was focused on getting back to his barn and a measure of oats.

CHAPTER TWENTY-NINE

The sun was setting with a spectacular display several days later, and Ruth was gathering in her clothes from the line.

Wolke and Heftig were lolling nearby on the dormant brown grass, keeping half an eye on the goats with their babies, out for the afternoon foraging in the enclosed meadow.

"I was glad to have this nice afternoon to do the laundry," Ruth commented to the dogs. "It may be lovely today, but Jonas says it's supposed to snow again later in the week. I don't know about you guys, but I'm ready for spring."

"Jonas is very smart. You should listen to him," came a deep voice from behind her. She spun around and laughed as Jonas, leaning against the nearby oak tree, grinned at her.

She shook her head, folding the last of the laundry and placing it on the basket of clean clothes.

"Careful, Jonas, that almost sounded prideful."

"I'll be careful." He looked at all the baby goats running and playing in the meadow. They were excellent climbers, and Ruth had placed a couple of wooden barrels and a few other items they could climb up on in the meadow to entertain them.

"They sure know how to entertain themselves, don't they?"

"Ja, they're very gut at that! I've been thinking about installing a small playset for them."

"Really? People do that?"

"Ja, you'd be surprised what serious goat owners do," she laughed. "Goats like seesaws and climbing walls and bridges. They can get pretty extensive, from what I've read." She picked up the basket and turned to head inside. He came to walk beside her and whisked the basket from her hands. She smiled her thanks and opened the gate to the garden, allowing him to precede her through.

"So, is the idea to keep them from getting bored?"

"Oh, ja." She nodded. "A bored goat is a naughty goat. And you'd be amazed at how gut they are at escaping enclosures. In the end, it's cheaper to give them what they need to keep them busy. I haven't done it before because I wanted to turn the profits back into the business. But putting a little playset in would be doing that, wouldn't it?"

"Seems like it to me, if it keeps them out of trouble." Inside, he set the basket on the floor and smiled wistfully at her. "Any chance of a cup of kaffi for a hardworking man?"

"I don't know, Jonas. We're alone here, without even Abby. You're the one who convinced me we don't want to invite gossip."

He frowned for a moment and then nodded. "Ja, you're probably right. So maybe you should come to my house for supper tonight and take a break from cooking for a day. Selma will have the meal ready when I get home."

"That sounds tempting," she admitted. "All right, I'll come. I can follow you home in my buggy so you don't have to drive me back after."

"Nonsense. I'll drive you back, sure enough. That way I can steal a good-night kiss at your door."

She blushed. "Goodness, Jonas."

He stepped closer to her. "Are you shocked?"

"Maybe a little."

"I haven't really kissed you in days." He took another step closer, and they stood toe to toe, her back against the sink.

"Jonas, I'm not sure. . ."

"Don't you want me to kiss you?" He raised a hand and ran his knuckles down her cheek. She leaned into the caress, her eyes drifting closed. And then she jerked with surprise when she felt his lips, softly brushing over hers. She opened her eyes to find Jonas gazing back at her with a look of such tenderness on his face that her eyes filled with tears.

"Tears? Ruth, I don't mean to upset or frighten you. I'm sorry, liebchen. I won't rush you."

She swallowed. "No, I'm not upset or frightened. It was the look on your face after. . .after you kissed me. You looked at me as if. . ." She stopped, unable to continue for fear of making a fool of herself. He smiled tenderly at her.

"As if I cherish you? As if I love you? Ruth, that's because I do."

"You do?"

"Ja. And I have to tell you that I know how I want this courtship of ours to end. I want it to end with a wedding next October, Ruth. I want us to be a *familie*—you, me, and Abby. And not because I want a mother for Abby but because I want you as my wife. Will you take us?"

She smiled, suddenly feeling wonderful, and reached a hand up to cup his cheek. "Oh, Jonas, I never thought I'd feel this again. I love you too. And I love Abigail. She's like the sunshine whenever she's near. Ja! I'll take you. I'll take you both! And your little cat too," she added with an impish grin.

"Thank Gott," Jonas said, gathering Ruth close in a tight hug. After a few moments, while Ruth was thinking how nice it was simply to be held close by someone again, he pulled away slightly and looked down at her. "Of course, now that we're officially betrothed, it's perfectly fine for me to kiss my fiancée, you know."

"You just kissed me a minute ago," she pointed out.

"That was no kiss. This is," he said, taking her lips in a tender kiss, a kiss that deepened enough to promise more one day, when they were man and wife.

When he lifted his head, she sighed. "Ach, ja, kisses are gut!"

Jonas threw back his head and laughed. "Ja! They are. But now we'd better head over to my house and have dinner with Abby and tell her she's going to have a new mudder."

"Do you think she'll want me to be her mudder?"

"Abby loves you. She'll be thrilled to have you as her mudder. In fact, we may find it difficult to keep our betrothal a secret until fall, because she'll want to tell everyone!"

"Ach, such things are perhaps for the young, Jonas. I don't mind if people know. If the word gets out, so be it."

"I've been thinking, Ruth," Jonas said, looking suddenly serious. "With the basket business here and your businesses, not to mention Lydia arriving in a few weeks, it would make sense for us to live here, in your home, don't you think?"

She nodded. "Ja, I confess I've thought about it. And I noticed Bishop Troyer assuming it the other day. I don't know if you caught that?" He nodded, and she went on. "So after the wedding, you and Abby can move in here. And Alaska, of course."

"Perfect. I'm not attached to my house as you are to yours. True, it was mine and Viola's, but it wasn't a family home like yours is. And your property is in a much better location, especially for safely raising bopplin! You never know—we may have more one day." Seeing that she was about to remind him that there was no guarantee she could have children, he raised a finger and placed it against her lips. "I know, you may not be able to have any. But life comes with no guarantees, as we both know. No couple embarking on marriage has the guarantee of children, or anything else."

Ruth's mouth fell open as she considered this. "You're absolutely right. Why didn't I ever think of it that way?"

"You're just lucky you're getting such a smart *mann*. Now, let's go tell Abby she's getting a new mudder!"

As they hurried outside, Ruth took a moment to silently thank Gott for all the blessings He had bestowed upon her, all her life. And for those yet to come.

Jonas handed her up into his buggy and smiled into her eyes. "Ruth Hershberger. I like the sound of it."

As he walked around to the driver's side, Ruth thought she did too. She settled back into the buggy seat and rode with the man she loved toward their shared future.

EPILOGUE

Two Years Later

Jonas sat in the kitchen of the house he shared with Ruth and Abigail since their marriage, staring at the battery-operated clock hanging above the sink. He wondered if the clock, which had been a wedding gift, was working properly. The minute hand was moving unnaturally slowly, it seemed to him. The midwife, Mary Beth Hudson, had instructed him to take a half-hour break, and it seemed like the longest half hour of his life. Lydia placed a cup of coffee in front of him and sat wearily down in the seat across from him. It was late, and neither of them had slept since the night before.

"This is taking too long," Jonas said.

"No, it's about normal for a first time. The midwife said she's progressing well, right?"

Jonas nodded.

"Then it shouldn't be too much longer," Lydia assured him. She took a sip of coffee and sighed with pleasure. "There's nothing like a fresh cup of kaffi to perk you up. Drink some, Jonas. You're dead on your feet."

"I'm not complaining, not while Ruth is going through so much to bring our child into the world." He stood. "I should be up there, not down here relaxing."

Lydia put a staying hand on his arm. "I know, I know. Fact is, you've been a rock for her all day and all night. But you need a little break, or you won't be worth anything later. Drink up."

"Fine." Jonas sat down, took a sip of the hot coffee, and blinked his eyes. "This coffee tastes like. . .cucumbers? What is it?"

"It's a new Sumatran varietal I'm trying out. I've gotten interested in different kinds of coffee from around the world. It's gut, right?"

Jonas took a second sip and moved it around in his mouth, then swallowed it thoughtfully. "Ja, I guess it is. I didn't expect to find my salad in my kaffi, though. But it's not bad."

Lydia looked pleased. "There's a new coffee shop in Berlin that's carrying different varietals and blends. I'm having fun trying them all out."

"Well, I'm always happy to be your guinea pig," Jonas said. He sipped his coffee and kept one ear trained upstairs, ready to bolt if he heard anything alarming.

"Did you hear anything?" he asked suddenly, sitting upright and sloshing a bit of coffee onto the table.

"No, Jonas. Relax. Ruth is fine."

He sank back into his seat and sighed. "I'm losing my mind."

"It's normal," Lydia said, patting his hand. "A combination of sleep deprivation, caffeine overdose, and adrenaline. You'll be fine. Have a cookie." She pushed a plate of peanut butter cookies toward him, and he absently took one and munched on it.

He remembered how happy he had been when Ruth had told him she was pregnant. She'd waited nearly three months to share the news with him, first because she hardly dared to believe it could be true and then because she was terrified she might lose the baby and didn't want to get his hopes up. But the pregnancy had gone well. Ruth had never suffered from morning sickness, which explained how she was able to keep her pregnancy a secret from him the entire first trimester. In fact, she'd felt wonderful the entire nine months, even as her belly became remarkably round. Then came labor. He'd forgotten how scary it was to watch a woman he loved go through that pain. And there was the terror of remembering that Viola, his first wife, had died following Abigail's delivery. If that happened to Ruth, he didn't know how he'd be able to survive. He'd even tried to convince her to have the baby in the hospital, but she'd convinced him to let her try having it at home. The hospital wasn't far, and if the midwife thought for a second she was in distress, they'd call an ambulance right away. He'd reluctantly agreed and then decided to read up on everything he could find about childbirth so he'd be ready to help if need be.

He'd gone through childbirth classes with Ruth and planned to be there with her the whole time. But at the twenty-hour mark, the midwife had insisted he take a break.

"I'll go down for a cup of coffee after you get back," she'd promised him. "We'll take turns."

He'd looked at Ruth, torn, and she'd rolled her eyes. "Go, Jonas. I'm fine, I promise. I'm not the first woman to have a baby."

So he'd gone. But he'd taken about as long of a break as he could stand. He had to know Ruth was okay. The midwife had a cell phone in case of emergency, but he had to see for himself that his wife was not in danger. He chugged the rest of the coffee, wincing when he burned his mouth, and jumped up from the table.

"Lydia, I can't stay down here when she's up there in pain. I'm going back up." He turned and took the stairs two at a time.

The bedroom door was closed, and he knocked, feeling awkward. "Come in, Papa!" the midwife called, and Jonas pushed the door open and looked cautiously inside. He was astonished to see Ruth resting quietly, while the midwife held a tiny bundle in her arms.

He gasped. "But I was only gone for about twenty minutes! I thought you had a long way to go yet!"

"You were making Ruth a bit nervous, so I suggested a break to allow her to focus," Mary Beth said, carrying the bundle toward Jonas. "And it sure worked! Ruth transitioned right after you left and only had to push for about ten minutes! Amazing for a first baby! And here's your beautiful, healthy son, Jonas."

Jonas felt tears rush into his eyes as he looked at the red-faced little boy peering up at him from the tightly wrapped blanket Mary Beth had placed him in after cleaning him up. He looked at Ruth, who was smiling at him with joy shining from her tired eyes.

"Isn't he beautiful?" she asked.

Jonas stared at his son, still held in Mary Beth's arms, and said, "He looks like a burrito with a face."

"A burrito!" Ruth gasped, craning her neck to get a look at the baby.

"Newborns always remind me of burritos too," Mary Beth said. "It's the way we wrap them up. Now, sit down there in the chair beside Ruth, and you can hold him."

Obediently, Jonas sat, and Mary Beth handed the tiny boy to him. He cradled the little bundle in his arms, careful to support his head with one hand, and studied his face.

"Well, what do you think of our little burrito?" Ruth asked.

"He's absolutely amazing, Ruth. Thank you so much." He leaned over and kissed her gently on the mouth, and she smiled.

"Well then, I may forgive you for the burrito remark," she said, sinking back into her pillows. Suddenly, a puzzled look crossed Ruth's face.

Jonas sat up. "What is it?"

She smiled at him. "Nothing, just a funny twinge."

"A twinge? What sort of twinge? Mary Beth, should she be feeling funny twinges at this point?"

Mary Beth approached the bed. "It could be afterpains from her uterus contracting to shrink back to normal. That takes about six weeks." But Ruth winced again, and Mary Beth frowned. "They can be strong but shouldn't be too bad." She bent over Ruth and placed her hands on her belly. "Huh. Why didn't I feel that before?"

"What are you feeling? Do we need to call an ambulance?" Jonas asked, becoming alarmed.

Mary Beth looked at him and smiled. "No, no, but you'd better give me the baby. I'll put him in his cradle for a bit. You and Ruth aren't quite done here yet."

She picked the baby up and walked across the room to place him in the cradle Jonas had brought from his old house—the cradle that had been Abigail's. Then she turned and came back to the bed.

Ruth gasped and placed her hands on her belly. "Oh! That feels like before!"

"Ja, that's because you're still in labor, apparently. I think you've got another boppli in there."

"What?" Jonas gasped, turning to glare at the midwife. "You never said anything about twins, Mary Beth! Isn't this dangerous?"

Mary Beth shook her head and moved down to the bottom of the bed. "No, Jonas. This is a surprise but not that out of the ordinary. I seem to recall that twins run in your family, Ruth, on your father's side?"

Ruth was breathing through a contraction, but she nodded. When it eased, she said, "Ja, I'd forgotten. There are a few sets in the last couple of generations."

Jonas was appalled. "I didn't know that! Mary Beth, are you sure we shouldn't call the doctor?"

The door opened, and Lydia poked her head in. "What's going on?"

"Twins! Twins! I think we need to call the doctor," Jonas said, looking to Lydia for support.

But Lydia smiled serenely. "Oh, how wonderful! Two for the price of one. Won't Abigail be thrilled?" She walked over to the cradle. "May I hold the first one while you take care of delivering the second? I just washed my hands."

Mary Beth nodded. "Ja. Okay, Ruth, looks like you're about ready to push this baby out. When the next contraction hits, push!"

Jonas sank onto the chair beside the bed. "Oh my goodness. How can I help?"

"Just take my hand, Jonas. I'm fine," Ruth ground out through clenched teeth as another contraction hit. She bore down and pushed, and Jonas gasped as he saw the baby's head crown. It took another couple of minutes for Ruth, with Mary Beth's help and Jonas' terrified support, to bring her second baby, this one a beautiful, healthy girl, into the world. The baby gave a lusty cry, and Jonas felt tears rolling down his face.

"Would you like to cut the cord, Papa?" Mary Beth asked, handing scissors to Jonas. Smiling tremulously, he carefully cut the umbilical cord, and Mary Beth tied it off.

A short while later, after Ruth had delivered the afterbirths and Mary Beth had made sure all was as it should be with her, she helped the new mother into a fresh nightgown while Jonas and Lydia changed her bedding. Then Jonas helped his wife back into bed and sank onto the bed beside her, exhausted.

"Now, Ruth, rest a bit with your mann while I get these babies cleaned up and weighed."

Ruth closed her eyes and rested as Mary Beth weighed the babies and administered the APGAR tests. Jonas turned his head on the pillow and looked at his wife in wonder.

"You gave me two beautiful babies, Ruth," he whispered. She nodded, not opening her eyes. "I've never seen anything as miraculous as when her head crowned! It was amazing. I love you so much. Thank you for these amazing gifts."

She opened her eyes and smiled at him and squeezed his hand. "I love you too, Jonas. But I'm so tired."

"Rest," he whispered, brushing a kiss on her forehead. "I'll be right here."

Mary Beth and Lydia came back over to the bed with their babies.

"Ruth, you should try nursing them both before you sleep," Mary Beth said. "It helps contract the uterus and prevent hemorrhaging. Plus it's important for the babies to try suckling right away. It's instinctive for them and gut to get mother and bopplin used to one another."

Jonas sat up straight. "You should do it now if it helps prevent hemorrhaging, Ruth," he said. "That's what killed Viola."

Mary Beth looked at Jonas and put a reassuring hand on his shoulder. "Jonas, Ruth is not Viola. She is not having the problems Viola had. This is all normal. But it's a gut idea to nurse. Of course, nursing two can be a chore, so you may need to supplement as well. You'll have to see. Some women have no trouble nursing multiples. Some do."

"Just like my nannies," Ruth chuckled.

Jonas took a deep breath and made a conscious effort to settle down.

"I'll hold her while you nurse him. He's probably hungrier, since he was born first."

He accepted his new daughter from Mary Beth and watched Lydia carefully hand his son to Ruth. Mary Beth showed her how to help the infant latch on to her breast. After a few moments, Ruth laughed. "Oh, he's a natural!"

"Greedy, like a healthy baby should be," Lydia laughed. "Make sure he leaves some for his sister!"

"They'll be getting colostrum for the first couple of days. It's full of nutrients and antibacterial and immune-boosting substances that help protect your babies while they develop immunity of their own."

"Sure, and in a couple days my regular milk comes in," Ruth said, smiling beatifically at her nursing son. She cradled him in her arms and looked into his face. "I don't think I'll ever get tired of looking at him. I can't believe I did this."

"With a little help from Jonas and God," Mary Beth said, bustling around and cleaning up the room. "You did very well. You didn't need stitches even though things moved quickly at the end there, and then there was the surprise bonus of your daughter! You'll recover fast. But no heavy housework or lifting for six weeks, got it?"

"Yes, ma'am," Ruth said. "Oh, he's falling asleep. Is that okay?"

"Sure. Now you can nurse his sister," Mary Beth said. "We'll burp him this time so you can feed her and then get some rest." Lydia had draped a cloth diaper over her shoulder, and she eagerly accepted the little boy, placed him on her shoulder, and gently rubbed and patted his back. A surprisingly loud belch emerged a few moments later.

"Ha!" Lydia said. "That's the way! You know, it always strikes me as funny that we spend the first year trying to get babies to burp and then the rest of their lives telling them it's rude."

The other women laughed, and Ruth cradled her daughter and put her to her other breast. The baby was rooting around, and Mary Beth watched as Ruth helped her latch on, supporting her head in the crook of her arm.

"You're a natural," she remarked after a few minutes of watching Ruth nurse the baby.

"It feels amazing, like I've been waiting to do this all my life!" Ruth said. "But it's making me sleepy." Her eyes drifted closed as the baby nursed hungrily, kneading at Ruth's breast with her tiny fists.

Lydia smiled in satisfaction. "*Ja*, a natural, just like I knew she'd be," she whispered, for mother and babies were all asleep. Mary Beth nodded. "Ja. They'll do just fine."

————————— 🌱 —————————

"Papa is fast asleep," Lydia said, nodding at Jonas, who'd finally succumbed to his exhaustion, now that he knew mother and babes were going to be fine.

"I figured it wouldn't take much to put him out. It's been a long day."

"You must be beat too," Lydia said. "I have the guest room made up. Why don't you head in and go to sleep. I'll sit here with them for a while and make sure they're fine."

Mary Beth shook her head. "Thanks. But we'll put the babies in the cradle—they're used to sharing, after all—and then we can all get a bit of rest. You're tired too. Tomorrow will be soon enough for visiting with the new bopplin."

Lydia laughed softly. "I'm that transparent?"

"I know you want to get your hands on them. Go ahead and take her and put her in the cradle."

Lydia smiled and carefully lifted the child from Ruth, who sighed but didn't wake up. She laid the baby in the cradle next to her brother, where she pursed her lips and made sucking motions before settling down to sleep.

"I am so happy for Ruth and Jonas," Lydia sighed. "I thanked Gott for her pregnancy and now for these two beautiful children. He has answered so many prayers."

"Ja, He has," Mary Beth said. "Now, off to bed with you. I'll be right behind you."

Reluctantly, Lydia left the room and headed for her bed in the adjacent dawdi haus. Tomorrow would be a busy day. She'd spoken with Ruth's parents earlier, when it was certain she was in labor. Then Jonas had called them and his own parents to announce the births of the two babies. And within a couple days, the eager grandparents would be descending on the household to see the new additions to the family.

As Lydia made her way quietly through the house, Ginger Snap mewed softly from his basket in the living room. He followed Lydia into the kitchen, and she stooped to pick the sleek cat up.

"Well, Ginger Snap, your peaceful life is about to be turned on its ear. There are two new babies in the house, and though they can't do much right now, just wait a few months. You and Alaska will be scampering for high ground, if you know what's best for you."

Ginger Snap purred and nuzzled Lydia. Alaska sauntered into the room and wound herself around Lydia's ankles. Lydia reached down and scratched the pretty, white, blue-eyed cat between her ears.

"Of course, you're both always welcome to come over to my place and spend time with your parents if things get too wild around here," she told them. "Well, I am tired, so I'll say good night."

She put Ginger Snap down and pushed to her feet. She walked the short distance to the door leading to the breezeway that led to the dawdi haus. She turned and looked back at the two cats, who sat quietly and looked back at her. "Good night, cats. This is a gut day. A gut day! Tomorrow, we'll see what mischief an old woman can get up to with two new bopplin in the house! I can hardly wait! Oh, I am so blessed!"

Turning, she opened the door and went to her snug little home.

RUTH'S RECIPES

RUTH'S GINGER SNAP COOKIES

INGREDIENTS:

2 cups sifted flour	¾ cup butter
1 tablespoon ground ginger	1 cup sugar
2 teaspoons baking soda	1 large egg
1 teaspoon ground cinnamon	¼ cup dark molasses
½ teaspoon salt	⅓ cup cinnamon sugar

INSTRUCTIONS:

Preheat oven to 350 degrees.

Sift flour, ginger, baking soda, cinnamon, and salt into mixing bowl. Stir to mix well. Sift again. Beat butter until creamy. Gradually beat in sugar. (Do not add cinnamon sugar. That's for later.) Beat in egg and dark molasses. Add one third of flour mixture into butter/sugar/egg/molasses mixture; stir thoroughly to blend. Stir in remaining flour mixture and mix together to get soft dough. Roll dough between your hands into one-inch balls. If sticky, butter your hands first. Dip dough balls in cinnamon sugar and place two inches apart on ungreased baking sheet. Bake about 10 minutes in preheated oven until tops show slight cracks. Cool on wire racks. If you're not eating them all at once or serving to friends, store in airtight container.

RUTH'S AMISH CHOW CHOW RELISH

Yields 6 Quarts

INGREDIENTS:

2 quarts fresh green beans, cut into two-inch pieces

1 large head cauliflower, broken into florets

3 cups lima beans

3 cups fresh or canned whole kernel corn

2 large sweet onions, chopped

1 red bell pepper, seeds removed, chopped

1 yellow bell pepper, seeds removed, chopped

3 green bell peppers, seeds removed, chopped

1 (15 ounce) can red kidney beans, drained and rinsed

2 quarts green tomatoes, chopped (if green tomatoes are not available, use any tomatoes)

3 quarts cider vinegar

4 cups cane sugar

⅓ cup salt

2 tablespoons celery seed

2 tablespoons yellow mustard seed

2 tablespoons dry mustard

1 tablespoon turmeric

INSTRUCTIONS:

Cook green beans, cauliflower, lima beans, and corn until just tender. Drain. Mix in heavy kettle with onions, peppers, kidney beans, and tomatoes. In separate pot, bring vinegar to boil, and add sugar, salt, celery seed, mustard seed, dry mustard, and turmeric. Stir to mix. Pour vinegar mixture over vegetables. Bring to boil and cook about 20 minutes, stirring occasionally. Pour into sterilized jars and seal.

If serving right away, pour vinegar mixture over cooked vegetables and turn off heat. Stir gently to mix, let cool, and place in covered bowl in refrigerator until time to serve. Ideal for canning or for serving to a large group of people.

(Note: original recipe called for half a cup of salt. Ruth was concerned with Lydia's blood pressure and cut it down to a third of a cup.)

RUTH'S AMISH PEANUT BUTTER

INGREDIENTS:

2 cups creamy peanut butter, any brand

2 cups marshmallow cream or fluff

½ cup hot water

½ cup real maple syrup (Ruth likes dark amber, but any variety will do)

¼ teaspoon real vanilla extract

INSTRUCTIONS:

Place all ingredients into large bowl and mix until smooth and creamy.

Ruth's Amish Peanut Butter can be stored in an airtight container (such as an empty peanut butter jar!) at room temperature for up to a week. Refrigerating it will cause it to become very difficult to spread. If it gets too thick, add hot water a little at a time, stirring to remix.

RUTH'S CORN CHOWDER

*Ruth's little secret: This recipe is so easy, she throws it
together on days when one of the goats gets sick and
she doesn't have time to cook from scratch.*

Yields 5 Quarts

INGREDIENTS:

6 (16-ounce) cans creamed corn

½ cup chopped onions (dehydrated onions work too—about a quarter cup.)

1 (12-ounce) can evaporated milk

1 (16-ounce) can chicken broth

2 cups water

1 box (7.06 ounce) sour-cream-and-chive-flavored dry mashed potato mix

INSTRUCTIONS:

Combine all ingredients. Cover. Simmer until hot.

(Note: If you have access to electricity, you can make this in a Crock-Pot. On High, it takes three hours. On Low, it takes six hours. Enjoy! Excellent with cornbread.)

RUTH'S AMISH PEANUT BUTTER COOKIES

(This was Ruth's Grandmother's Recipe)

Yields about 4 Dozen fluffy PB cookies

INGREDIENTS:

1 cup lard

1 cup sugar

1 cup brown sugar

2 large eggs

1 cup creamy or chunky
   peanut butter

½ teaspoon salt

2 teaspoons baking soda

1½ teaspoons vanilla

3 cups flour

INSTRUCTIONS:

Preheat oven to 350 degrees.

Ruth likes to use pork bacon grease she's saved in place of lard. You have to strain it to get the little bacon bits out. It's amazing in peanut butter cookies! You can substitute butter for lard, but the cookies won't be as fluffy.

In large bowl, cream together lard, sugar, and brown sugar until light and fluffy. Mix in eggs, peanut butter, salt, baking soda, vanilla, and flour, stirring to mix well. With your hands, roll dough into one-inch balls, then roll balls in sugar. Place balls on cookie sheets, and use the tines of a fork to flatten slightly, first one way, then another, to get that classic crisscross pattern. Bake until cookies are browned at the edges, about 10 to 12 minutes.

Anne Blackburne lives and works in Southeast Ohio as a newspaper editor and writer. She is the mother of five grown children, has one wonderful grandchild, and owns a spoiled poodle named Millie. For fun, when she isn't working on Amish romance or sweet mysteries, Anne directs and acts in community theater productions, and she writes and directs original plays. She also enjoys reading, kayaking, swimming, searching for beach glass, and just sitting with a cup of coffee looking at large bodies of water. Her idea of the perfect vacation is cruising and seeing amazing new places with people she loves.

THE HEART OF THE AMISH

Full of faith, hope, and romance, this new series
takes you into the Heart of Amish country.

The Flower Quilter
By Mindy Steele

Barbara Schwartz was born into a family of quilters, but she would rather eat dirt than partake in another quilting frolic or sew on another binding. When her parents send her to Indiana to help her grandmother in her quilting shop, she finds herself among a very different community where she is able to help landscaper Melvin Bontrager with a special project that leads to a romantic friendship. Could gardening also lead to an expression of artistry Barbara never knew she possessed?

Paperback / 978-1-63609-642-1

The Quilt Room Secret
By Lisa Jones Baker

Jacob Lantz asked Trini Sutter to marry him when he was five. The mature nine-year-old thoughtfully responded that she'd consider his proposal when they were older. Now, nearly two decades later, the Amish farmer returns to the beautiful countryside of Arthur, Illinois, to take the independent Quilt Room owner up on her promise. Quiet, handsome Jacob is truly in love with the spirited "list maker," and Trini finds herself falling in love with Jacob, but the youngest of eleven has big plans of her own. Will she forfeit her plan for the man of her dreams?

Paperback / 978-1-63609-775-6